Abode Of The Clouds

A Sequel To
In Our Image

Susan Alan

DEDICATION

In reflection on the story woven through this book as well as my prior book "In Our Image", it became apparent to me that my mother played a consistent role. Whether it was seeing UFOs together, discussing religious beliefs together, shopping together, making Christmas ornaments together or baking and cooking together, those memories have greatly influenced my life and thus this story. I started reading some of the books in her library when I was in my teens and continue reading them all these decades later. The books she accumulated reflected her open mindedness and inquisitiveness. The subjects ranged from religion and spirituality, extraterrestrials and UFOs, the power of the mind and health. I couldn't have asked for a better role model and I am thankful to have had her for my mother.

CONTENTS

PROLOGUE

The coffee that morning tasted putrid. It had a metallic flavor with a hint of a chemical aftertaste. I tried a second sip, just to make sure that my taste buds told me what I thought they had told me. That second sip confirmed it, and that was the end of the morning coffee.

I sat there staring at the television as Alex was clicking from channel to channel watching the various special reports on the overnight worldwide UFO sightings. All of the major channels were covering this. There had been sightings on every continent. The reports were pretty much consistent. There were large triangular shaped ships with smaller craft which were seen to come and go from the larger. The large ships were reported as having white, amber and blue lights, but some reports indicated they were completely dark as they moved silently across the sky. A woman in Australia reported that she saw a smaller ship with white lights leave the large ship and after watching it zoom toward her, it just disappeared. Others also reported seeing the ships just vanish in the sky.

Jane had called earlier just after I had seen the first special report on the TV screen. She and Joshua were on their way over. I had to go shower and dress, but I felt so lethargic. I really think I could have stayed in my nightgown and robe all day and just stare at the television. I managed to get myself pulled together just before the doorbell rang.

Alex escorted Jane and Joshua into the den. Jane handed me a tin of red raspberry leaf tea, and asked "Did coffee taste awful this morning?"

"Vile. You too?"

"Uh huh. I happened to have a supply of this raspberry tea on hand, and it seemed to taste very good to me. Why don't you try it?"

I put on the kettle, and got a teapot down from the shelf. Everyone was settled in around the TV watching the special reports.

"At least this is being reported as legitimate news," Joshua commented. "There is no snickering or cynicism."

I brought the teapot and the coffee carafe over to the table and poured coffee for the guys and tea for Jane and me.

"I hoped I would live to see this day," Jane said. "It's surreal. We had asked for their aid, and I truly believed we would receive it. But I didn't anticipate such a tremendous worldwide showing of their craft. I thought it would be their 'cloaked in clouds' modus operandi."

"You know what? It just dawned on me that I haven't looked at my blog this morning! I was so befuddled by the full moon thing last night and the news this morning that I didn't even think to look."

"I completely forgot all about it too!" Jane exclaimed.

I walked over to the computer, turned it on, and went directly to my blog. Jane, Joshua and Alex were standing behind me looking over my shoulder.

All hell had broken loose in the chat room. In addition to the news on the UFO sightings overnight, there was also chatting going on about individual experiences connected with the phenomenon.

"It's a good thing that I changed the privacy setting a while back and opened this only to our core group members and no one else."

"A very good thing," Jane concurred.

"I guess we had better dive right into this, don't you think?" I asked Jane.

"Dive! Dive!"

I started my chat with "Jane and I are together right now watching the news on television, similar to many of you I'm sure. We both thought there was a full moon last night..."

Jane and I sipped red raspberry tea and chatted along with everyone else on my blog well into the afternoon. The consensus was that we received what we had been asking for. We didn't know exactly what to expect, but we agreed that we were all in this together and would stay united.

Alex suggested that Jane and Joshua stay overnight, as it didn't appear there would be any letup on the news coverage in the near future. I had a nightgown and robe that Jane could borrow and Alex had some sweat pants and shirt that Joshua could borrow. To my delight, they said yes.

I made a couple of martinis for Jane and myself, while the guys grabbed a couple of beers. I took a sip of the martini and thought to myself, "Oh no, not martinis too!"

I looked at Jane as she took a taste, and I could tell from her expression that it tasted as revolting to her as it did to me. She put her glass down on the counter and announced "Well it is evident that these little extraterrestrial babies don't want us drinking anything with caffeine or alcohol in it. At least our suffering is for a good cause."

"Right, we're suffering for a noble cause, the good of the planet."

"No point in letting those martinis go to waste," Alex proposed. "How about it, Joshua, you're not driving home tonight?"

"I'll drink to that," Joshua agreed and picked up Jane's glass. "To the good of the planet!"

Chapter 1 – No Sequel

It had been almost three months since the spring equinox and the UFO sightings. Jane and I were definitely pregnant as were many of the women with whom we corresponded on the blog. All of us were post menopausal, similar to those women in the bible like Sarah and St. Anne.

The tricky part was how to keep these "miracle" pregnancies out of the news. The good thing was that all of the women involved were in their late 50's. It was extremely unusual for a woman of that age to give birth, but it wasn't impossible. Actually, I had read about a woman in India who gave birth to twins at age 72 as a result of in vitro fertilization. Why she would want to have twins at 72 years of age, I haven't a clue.

Jane and I were the only two women who lived in close proximity to each other. The remaining twenty two women were spread out around the globe. We all managed to convince our doctors and/or caregivers that it was a natural occurrence; unusual but natural, nothing to be alarmed about. It seemed to work.

The midwife route, with the hope of giving birth at home, appealed to Jane and me. I guess you could call that home delivery? Our ages put us in a high risk group. However, Jane and I were healthier now than we had ever been. We craved fresh fruits and vegetables, whole grains and beans. The consumption of a healthy diet coupled with the absence of caffeine and alcohol contributed to our physical wellbeing. We experienced no morning sickness. We had more energy than ever and I swear we even looked younger.

After interviewing several midwives, I decided on one with whom I was extremely comfortable. Her credentials were impressive. We discussed my age factor as a potential problem, but the decision was made that we would monitor my condition as the pregnancy progressed. If at any point she felt that I needed to be referred to a medical doctor, I would comply with her recommendation. Likewise, Jane found a midwife with similar qualifications with whom she was very happy.

Alex and Joshua must have felt guilty about drinking beer in front of us, so they stopped drinking. They ate pretty much what Jane and I ate, and as a result they lost weight and felt better. This was a win/win situation all around!

The only downside to the general state of events was the amazing lack of positive response to the mass UFO sightings earlier in the year. This had been THE major news event of the decade, maybe even the century, maybe even in recorded history. However the story was hot for a week or two, and then it pretty much died.

Alex and I were having lunch with Jane and Joshua and the UFO topic came up; actually I brought it up.

"Can you believe that basically nothing changed after the UFO appearances back in March? Oh, a presidential commission was formed to investigate the UFO phenomenon, but what can we expect from that?" I asked.

"Several countries have initiated full disclosure policies on UFO's, that's something at least," Jane said.

"That's nothing! There are those within the government, within the military industrial complex, within the media and scientific communities, within organized religion, who already know the truth. They've known the truth for decades, if not longer. And they're keeping their mouths shut. They're hoping that this will all go away, that there won't be any more mass sightings, or heaven forbid, actual landing and contact," Joshua responded.

"Right, if there were an actual landing and/or contact, it might be a little more difficult to sweep under the carpet," Alex retorted.

"And what I find fascinating is the posturing being done by organized religion. Actually, they were way ahead of the curve on this. Remember that monsignor what's his name talking about extraterrestrials?" I asked.

"Monsignor Carrado Balducci," Alex interjected.

"Right, Carrado Balducci. How do you remember this stuff? Anyway Monsignor Balducci said something to the effect that if extraterrestrials exist, they have to be better than humans, because humans are the worst. And if extraterrestrials do exist, they will come to our aid."

"And do you remember there was a priest named Jose Gabriel Funes who stated that there is a possibility that extraterrestrials could have remained in full friendship with the father and might not need redemption?" Alex added.

"So representatives of the Roman Catholic Church were out there talking about ET's to kind of set the stage for the church's acceptance of these beings, should they suddenly show up some day," Joshua said.

"Correct, and supposedly the telescopes at their two observatories are set toward the southern hemisphere, as that is where the starships were first supposed to appear," Alex continued.

"Where did you get that idea?" I asked.

"I don't know, but I'm pretty sure I read that somewhere. You know my mind is like a steel trap."

"Right, steel trap."

"And, if you recall, the ships recently sighted did first appear in the southern hemisphere and headed north."

"Yes, I do recall that." I responded. "Did I tell you our fellow ladies in waiting were talking about the lack of response from the world community?"

"Something sounds weird with that phrase 'fellow ladies in waiting', don't you think?" Jane asked.

"Okay, how about our comrade ladies in waiting?"

"Better. But how about comradette, it sounds more feminine."

"I like the sound of that, comradette ladies in waiting. Anyway, remember Alice?"

"Of course, how could we forget Alice," Joshua joked.

"Well she was so annoyed by the lack of response from world leaders that she suggested we band together and make a public statement that we were all impregnated by extraterrestrials during the night of the sighting."

"You're kidding!" Joshua almost shouted.

"No, we're not kidding," Jane exclaimed. "Alice was pretty much by herself with that sentiment, and there was a heck of a lot of chatting that ensued before we finally convinced her that it definitely was not a good idea."

"Didn't she realize that she would be putting each one of you women in physical jeopardy? You'd be in danger now and for the rest of your lives, the children too," Joshua said.

"There are lots of people who would look at you and your offspring as threats, freaks, monsters or demons or some such thing. They would be doing the world a great service by getting rid of the lot of you, or so they would think," Alex declared.

"We explained that to Alice, and once it sunk in, she was fine with it. She was just annoyed that the mass UFO sighting didn't change the world as we know it. She expected something to happen, something really major to happen, and it didn't," I replied.

"I'm sure there have been changes, it's just that the rank and file population on this planet doesn't know about it," Joshua proposed.

"What do you mean?" Jane asked.

"Was there a sequel to 'Close Encounters of the Third Kind'?" Joshua asked.

"Okay, I'm asking again, what do you mean?"

"Remember in 'Close Encounters of the Third Kind'

how the US Army spread the story that a train had derailed near Devil's Tower, Wyoming, spilled nerve gas and they closed the area off? The population never knew what was happening. They were told a lie. And I'm certain, if the story continued, they would never have been told the truth.

"Yes; and your point is what?"

"There was no sequel to 'Close Encounters'. In the movie, the populace was kept completely in the dark. The government, scientists, military, and all others directly related to the phenomenon knew what had happened, and were most likely sworn to secrecy, but average humans were intentionally kept in the dark. And that is what is happening now."

"Excuse me for being dense, but exactly what do you mean?" Jane asked.

"Today those with power within the government, media, military, religion, industry, science and industry are all scrambling to get ready for the next step, whether it be another mass sighting, landing or contact. They're all preparing to cover their butts. They're all concocting a good spin. They need to survive, no matter what happens, and they're preparing for that eventuality. So that's why there was no sequel to 'Close Encounters'. Do you think government officials or that French scientist character told the truth to the public about what really happened at Devil's Tower? Of course not. If they had, if the truth had leaked out, then that would have been the sequel. But that was the end of the story. Today's real story is taking place in the shadows and will never see the light of day."

"They're all holding their breath and keeping their fingers crossed that nothing happens again," Alex said.

"Right, they don't want a sequel to this story."

Chapter 2 – They're Back

"What time does your sisters' plane come in?" Alex asked.

"2:55."

"And we're having Peruvian spaghetti made with brown rice pasta?"

"Yup, I've got the vegetables all diced and sliced and ready to go. I'm making it with shrimp instead of beef."

"We haven't had that for months. I'm salivating already. And tomorrow we're having lunch at Jane and Joshua's, right?"

"Right."

"I'll be working on their patio tomorrow, so I'll meet you there."

"How is that progressing?"

"Good, we're almost finished. I'm going to miss working at their place."

"I bet. I'm sure Jane fed you all kinds of healthy snacks and drinks."

"Let's just say she took very good care of both me and the crew."

"Good, I wouldn't want you boys starving to death. I'm going to head outside and see what's happening in the yard."

"Okay, I'll be leaving in a few minutes, so I'll see you later this afternoon. I should be here by the time you get back with your sisters. Drive carefully."

I walked out the terrace door and took a deep breath of incredibly sweet air. It was a beautiful June day. I had several urns out on the patio filled with verbena, wild yam vine and lantana. The verbena was dark purple, the wild yam was both the chartreuse and the almost black variety and the lantana was a bright orange. It was hard to find lantana up in Vermont, as it is more of a tropical plant. There was one nursery that had it last year, and I made sure to tell them that I loved it and hoped they continued to carry it. Once you got past any danger of frost, the plants did great. You never had to deadhead them and they bloomed like crazy until you got your first hard frost in the fall. They said they'd make a note of it and be sure to have some for me again this season. They even gave me a call when the shipment arrived. Such nice people.

I stopped by the potting shed for a pair of snips and a basket, and then headed toward the backyard. To me, this place was heaven on earth. What could be better? The lilacs were still in bloom; I had white, dark purple, periwinkle and lavender varieties and they were all grouped together off to the right side of the stone foundation. The yellowwood tree was abloom with clusters of pea-like creamy white flowers. The fragrance of the sweet mock orange rode on the breeze. Spireas dotted the landscape with various shades of pink and plum.

And the peonies! Words couldn't describe how extraordinary they were this year. The tree peonies as well as the herbaceous variety were loaded with magnificent blooms ranging from the reddest of red to the palest of pinks, along with peaches, yellows and whites. The foliage of the heuchera, tiarella, hosta, astilbe and daylilies all added texture and color. The early blooming Stella d'Oro daylilies were ablaze with their golden glow.

I headed over to the cutting bed and selected a variety of peonies for an arrangement. I was on my way back to the house when I decided to make a detour over to the lilacs and cut some of them for a separate arrangement. I included all the various colors and threw in some mock orange as well. What a spectacular fragrance!

A few hours later I was heading toward the airport and thinking about "the morning after" as we now referred to it. Jane was the first to call that morning, and my sisters called a little later after Jane and Joshua arrived. Anne had gone over to Mary's house so they could watch the news together. They had been following my blog, so they weren't shocked by the news, at least no more shocked than the rest of us. And of course, they suspected that "it" happened and wanted to know if "it" really did happen. I told them about the "full moon" and the vile tasting coffee. They thought for sure that these were signs that "it" did happen. They were disappointed that I couldn't remember any details of exactly what had happened, only that I remembered it was so bright outside that I thought there was a full moon.

Actually, the women on the blog also discussed what they remembered from that night. Very few women remembered anything unusual at all. A couple did seem to recall that they were floating through their windows and out over their yards, but nothing else. These women, however, reported that they had experienced "floating" dreams quite often, so this was no indication to them that something unusual had happened.

This prompted a discussion as to the possibility that these individuals might have been visited by extraterrestrials their entire lives, and taken aboard spaceships previously. They both thought that this might be a possibility.

Alice, however, had a detailed remembrance of the events of that night. She related that she was awakened by something, but she wasn't sure what it was. She didn't open her eyes, as she thought she would fall back to sleep within a few seconds. But as she lay there, she felt a presence and she reluctantly opened her eyes. Standing next to the bed was a man and he was looking down at her. She said he was tall and of slim build, blond hair, nice looking and casually dressed.

For whatever reason, she did not feel fear. He reached for her hand, and she extended it, and the next thing she knew she was inside a room which she thought to be within a spacecraft. She didn't see the outside of the ship and she had no recollection of how she got there. She was in her bed one minute and in what she assumed to be a spacecraft the next. She remembered nothing else of the happenings of that night. When she awoke in her bed the next morning, she thought it was all a dream. It wasn't until she got up and put the news on that she realized it wasn't a dream.

I have to admit that I was glad that I didn't remember anything about that night, other than the bright light which I assumed to be the moon. Jane and I wondered if the so-called 'father' of our children was one entity, or were there multiple extraterrestrial 'fathers', a separate one for each of the 24 of us. Perhaps embryos were implanted in us, and we were only hosts and not the biological mothers. There was so much we didn't know. The only thing that each of us knew for sure was that we were with child and the father of that child was not from this planet.

I reached the gate just as my sisters were arriving. It was so good to see them again. The last time I saw them was in late November and now it was just about seven month later. And here I was three months pregnant with the child of an extraterrestrial. Truth is really stranger than fiction. There was no way I could have remotely envisioned this when I last saw them. Actually, it was hard for me to believe it was real now.

"Connie, you look wonderful!" Anne exclaimed. Mary chimed her agreement. There were hugs and kisses all around. We collected their luggage, and off we headed toward home.

"You're not showing yet, and if anything, it looks like you've lost weight," Mary declared.

"Not taking in all those alcoholic calories makes a difference. Plus I'm eating lots of fruits, vegetables and whole grains; it really makes a difference. I feel better than I have in decades."

We reached the house just before 4 p.m. and Alex was already there, ready to assist with the luggage. Again, more hugs and more kisses.

"And even you look great," Mary proclaimed to Alex. "You're svelte!"

"Thanks, Mary; I think you're swell too." Alex joked.

"Svelte, svelte! You've lost weight."

"Yup, got rid of that beer belly."

Alex brought their luggage upstairs, and the girls followed me into the kitchen.

"Glass of wine?" I asked.

"Love it," Anne replied.

"Me too!" Mary chimed in.

"Look at that bouquet of lilacs on the table," Anne observed. "What is that other white flower mixed with them?"

"Mock orange. Doesn't it smell great? Walk into the living room and take a look at the vase full of peonies."

I poured the wine and served it to them in the living room. The French doors were open and the afternoon sun was streaming across the lawn and into the room. Alex joined us just as I suggested we go outside. We took a stroll around the backyard and then over to the stone bench with the word "Meghalaya" carved in it. The view of the lake and mountains was spectacular from that vantage point.

"Remind me again what 'Meghalaya' means," Mary said.

"It's Sanskrit for 'Abode of the Clouds'," Alex responded.

"Perfect name for this spot," Anne commented as we headed back toward the patio.

"I'll bring the bottle of wine out," Alex volunteered. "Connie, want a glass of iced raspberry tea?"

"That would be lovely. Could you please put a wedge of lemon in it?

"Sure thing."

"How do you think Gene and Hilda knew a Sanskrit

word?" Mary asked.

"I have no idea. The only thing I know about them is that they were into horticulture and loved to play cards and ride their horses."

Alex walked back out onto the patio and inquired, "Oh, talking about Gene and Hilda?"

"Yes, Mary was wondering how they knew that Sanskrit word 'Meghalaya'."

He refilled the girl's wine glasses, put my iced tea down in front of me and advised, "Don't drink that tea, I want to get a sprig of spearmint to put in it," and he disappeared around the corner of the house. He reemerged a minute later with the mint, crushed it a bit in his hand, and put it in my glass. "Okay, take a sip."

I don't know why I never thought of putting mint in my tea. It was growing like crazy in the herb garden. Actually it was taking over the herb garden and I didn't use it at all. I took a sip and, wow! "This is incredible. What a difference it makes."

"I'm going to make one of those for myself. I'll be right back."

A couple minutes later he was back out and joined us at the table.

"Connie and I thought it was synchronistic that we should be drawn to this property named 'Meghalaya' considering our relatively recent research and current situation," Alex noted.

"What do you mean?" Anne asked.

"Well, when Connie first started connecting the dots in the bible…"

"I wasn't connecting the dots alone. If anyone was the chief dot connector, it was you."

"Okay, when we first started connecting the dots in the bible, the phrase 'glory of the Lord' came up over and over again in Exodus. Like 'the glory of the Lord' settled on Mount Sinai for example. I looked up the word 'glory' in the dictionary and one of the definitions was 'nimbus'."

"Nimbus, like cloud?" Anne asked.

"Right. So then Alex looked up the word 'nimbus', and the definition stated that it was a luminous atmosphere believed to envelope a deity; glory; or low formless dark gray cloud. Did I get that right, Alex?"

"You nailed it. So here we are coming to the belief that a spaceship is enveloped in the glory of the Lord, and the word 'glory' means nimbus and nimbus is a cloud. And we are living in a spot called 'Meghalaya' which means 'abode of the clouds'. Kind of weird, don't you think?"

"Weird...." Mary and Anne said in unison.

"And then it gets even weirder when Alex and I meet Jane who is obsessed with painting clouds cloaking spaceships within them."

"Weird..." Mary and Anne again said in unison.

"And the weirdest thing of all is that I am now having an alien's baby!" I exclaimed.

"Weird!" Mary and Anne shouted in unison this time, and then we all broke out into laughter.

"Okay, folks, I've got to go make dinner," I proclaimed and got up.

"We'll help," Mary offered.

"There's nothing to do. We're having Peruvian spaghetti and everything is all chopped up and ready to throw in the wok."

"Peruvian spaghetti, I haven't had that in years!" Anne exclaimed.

They followed me into the kitchen anyway and watched me get dinner going.

"We're all going to Jane and Joshua's tomorrow for lunch," Alex said.

"Marvelous!" Anne chimed, "I can't wait to meet them."

"It's hard to believe that we've only known them about seven months ourselves," I commented. "We met them shortly after you left right after Thanksgiving last year."

"And now Jane is also having an alien's baby!" Alex shouted.

"Weird!" Mary and Anne said and squealed with laughter.

Chapter 3 – Mystery Man

The next morning I thought I had overslept. The birds were chirping, the sun was up and I jumped out of bed with a start. I looked at the clock and it was only 5:40. It seemed more like 7 o'clock to me. Anyway, I was up and wide awake, so I put on my robe and slippers and quietly made my way downstairs. I thought to myself that tomorrow was the summer solstice, so we were experiencing the longest days of the year right now.

Alex was wide awake, watching television in the den and Itzy seemed to be ravenous. I fed Itzy first, then got the coffee going and put on the kettle.

Alex walked over to me and whispered "Good morning."

"Good morning to you! What are you whispering for?"

"I don't want to disturb your sisters."

"You know Anne is going to be down here any minute; don't worry about disturbing them."

I put steel cut oats on to cook, as it would take 30 to 40 minutes and I figured even Mary would be up by then. I ate oatmeal just about every morning now. It was high in fiber, low in fat, had protein, iron and no cholesterol. In fact, studies showed that it even lowered cholesterol. Although the steel cut oats took longer to cook, I felt it was worth it. The texture was creamy yet chewy at the same time.

"It's going to be another beautiful day today, just like

yesterday," Alex declared.

"Great, maybe I can convince my sisters to go for a walk with me after breakfast. We have to be at Jane's at noon. And I was thinking we could stop at Champlain Orchards on our way home."

"That sounds good."

The coffee was just finishing when Anne came around the corner.

"Good morning! How'd you sleep?" I asked.

"Wonderfully. I always sleep well when I'm up here. And Itzy slept with me! She usually sleeps with Mary, so I feel very flattered that she chose me this time."

I poured coffee for Anne and Alex, made some red raspberry tea for myself, and gave the oatmeal a stir.

"Before I fell asleep last night I was thinking about the mass UFO sighting. You said you thought there was a full moon because of the bright light shining in the window. That must have been a UFO, right?"

"I would assume so."

"Do you think it actually landed on your property, or do you think it hovered?"

"We didn't find any evidence on the ground. But we did have some unexplained damage to a limb on the yellowwood tree," Alex said.

"What kind of damage?" Anne asked.

"The tips of the branch were slightly singed. Come here and look out the window," Alex got up and Anne and I followed him to the window.

"See that tree out to the right that has those clusters of white flowers? That's a yellowwood tree. Do you notice that every branch of that tree is loaded with flowers, except for one on the right side? There's not one flower on the branch."

"That's the one that was damaged?"

"Right."

"Hey, what's everyone looking at?"

We all turned around and saw Mary standing there

with her lavender robe and slippers.

"We're looking at a branch of a tree that the UFO scorched when it was here in March!" Anne exclaimed.

"What?"

"Come over here and look. I asked Connie if she thought the UFO had actually landed on the property or if she thought that it hovered," Anne explained. "There was no evidence that it had landed on the ground, but there was one branch that was damaged. See that tree with the white flowers out there to the right? See that one branch that has no flowers at all? That's the one that got scorched!"

"Holy moly!" Mary murmured, staring out at the tree.

I ran to the stove to stir the oatmeal, which was just starting to stick to the pot. It was almost done.

I poured Mary a cup of coffee and brought it over to her. She was standing there speechless staring out at that tree.

I got the soy milk and blueberries out of the refrigerator and the maple syrup out of the pantry.

"Breakfast is ready," I announced.

Mary and Anne were still staring out the window when I put the bowls of oatmeal on the table.

"Ladies, attention please, breakfast is served," Alex said in a loud voice.

They seemed to reluctantly turn their gaze away from the tree, walked over to the table and sat down. Apparently still lost in thought, they started to eat their oatmeal. After a few spoonfuls, Anne stated, "This is the best oatmeal I've ever had. What kind is it?"

"Steel cut Irish oatmeal."

"It's so much better than regular oatmeal. What a wonderful texture! And the fresh blueberries and maple syrup go perfectly with it," Mary piped in.

"That's Vermont maple syrup. Remember Herbert and June who live down the road? You know, the couple we had the Old Krupnik with on Thanksgiving? This syrup came from their maple trees," Alex remarked.

"You're kidding? This is incredible," Anne marveled.

It got quiet as everyone was savoring their oatmeal. Breaking the silence I asked, "So what's the big deal with one singed branch on a tree? I'm sitting here with a little alien baby growing inside of me and that doesn't seem to faze you two in the least!"

"You know what it must be?" Mary proposed. "It must be that we can actually see the damage done to that tree by a spaceship. Actual physical evidence is sitting out there in your yard. But you, although you are three months pregnant, you don't look pregnant. Do you know what I mean? A few months from now it will be different."

"I guess I can accept that," I responded.

Soon after breakfast, Alex left to go to work at Jane's and Joshua's. Fortified by a hearty breakfast, Mary and Anne and I headed out for a walk. First, however, they wanted to walk over to the yellowwood tree for a closer look.

"Some of the leaves on that branch seem to have been damaged as well," Mary noted. "They're smaller and curled a little."

After a few minutes of staring at the tree, I managed to pull them away and we headed down the driveway. Mary and Anne were still talking about that tree and how they would have loved to have seen the UFO hovering. We reached the road and turned right. We passed Herbert and June's house and kept on going for about half a mile when I saw Mark and his dog Fallon approaching.

"Hey, Mark, good morning! Hi Fallon." Fallon was a Swedish Vallhund, a very friendly and intelligent little dog. He knew me, and came right up for a pet. He kept his distance from my sisters, though.

"Mark, these are my two sisters, Anne and Mary, up from Hilton Head for a visit."

Greetings were exchanged and Mark commented that he had been to Hilton Head on several occasions and loved it.

After a little chit chat, Mark asked "Have you heard

that Russell is back in town?"

"Who?" I asked.

"Russell, you know, Gene and Hilda's son."

"I didn't know Gene and Hilda had a son. Hilda's nephew Richard never said anything about him. I had no idea!"

"Well, I guess you could say he was the black sheep of the family. Some of the town folk considered him a little strange."

"Strange how?" I asked.

"I was two grades ahead of him in school, so I don't really know; all I know is that he was a loner. He went to college, a good college, but I can't remember which. After that he travelled. I don't know where he went all those years ago, but I think he just came back from India."

"Have you seen him since he came back?" I asked.

"Yes, I saw him at the general store yesterday. He looked different, of course. I'm sure I looked different to him, too. After all, it's been many years since we last saw each other. It's really weird, because I was sure you knew about him."

"So he left this area after high school and hasn't been back?"

"Right, and that was maybe 28 years ago or so."

"And he never came back to see his parents, even when they were older?"

"Not that I know of. Hilda had him rather late in life. I remember my mother saying that the word was Hilda couldn't have children. She and Gene traveled the world during the first few decades of their marriage. Apparently it created quite a stir in town when she gave birth to Russell."

"Well, thanks for the info, Mark. Maybe I'll have the opportunity to meet Russell."

"You probably will, as I can't imagine why he would come back here except to see his parents' property. He was never close to any of his relatives and he never had any friends here."

We said our goodbyes and walked toward home. Why hadn't Russell inherited the property? What was the real story? Now I was both curious and also agitated by the whole thing.

Anne asked "Are you okay? You seem upset by that conversation."

"I didn't know Gene and Hilda had a son, and I don't understand why this property didn't go to him. And it's bizarre that Richard never mentioned a word about him."

A little later we were headed down toward Shoreham to Jane and Joshua's house. My sisters enjoyed the ride and the scenery and the setting of Jane's house amazed them.

"They're directly on the lake! What a location!" Anne exclaimed.

When we pulled up, Alex walked around from the back. Jane and Joshua came out the front door, and I introduced them to Anne and Mary. We walked through the front door and I could tell my sisters were impressed. It was a spectacular house. Jane showed them the dining room and the transferware collection, and then brought them into the living room. They noted the cloud picture over the mantel which Jane had painted. And then Joshua proposed, "Why don't you ladies come out onto the patio?"

We followed him through the back door and to my amazement, the patio and steps were complete. The urns were filled with plants, the dining table and chairs and lounges were out there and it was incredibly beautiful. I looked at Alex, and he winked back at me.

"It's finished!" I exclaimed.

"We wanted to surprise you. Isn't it marvelous?" Jane asked.

"It's even better than I envisioned. Alex, you did an incredible job with this. I'm so proud of you. You know, it's seldom that I get to see the actual finished project, and this is amazing. Nice work. Better than nice work, spectacular work," I remarked.

"Thanks. There were just a few things I wanted to finish up this morning. The table and chairs were also delivered a few hours ago and I wanted to help Joshua set them up and get them in place," Alex responded.

"Why don't you sit down at the table and I'll bring out lunch?" Jane asked.

Within a few minutes we were munching on avocado and sprout wraps with soy bacon, spinach and natural cheddar cheese. Jane had made a wonderful dilled cucumber salad as an accompaniment.

"These wraps are absolutely delicious, Jane," Mary commented. "I had steel cut Irish oatmeal for breakfast and now this; I feel healthier already. I really do."

"Funny, I was just thinking the same thing," Anne agreed.

"We've been eating this way for almost three months now, and it has made a tremendous difference in how we feel," Jane said.

"And I think we all look younger!" I chimed in.

"Right, you should have seen us three months ago, we all looked decrepit," Joshua joked.

"It's kind of like the 'Portrait of Dorian Grey' only we didn't sell our souls to the devil," Alex responded.

"Or at least we hope we didn't sell our souls to the devil," Jane whispered.

"I met Mark during our walk this morning," I said to Alex.

"How is he? How's the family?"

"Oh, they're fine. However, he mentioned to me that Gene and Hilda's son, Russell, was back in town."

"Who? Russell? We never heard of him, have we?"

"No, the attorney at the closing never mentioned that Gene and Hilda had a son, and Richard never mentioned that he had a cousin."

"Well, that's weird," Alex muttered.

"Weird…" Mary and Anne muttered simultaneously.

"And Mark said that Russell was strange, that he was a loner and that after college he travelled and Mark thought that he had just come back from India. Mark also thought that it was possible that Russell would like to see the old family homestead."

"Everything happens for a reason, so if Russell shows up at our door, I'm sure there's nothing to worry about. It is all meant to be," Alex said.

We continued munching on our wraps, and Jane said "Tomorrow is the summer solstice, I think it happens around 7:15 or so tomorrow evening. How about you come back late in the afternoon tomorrow and we'll have an early dinner down by the lake?"

"Sounds great to me, how about you girls?" I asked Mary and Anne.

"Fantastic, we'd love to!" Mary answered.

"Absolutely, sounds great," Anne added.

We left mid-afternoon. Alex went straight home and my sisters and I headed over to Champlain Orchards. I knew Anne and Mary would love it, and they did. Of course they zeroed in on the sauerkraut.

"Do you know how to make those little potato dumplings that mommy used to make?" Mary asked.

"Yes, would you like me to make some to go with this sauerkraut?"

"I don't want you to go to any trouble…"

"If you peel and grate the potatoes, I'll make the dumplings."

"It's a deal."

I pulled into our courtyard a little while later. On the other side of the stone wall, I could see Alex sitting out on the patio with another man. There was no vehicle parked out front. How did this person get there? And who was he? Then it dawned on me, it must be Russell.

Chapter 4 – Really Weird

"Who's that guy with Alex?" Mary asked.

"One guess," I sighed.

"Russell?"

"Bingo," I responded.

"Well that's weird, because just a few hours ago Alex said that if Russell showed up at your door, he was sure there was nothing to worry about. And here he is," Anne mused.

"You know ladies, I've come to the conclusion that there is some great force controlling my life and I'm just sitting back and going along for the ride," I said.

"Good thing, because I don't think there is anything you could do about it anyway," Anne concluded.

"Right you are!"

I parked the car and we headed straight to the patio.

"Ah, here are the ladies now," Alex announced.

Russell, or at least the man whom I assumed to be Russell, stood up and Alex said, "Connie, let me introduce Russell."

Russell extended his hand and when I touched it I got a faint electric shock. His hand was warm and his grasp was firm. I looked into his dark brown eyes and I was thinking to myself, "I like this man."

"Connie, it's a pleasure to meet you."

"The pleasure is mine, Russell," I answered. "Let me introduce you to my sisters, Anne and Mary."

He shook hands with each of them and I could see they were both mesmerized by him.

"Please, sit down," I urged. "Can I get you anything to eat or drink?" I asked.

"Alex was kind enough to get me a glass of water, that's all I needed, thank you."

"You know, it's quite a coincidence that I met Mark Mason this morning when I was out for a walk, and he mentioned that you were in town. I have to confess that I didn't even know you existed. I had no idea that Gene and Hilda had a son. Your cousin Richard never mentioned it to us. And here you are sitting on our patio," I declared.

"I left to travel when I was a very young man, and I don't think anyone expected me to ever return, so why mention me? But I had learned that my parents' house had been purchased and I did want to meet the new owners, so I thought I'd drop by. I hope I'm not intruding."

"No, not at all, we're glad to meet you," Alex responded. Alex continued to tell Russell how Richard had told us a little bit about Gene and Hilda, and how their ashes were strewn on the property.

As Alex talked, I took in Russell's appearance. He was dressed in worn khaki pants with a cream colored shirt. He was a tall man, over six feet I would guess and slim build. He had a rugged look to him, tanned face and arms. His hair was shoulder length and dark brown with a slight bit of grey. He had a longish beard with a touch of grey in it as well. But it was his eyes that were astounding. They were wide set and the darkest brown I had ever seen. When he looked at me, I felt that he was actually looking into my soul. I never had another human being look at me like that. I got the impression that those eyes had seen the entire human experience, maybe even more.

"From what I see, you've taken very good care of this property. This patio is a wonderful addition. It looks like it has always been here. And I noticed that cairn up on the hill; is there special significance to that?"

"Funny you should ask," Alex answered, "I built that

as a memorial to your parents. I gathered the stones from this property, and their ashes are here, so I thought it would be appropriate to memorialize them with that structure."

"Thank you for that, Alex."

"I know we've just met, and this might sound a little strange to you, but I do believe your parents are still here with us at times," Alex confessed.

Russell nodded, almost as a sign of encouragement.

"The first summer we were here, I was doing some carpentry work; actually it was for the dining room. I'll show you that in just a bit. In any case, I had saw horses set up outside the backdoor, and I had worked late into the evening. Connie was making dinner. It was almost dark. I was gathering up my tools when I suddenly felt electricity in the air. The hair was standing up on my arms and the back of my neck. And then I heard a female voice say 'Why don't you...' and then a male voice interrupted her and said 'Shhhh...', and we believed those voices belonged to your parents."

"It's quite possible. But you didn't feel threatened or afraid, did you?" Russell asked.

"No, if anything it was comforting to believe they were watching us. I'm sure if I screwed anything up, they'd make certain to let me know."

Russell laughed; a deep easy kind of laugh.

"Why don't we take Russell inside and show him how little we've changed his old homestead," I suggested.

"Okay, thanks very much, but just for a few minutes, as I really have to be on my way."

"So soon?" I asked.

"Yes, although this is almost the longest day of the year, we'll be losing sunlight in a few hours and I've got a way to go."

"Can we drive you somewhere?" Alex asked.

"That's so kind of you, but no thanks. I do appreciate the offer, however."

"Then come into the house for a few minutes, please,"

I motioned and got up.

Russell and the group followed me through the open French doors.

The oak table to our right was still covered with stacks of books, but mercifully he didn't look at them, or at least it didn't appear that he looked at them. What he was looking at was the reproduction of "The Baptism of Christ" painting hanging on the back wall.

"That's one of my favorites," he asserted.

That comment pretty much blew me away. I managed to say, "You're familiar with that?"

"Yes, it's 'The Baptism of Christ'. The artist is Aert De Gelder and I believe it was painted in the early 1700's. The original is housed at the Fitzwilliam Museum in Cambridge. I've seen the original."

This was just too incredible, but as I said to the girls earlier, some unseen force was in control. He then spotted Jane's painting over in the other corner and walked over to it.

"This is an amazing work of art. There's a sense of mystery to it. Who is the artist?"

"It was painted by a friend of ours, Jane," I responded.

"Well please tell Jane for me that I greatly admire her work."

Alex brought Russell into the dining room and showed him the paneling he had put up and the little niche he had made for my smaller pieces of transferware.

"Nice work, Alex. You would never know this wasn't original to the house either. Actually, I feel right at home here. You've kept the same feel to the house as it had when I was growing up."

"Thank you, Russell," Alex replied.

"So now I must be off," Russell said and retraced his steps back through the living room.

"Are you sure you won't stay for dinner?" I asked.

"Thank you, but no, I really must leave."

We were back on the patio and Russell picked up his

duffel bag and slung it over his shoulder.

"Will you be coming back this way?" Alex asked.

"Not for a while, probably in a year or so I should be back in this area."

"Where are you headed? Oh, I'm sorry, I shouldn't be so bold as to ask," I apologized.

"No apology needed. I'm heading back to India."

"Which region?" Alex asked.

"Oh, it's a small state in north eastern India. The name might be familiar to you; it's Meghalaya."

Okay, we were all floored by that response. You could hear a pin drop. We were speechless.

"Yes, this is not the only Meghalaya in the world. There is also a state in India called Meghalaya," Russell chuckled. "Sorry to shock you."

He extended his hand and shook each of ours, and turned to leave.

"Please come back when you return to this area," I said. "We'd love to see you again."

"Thank you, I will. You can count on it."

He walked out into the courtyard and turned and called back "Do you know what 'Meghalaya' means?"

"Yes, 'abode of the clouds'," I called back.

"Correct you are!" he shouted. "Clouds being the operative word in that phrase..." And with that he turned and headed down the driveway. We stood there and watched until he disappeared from sight.

"If I were a drinking woman, I'd make myself a martini right now," I whimpered.

"Well I'm a drinking woman, and I'm going to get myself a glass of wine!" Anne exclaimed.

"Oh, sit down ladies, I'll get drinks for all of us," Alex said and headed into the house.

"Is Russell the most charismatic man you've every met in your life or what?" Mary asked.

"I couldn't take my eyes off of him, there was

something almost hypnotic about him," Anne responded.

"I've never had another human being look at me the way he did, as if he were peering into my very soul," I sighed.

"Well, I guess that Russell fellow was a big hit, huh?" Alex said as he emerged from the house with a bottle of wine in one hand and a tray with glasses in the other. He put the tray down on the table and poured wine for both Mary and Anne. He had sparkling cider for himself and me.

"He's got the female vote, that's for sure," Anne said.

"What did you think of him?" I asked Alex.

"I took an immediate liking to him. It was weird because he was here when I arrived home."

"Weird..." Anne interrupted. "Oh, I'm sorry, I just couldn't help it."

"He was sitting out on the patio. I found it a little unsettling to drive in and see someone sitting out there. And then I thought to myself, 'That must be Russell'."

"I parked the truck and he was walking to meet me. He introduced himself, and extended his hand, and I thought 'I like this guy'. There was just something about him that drew me to him."

"I felt exactly the same way," I agreed.

"So I invited him to sit down on the patio and asked if I could get him something to drink, and the only thing he wanted was a glass of water. We talked about his experience growing up on this property, and how he had a wonderful childhood here. Then he asked what I did for a living, and I told him I was a stone mason and garden designer. He asked if I had built the patio, and I said yes. We talked about building with stone the entire rest of the time until you arrived."

"He mentioned that he heard someone had purchased this property, and he made it almost sound like since he was in the neighborhood he wanted to drop by and meet us. But he was in India, how could he have heard that someone purchased Meghalaya? And is that just a coincidence that he has been living in Meghalaya, India? Is that weird or what?" I asked.

"Really weird," Mary concurred.

"And what was with that comment 'clouds' is the operative word in that phrase...'?" Alex asked.

"And is it just synchronicity that he has seen the original 'Baptism of Christ' painting in Cambridge?" I asked.

"No," Mary said, "it's not synchronicity, it just plain..."

"Weird..." Mary and Anne shouted in unison.

"Okay, enough weirdness for one day. I've got to get our purchases out of the car," I said.

"I'll get them," Alex said. "What did you get?"

I gave him a look, and he moaned, "Oh no, not sauerkraut!"

"Come on, you love those little dumplings with sauerkraut," I kidded.

"What were they called in Slovak?" Anne asked.

"Halusky," I said. "And Alex only pretends to detest them. Watch, tonight he'll have a second helping."

"And we also bought oatmeal crumble apple pie," Mary said. "So if you're a good boy and eat all of your dinner, you can have dessert."

We went into the house, and Mary peeled and shredded the potatoes as she had promised.

I have to say, I outdid myself with the halusky. Alex wasn't the only one who had seconds.

Chapter 5 – Solstice Celebration

The solstice turned out to be another incredibly beautiful day. I was so glad that the weather was cooperating for our picnic by the lake. I called Jane right after breakfast and told her I was bringing a Champlain Orchards apple pie for dessert, as I had picked up two yesterday, and asked if there was anything else I could bring.

She said the apple pie would be great, and I didn't need to bring anything else. We would be having grilled salmon, a dilled wild rice salad and also spinach salad. Yum.

Mary and Anne were sitting out on the patio sipping coffee. I took my tea out and joined them.

"We have something to propose to you," Anne stated.

"Okay, shoot."

"We'd like to come back and help with the baby for a couple of weeks after it's born. Would that be okay with you?"

"I'd love it, and I'd appreciate the help as well. After all, I haven't had a baby in about 40 years. That is really very considerate of you."

"Okay, then we'd like to pass something else by you. We'd like to ask Jane if she would like one of us to stay with her, while the other is here with you," Mary proposed.

"Jane has no family in the area, and I'm her only friend, so I'm sure she would be very receptive to your suggestion," I responded.

"So it's alright if we bring this up when we see her today?" Anne asked.

"Absolutely! Actually, I have a feeling this baby is going to be born on the winter solstice, so maybe you could plan on arriving the day before, and then you'll be here for the birth, how does that sound?"

"Great. We didn't want to intrude, and we were hoping we could be here for the birth. But we didn't want to be pushy, you know," Mary said.

"You have no idea how much I appreciate your offer. Thank you very much."

"Have you given thought to names for the baby?" Anne asked.

"Well, if it's a girl, her name will be Hope."

"How perfect! It's a beautiful name with much meaning." Anne replied.

"And," I continued, "if it's a boy I think it will be either Stephen or Michael; we're still uncertain."

"And what about Jane, has she decided on any names?" Mary questioned.

"If it's a boy, it's Seth. And if it's a girl, it's Faith."

"Lovely names," Mary commented.

"What's Alex doing out there by the old stone foundation?" Anne asked.

"You know that old saying about the cobbler's children going barefoot?"

"Yes," Anne responded.

"Well that foundation was deteriorating. It would be a mass of rubble at some point. He's rebuilding part of it."

"Want us to do some weeding?" Anne asked out of the clear blue.

Mary looked at Anne like she had lost her mind.

"Why that would be great, thanks."

I gathered three baskets and in no time we were out there weeding. I loved to weed; feeling the initial resistance and then release as the roots surrendered their hold was somehow satisfying to me. Alex always said there was no such thing as a weed, only a plant that was growing in the wrong place at the wrong time. How could you argue with that?

We broke briefly around noon for whole grain bread and organic peanut butter and apricot jam sandwiches, and then we went back out. I got the edge trimmer, and did the edges of all the planting beds. By the time we were finished, the yard looked wonderful.

Around 2:30 or so we went in, cleaned up and got dressed. On the way to Jane and Joshua's we stopped at a wonderful wine shop and the girls bought wine for themselves and organic non-alcoholic wine for the rest of us.

We arrived at our host's at exactly 4 p.m. Jane met us at the front door and hurried us to the back door to see what Joshua had done. What we saw was a fire pit of sorts not far from the edge of the lake. There were stones piled around the edge of a circular shallow pit, with six smallish stone pillars protruding upward from the base of the pit holding a round grate. A fire was already burning nicely. Six dark green Adirondack chairs were positioned in a semi-circle around the fire, facing the lake. Quite industrious of Joshua, I had to admit. He was still out there surveying what he had accomplished.

Off to the right side, under a big old maple tree, the only tree that was down by the water's edge, was a round table with a white tablecloth, dinner plates, wine glasses, utensils, napkins and a vase full of lilacs.

"Where did he get those chairs? They must have been heavy to carry down there," Alex commented.

"They're vinyl, so they're fairly light. We had them in the garage. Joshua just hosed them off and carried them down. I really like the way they look there," Jane said. "Let's go join Joshua."

"How about I bring the wine down?" Alex asked.

"Thanks, that would be great," Jane replied.

We descended the steps off the back patio and walked down the gently sloping lawn toward Joshua.

"Wonderful job constructing the fire pit, Joshua!" I

called as I approached.

"Thanks, I don't know why I didn't do this years ago, because I think we're going to get a lot of use out of it."

"I agree," Jane said. "Especially now that it is so easy for us to walk out the back door, across the patio and down the steps. Look at how nice that patio looks from down here."

We turned just as Alex was descending the steps with wine bottles in hand. I was so impressed with his design of that curved patio and steps. It fit perfectly with the house and seemed to highlight that Palladian window in the middle of the second floor.

"We're enjoying the view of the patio from down here," Joshua remarked as Alex approached. "You outdid yourself."

"Thanks, but if anyone outdid himself, it was you constructing this fire pit. Nice work!" Alex responded.

"Okay, everyone, let's sit down and relax," Jane suggested.

We took our seats and Alex poured real wine for Mary and Anne and the non-alcoholic version for the rest of us.

"How comfortable these chairs are!" I exclaimed. "The angle of the back with the seat seems to stretch my spine. I don't think I'll be moving from here for a while!"

Anne was giving me a look, like she wanted to bring up the proposal to assist Jane after the baby was born, and I segued into that by continuing with "In fact, I think these chairs would be almost therapeutic as we get further along into our pregnancies. Speaking about getting further along into our pregnancies, my sisters have a proposal to make to you, Jane."

Anne cleared her throat and said, "Mary and I have suggested to Connie that we come back to Vermont and help out for a couple of weeks after the birth of the baby. What we'd really like to do, is for one of us to stay with Connie and the other to come and stay with you to help as much as we can. Connie thought this was a great idea. What about you, Jane? Will you accept our offer?"

I could see Jane was tearing up. She nodded and said "That would be wonderful. Although Joshua knows a great deal about antiques and furniture restoration, he doesn't know anything about babies; for that matter, neither do I. What is it that Butterfly McQueen said in 'Gone with the Wind', 'I don't know nothin' 'bout birthin' no babies…'? Well, that goes for me as well. Thank you, ladies, I accept your very kind offer."

"Well, that's a relief," Joshua sighed. "You have to take a test to get a driver's license, but there's no test to see if you're qualified to have a baby. You're not even given an instruction manual. You're just flying solo, hoping you don't make any mistakes."

"Do you know which one of you will be staying with me?" Jane asked.

"I'll be staying with you," Anne answered. "Although it was decades ago, I have had five children. I'm sure it's just like riding a bicycle, it will all come back to me."

"Thank you again, Anne. This is a real weight off my mind," Jane confessed.

"And mine as well," Joshua added.

"So, not to change the subject," I interjected, "but guess who came to visit us?"

"Don't tell me it was Russell?" Jane asked.

"Yep, he was waiting for me when I got home yesterday," Alex replied.

"You're kidding! He was there waiting for you?" Joshua asked.

"He was sitting out on the patio when I drove up. I had to say it was a little unnerving to see a stranger sitting there, but I suspected that it was probably Russell. As soon as we shook hands, I was at ease. He is a very likeable fellow," Alex affirmed.

"He is very charismatic," Mary murmured.

"Almost hypnotic," Anne sighed.

"His eyes are amazing," I just about gushed.

"Sounds like he has a fan club already," Joshua

laughed.

"Okay, tell me what he looks like," Jane pleaded.

"He's tall, nice build, rugged looking, tanned face and arms, shoulder length dark brown hair with a few strands of grey, full beard, and incredibly expressive dark, dark brown eyes," I replied.

"We had him come into the house for a few minutes and he stopped and commented on 'The Baptism of Christ' picture. He said it was one of his favorites, and that he had seen the original at the Fitzwilliam Museum in Cambridge," Alex said.

"Then he went over to your cloud picture and said it seemed to have some mystery to it, and that it was an amazing work of art. He asked who had painted it, and I said it was painted by my friend, Jane. He said to make sure I told you that he greatly admired your work."

"I like this fellow already," Jane giggled.

"Wait 'till you meet him…" Mary proclaimed.

"Am I going to meet him?" Jane asked.

"Not for a year or so, but I have a feeling that you will meet him," I said.

"He had no car. He apparently walked to the house, and he turned down my offer to drive him somewhere," Alex said. "He just walked down our driveway and disappeared from sight. He was returning to India, that's where he's been living. Guess where he lives in India?"

"Mumbai. I don't know, where?" Joshua asked.

"Meghalaya," Alex responded.

"No way," Jane protested.

"Way," I said.

"Actually, this morning I went online to see if Meghalaya actually was an Indian state, and it is," Alex added.

"You actually doubted that nice man?" Anne asked.

"I just wanted to check; it was hard to believe, wasn't it? I mean it is an amazing coincidence, isn't it?"

"And the last thing he said as he was walking across

the courtyard was a little cryptic, wasn't it?" Anne asked.

"Oh, right, I almost forgot. He asked if we knew the meaning of 'Meghalaya' and I responded, yes, it meant 'abode of the clouds'. He came back with 'clouds being the operative word in that phrase...' and with that he just disappeared down the driveway."

"Weird..." Jane said.

"Very weird," Anne and Mary added.

We all sat there sipping our drinks for a while in silence. Then Jane said "Okay, I think it's time to throw the salmon on the grill."

"I'll get it," Joshua said and got up.

"You might as well bring the two salads down because the fish will only take a few minutes to cook," Jane responded.

"Okay, Alex, your assistance is required," Joshua said, and the two of them headed toward the house.

"Ladies, you have two very nice men there," Anne remarked.

"Don't we though," Jane responded.

"It's like I said yesterday," I added "I have a feeling a great force is controlling my life, and I think that great force is controlling Jane's life as well. That force brought us together with those men for a reason."

"Absolutely!" Jane exclaimed.

The four of us women sat there in those incredibly comfortable chairs for a few minutes, sipping our drinks and chatting, when the men reappeared with salmon and salads. Joshua put the fish on the grill and refreshed everyone's drink.

"What is the exact time of the solstice?" he asked.

"7:18," Jane responded.

A short while later we were enjoying the salmon, rice salad and spinach salad.

"How did you make this spinach salad? It's delicious," I asked.

I sautéed soy bacon strips in a little olive oil, and when they were done, I removed them from the pan and sautéed chopped onion and sliced mushrooms in the same skillet. Once they were through cooking, I put them in the serving bowl and drizzled some poppy seed dressing over them. Then I put spinach leaves over the top, put chopped hard boiled eggs over that, and then sprinkled the salad with the crumbled soy bacon. I didn't toss it until just now before I served it. Easy or what?"

"Easy and delicious," I said.

After dinner we sat for a bit and took in the incredible scenery of the lake and mountains. Then we had some of the oatmeal crumble apple pie. Such a wonderful meal it had been!

It was now almost the stroke of summer solstice and we just sat back in our chairs, staring at the view.

"What a day, not a cloud in the sky," Alex commented.

"Except for that one over there," Mary proclaimed.

"Where?" Alex asked.

"It just came up over the mountain pretty much straight ahead," Mary responded.

Sure enough, in a perfectly clear blue sky without one other cloud in it, a moderate sized dark cloud had suddenly appeared over the Adirondacks straight ahead of us.

"That's strange, isn't it? Not another cloud in sight and this dark cloud suddenly appears. And what's really bizarre is that there is not a breath of wind, but that cloud is really moving quickly," Joshua remarked.

We sat in silence and watched. The cloud moved at a very fast speed to about the middle of the lake, and then it just stopped. I mean it stopped dead. How could it have moved so quickly over the mountains and then just come to a dead stop like that?

Although stationary in the sky, the formation of the cloud seemed to swirl and have a life of its own. Then suddenly there were flashes of what appeared to be multicolored lights illuminating the cloud from within. This wasn't normal lightning; the flashes were contained within the cloud and didn't extend beyond. There was no thunder. And then a slight opening appeared toward the center of the cloud and within that opening I swear I saw a metallic flash for a few seconds. The cloud swirled some more and the opening closed. The flashes of lightning stopped and the cloud started to move again. It took off at a rapid pace directly over us, toward Jane's house and was lost from sight.

"Did anyone else see that?" Anne asked.

"Yep," Alex said.

"It looked almost like some of my cloud pictures!" Jane exclaimed.

"I'm pretty sure we just saw the glory of the Lord pass by," I stated.

"AKA a spaceship," Joshua responded.

Chapter 6 – The Day After

It was overcast the next morning. I was surprised that I had slept so soundly, considering the events of the prior evening.

When I reached the kitchen, Alex and Anne were seated at the table, sipping coffee.

"Good morning," Anne greeted. "Sleep well?"

"Yes, surprisingly so. How about you?"

"Like a log," Anne replied. "Alex and I were just talking about last night. I am so glad I was there to see that. And the funny thing is, I had no fear. I felt almost serene. It seemed to me that they came to assure us."

"Assure us about what?" Mary asked as she came around the corner.

"Assure us that we were on the right path. That everything was proceeding as it should. That they were watching over us and guiding us. And I felt what I could only describe as an overwhelming sense of love; love emanating from them toward us and love emanating within me outward. I felt there was absolutely nothing to fear. Like Connie says 'there is a great force controlling my life…' Now I know that there is a great force controlling all of our lives. I have a tremendous sense of well-being. All is right with the world."

"I don't think I could have expressed that as eloquently as you did," Mary said. "But you succinctly described how I feel as well."

"I think Anne described what we are all feeling," Alex

added.

"Most definitely," I concurred.

Mary poured herself a cup of coffee and joined Anne and Alex at the table.

"How about an asparagus and Gruyere cheese frittata this morning for a change?" I asked.

"Sounds great," Alex answered. "I'll take a walk to the mailbox while you're getting that together."

He took another sip of his coffee, and headed toward the front door.

"You know what they say about truth being stranger than fiction?" Mary asked. "Well if our current experience isn't confirmation of that statement, I don't know what is."

"If you wrote a book about it, no one would believe it was non-fiction," Anne retorted. "It would make a good science fiction novel, though."

I took a sip of my tea and said "If someone had told me this story a year ago, I honestly don't think I would have believed it. Would you?"

"Probably not," Mary replied.

The oven was hot enough and I put the frittata in to bake.

I sat down at the table with the girls and we started to discuss their next visit, when Alex came back in with mail in hand. He had a peculiar look on his face.

"Is something the matter?" I asked.

"No, not really," he said as he put the mail on the table, reached into his shirt pocket and took out a folded piece of paper.

"I found this in the mailbox. Russell left it there. It says ''Of' is the other operative word. See you next year. Russell.' What do you make of that?"

"Let me look at that," I said.

He handed me the note.

"What beautiful penmanship he has," I commented. "So fluid, so strong…"

"Let me see," Mary requested.

I handed her the note and Anne leaned over to look at it too.

"Lovely…" Mary murmured.

"So what do you think about that 'of' being the other operative word comment?" Alex asked.

"Well, the phrase is 'abode of the clouds'. 'Clouds' is an operative word, and as we've just learned, so is 'of'. I can understand 'clouds' being an operative word, but 'of' is a preposition. I don't get what he means," I pondered.

"Remember the other day when I asked you to tell me again what 'Meghalaya' meant?" Mary asked.

"Yes."

"And you said it meant 'abode of the clouds'? Well I thought to myself that it would make more sense if it were 'abode in the clouds', because the house was located high up on a hill and I was sure clouds would settle on this high elevation from time to time. So the house would literally be 'in' the clouds not 'of' the clouds. Do you follow?"

"I do. So what does 'of the clouds' mean?" I asked.

"I think it's time to get my trusty old dictionary out," Alex announced

He poured himself a little more coffee, took a sip, walked over to the bookcase and came back to the table with the dictionary.

"Okay, let's look at 'in' first. A few seconds later he was reading 'a function word indicating inclusion, location or position within limits'."

"Right, so my thought that the phrase 'in the clouds' was correct, as I was thinking the house was located or positioned within the clouds," Mary said.

"I follow what you're saying; it makes perfect sense," Alex said. "Now let's look at 'of'."

He flipped the pages back to the 'O' section, located 'of' and read, "function word indicating belonging or a possessive relationship".

"Belonging or possessive relationship, what the heck does that mean," I asked. "The house belongs to the clouds?"

"Oh, I know…" Anne murmured.

We all turned to her expectantly.

"I don't know why we didn't think of this before, but you know what is enveloped in those clouds?" Anne asked. "Spaceships! And the word 'clouds' could be used in this phrase as a substitute for 'spaceships'. I think it means that this house, or this property, belongs to the spaceships, or the beings in the spaceships."

We stared at her speechless. It seemed we were speechless a lot lately.

It made perfect sense, though. At least as much sense as anything else. This was home to the spaceships, to the extraterrestrials. It was their abode.

"Do me a favor, Alex," I asked, "could you please look up the definition of 'abode'? You know how we assume we know the meaning of a word, and then when we look it up, it has alternate meanings that we didn't consider."

"I know exactly what you mean," he reassured and started flipping back to the 'A' section.

I could smell that the frittata was done, and I took the old cast iron skillet out of the oven and put it on a wooden cutting board on the table. In a few minutes it would be cool enough to be served.

"This looks fantastic, Connie," Mary declared. "Someday, when you have lots of spare time, I'd really appreciate it if you'd put all of your recipes down in writing for me."

"I have a feeling it's going to be a long, long while before I have free time," I responded.

"Okay, ready? 'Abode', the first definition indicates that it is now obsolete, but it's 'wait, delay'; the second is 'a temporary stay, sojourn' and the third is 'the place where one abides, home'.

"We assumed that it meant home," Anne said.

"But it could mean this is where they waited or temporarily stayed," I hypothesized. "That dictionary is the most valuable book in this house. Here we thought 'abode of the clouds' meant that this house was literally in the clouds, and instead it meant where the spaceships sojourn or temporarily stay."

"What puzzles me is Russell," Alex commented. "He knew. He told us that 'cloud' and 'of' were the key words in that phrase. He knew exactly what that meant. He knew it meant extraterrestrial spacecraft. And most likely he anticipated that we'd figure out the 'abode' part as well."

"You're correct about Russell. But have you thought about Gene and Hilda?" I asked.

"What do you mean?" Mary inquired.

"Gene and Hilda called this spot 'Meghalaya'. They named it. They must have known about the cloud and spaceship connection as well."

"Wow!" Anne exclaimed.

"And Russell is now living in another Meghalaya. Is it possible that the other Meghalaya is also an 'abode of the clouds'…in the biblical sense?" I asked.

"A little humor there, Connie? In the biblical sense?" Alex laughed.

"Yes, a feeble attempt. But the cloud-spaceship connection did originate in the bible, so I thought it was appropriate. Anyhow, to summarize, Gene, Hilda and Russell were/are all somehow connected with extraterrestrials. We were drawn to this house for some strange reason and knew without a doubt that this is where we belonged. I opened the bible one morning and read the words 'in our image' in Genesis, started a blog, and now I'm pregnant with a little ET baby, as are 23 other women around the globe. Does that pretty much sum up the situation?"

"You forgot one thing," Anne reminded. "Russell came back, and Russell said he will come back again in a year or so. Russell is still very much a part of this story, at least that's my guess."

"And I think we'll just have to wait for this story to be continued," Mary said.

Chapter 7 – Six Month Checkup

Anne and Mary left the next morning. And now the wait began.

I spent much of the summer outside working in the yard. I continued to be energized with no ill effects from the pregnancy.

Alex supervised his crew on several landscape jobs in various parts of the state, but he still had time to work on shoring up part of the stone foundation out back. Late one afternoon he came into the kitchen holding what appeared to be a green stone.

"What's that?" I asked.

"I found it buried out back near the stone foundation. You're the gem expert here; what is this?"

I took it and rinsed it off with water and went over to the window and held it up to the light. It was a beautiful glowing emerald green translucent stone. It was roughly the size and shape of an egg and had a rough exterior that looked like tiny little feathers jutting out all over it. I knew what it most likely was.

"I think it's a tektite. Actually, I think it's Moldavite."

"Moldavite? Don't you have a couple Moldavite rings?"

"Actually, I have quite a few pieces of Moldavite jewelry. I've got one of the rings on now." I extended my hand to show him a marquis shaped Moldavite ring.

"But the quality of this stone that you dug up in the

backyard far exceeds the quality of the stone in my ring. Look how the Moldavite in my ring is more of a darker grey green color, and it is not as translucent? It looks to me that what you have found is museum quality. It is very rare and I think they call this color poison green. It is only found in the Czech Republic. How did it get here, buried in our backyard?"

"I miss your sisters," Alex said.

"That's nice, but why are you saying that now?"

"Because they'd probably shout in unison 'weird...'.'"

"You're right about that. But this is truly a mystery, as someone had to have brought this stone here. It doesn't occur in this area. If my memory serves me correctly, Moldavite is believed to have been formed 15 million years ago in the Moldau River Valley region of what is now the Czech Republic. Supposedly it was created by a fusion upon impact of a meteor or some substance from space with earth."

"You're saying this stone was created by something falling from outer space?"

"Yes, that is my understanding."

"I don't know why I continue to be amazed by what we seem to uncover," he sighed. With that he walked outside and headed toward the stone foundation.

Later that afternoon, I called Anne to tell her what we had discovered, and Mary was with her. Alex had just walked back into the house and I called him over to the phone and told him my sisters wanted to talk to him. He picked up the receiver and they chimed in unison, "Weird..." He responded, "Thanks, I needed that."

Jane came over the next day for lunch. We were both now almost six months pregnant and we were definitely showing. Joshua was out doing appraisals, so he didn't join us. I showed Jane the Moldavite. She had never seen or heard of Moldavite before. I filled her in on the background. She, too, was taken with the fact that it was created by something falling from the skies.

"Don't you think you should put it back outside where

it came from? There must have been some reason it was out there in the yard."

"You've got a point; maybe we should."

"Have you ever explored all of your property?

"I've got twenty acres here, and it's all on the side of a hill. I've walked the cleared area, and the area immediately adjoining the cleared area, but I haven't walked all of it."

"Don't you think it would be a good idea to survey the area?"

"Okay, let's take a walk after lunch."

Alex was away at a job site, so it was just the two of us having lunch. We had egg salad sandwiches with tomato and sprouts on pumpernickel bread. After that we headed off across the yard toward the edge of the woods, depositing the Moldavite on the stone foundation as we passed by.

The property sloped down to the right, toward the lake. We both had walking sticks with us. There was no path through the woods, so the going was extremely slow. We walked for about a quarter of an hour and reached a clearing. The view toward the lake was stupendous. I wondered why there would be a clearing in that location. When I say clearing, I mean there were no trees in this area. There was brush and some shrubs, but no tall trees. It appeared that someone had kept this area open and cleared on purpose in years past. Jane and I found a large rock just to the north of the clearing and sat down to rest.

"This area was kept cleared by someone," I observed.

"Yes, it appears that way."

"It must have been Gene and Hilda. Who else would have done it?

"Why do you think they maintained this area?"

"I have no idea. There's no evidence that they had farm animals other than their two horses, and it's not easily accessible from the house. This area isn't even visible from the house as it's blocked by tall trees."

We got up off the rock with the intention of continuing

further into the woods at the other side, when I spotted something further up on the east side of the clearing. I pointed it out to Jane.

"It looks like it's a cave of some sort," she said. "Let's take a look."

We walked toward the far side of the clearing, which was the southeastern side, and there in the side of the hill was a cave. It wasn't just a natural cave; it appeared to be a manmade chamber. The opening was about 8 feet high and 8 feet wide and it was built into a mound on the hillside. There was a single large stone that crossed the entire top of the opening, with similar large stones holding up the sides. The slope of the mound seemed to have been cut away for a distance of several feet on either side of the entrance, and covered with stone that looked almost like a stone retaining wall on both sides of the entrance.

Jane and I cautiously approached the opening and peered in. The sun was low enough in the western sky to illuminate some of the interior. I could see there were stone walls and a massive stone ceiling.

"I don't think we should go in there," Jane cautioned.

"Believe me, I have absolutely no intention of going in there," I responded.

"What do you think it is, a root cellar?"

"Maybe, or perhaps it's a burial chamber of some sort?"

"Could be. I think the guys should take a look at this."

That was the last thing I remembered before I woke up on the ground. I was laying flat on my back and when I opened my eyes, I was looking at the sky. What happened? How did I get here?

I heard Jane say, "Connie"?

I turned my head, and there she was lying right next to me.

"Why are we lying down? The last thing I remember was you saying that the guys should come take a look at that cave thing and the next thing I know we're laying side by side on the ground."

I sat up. I felt a little disoriented, but fine.

Jane sat up.

"Are you okay?" I asked.

"I guess so."

We both got to our feet and I realized the sun would be setting soon.

"It's late," I gasped. "It's got to be around 6 o'clock."

Jane looked at her watch and said "6:06".

"We left the house no later than 1:30, and it took us about a quarter of an hour to reach this spot. We've lost over 4 hours. Alex must be a basket case by now wondering where we are."

We took off toward the house. The good thing was that it was simple to tell we were headed in the right direction, as the lake and setting sun were now toward our left. Jane and I discussed our experience on the way back and the missing time. Obviously we must have been taken by the extraterrestrials.

"I'm thinking that it was just a little medical checkup to make sure everything is going okay, don't you agree?" Jane asked.

"Right, it was our routine six month checkup."

"Funny, I never even saw the cloud coming."

We both felt really good now, like we were energized, almost euphoric. We joked and laughed all the way back. I could see through the trees that we were almost to my backyard. I reached inside my pants' pocket to grab the house key, just in case I got lucky and Alex wasn't home yet. I felt a tiny little piece of paper in there. I pulled it out and read 'Inspected by No. 443' and started to laugh.

Jane looked over at me and I showed her the paper. She started to laugh. We emerged from the woods laughing like two lunatics. The laughing stopped abruptly, however, when I saw Alex running toward us and the look on his face.

"Where the hell have you two been? I was just about to call the police," he shouted.

"Well, we were talking about finding the Moldavite in the yard, and then we thought it might be a good idea to explore more of the yard, and I had never been in the area further back in the property, so we went exploring..." I rambled on.

Just then I could see Joshua come around the corner of the house and start running toward us. He reached Jane and grabbed her in a big bear hug.

"The two of you went exploring in the woods? Are you crazy? You're six months pregnant and you're traipsing through the woods! You could have been killed! You could have fallen into an old well! You could have been bitten by a snake!"

"Alex, calm down," Joshua urged. "The important thing is that they're fine."

He was still fuming when I said, "The only thing that happened was that we found a very strange manmade cave back there, and then we were abducted."

Jane just burst out laughing, and I really had to control myself in order to keep a straight face.

"Are you serious?" Alex asked.

"We sure are," Jane said, still giggling a little.

"Let's go inside and sit down," Alex muttered.

When we got inside, I made some tea for Jane and me, and Alex and Joshua were splurging on some non-alcoholic beer. I'm sure if we had the real thing, they would have been drinking that.

"So tell me exactly what happened," Alex demanded.

"Okay," I started, "at around 1:30 we walked straight back into the woods, and walked for approximately a quarter of an hour. At that point we reached a clearing. It was good sized, maybe like the size of a football field. We saw something to the left side that looked like a cave entrance. We went over to take a closer look and what we saw appeared to be a manmade chamber of sorts built into a mound that was on the side of the hill. The opening was about 8 feet high and wide. The lintel stone was one really large stone, as were the two side supporting stones. We could see inside to some extent as the afternoon sun was providing light. The walls were also made of stone and the ceiling was one huge flat stone. We didn't attempt to go inside as we thought it would be a good idea for you guys to check it out."

"And the next thing we knew," Jane divulged, "we were flat on our backs on the ground. I looked at my watch and it said it was 6:06. We hurried to get back. I think we both felt strangely invigorated…"

"Sure, we had a four hour nap," I giggled. I could tell Jane was trying to keep a serious tone, so I shut up.

"It's hard to explain," Jane continued, "but we were in a euphoric state. We didn't have any ill effects from what we assumed to be a little checkup by our extraterrestrial friends. We chatted and joked all the way back."

"And then I felt a little note in my pocket," I revealed.

"A note? What did it say?" Alex asked.

I pulled that little piece of paper out of my pocket and read out loud, "Inspected by No. 443."

Joshua almost choked on his make-believe beer, and started to laugh. Even Alex had a smile on his face.

Chapter 8 – Portal to Other Dimensions

The next morning Jane and Joshua were over bright and early to go exploring with us. The men carried flashlights, knives and rope. I didn't know what the rope and the knives were for, and I didn't ask. No point in antagonizing them so early in the day; I was sure there would be time for that later.

We walked straight back into the woods and kept on walking until we reached the clearing. I think Alex thought I had exaggerated about the size of the clearing, but I hadn't. He was amazed.

"I guess you never looked at this property on Google Earth," Joshua chuckled.

"No, but I will when I get back. I want to see if there are any other surprises," he responded.

"The cave is over there," I said and pointed to the left side.

We made our way over to the cave entrance and I could tell the guys were impressed.

"This is no root cellar," Alex declared.

It was a good thing that we had brought flashlights with us, as the morning sun was now on the other side of the mountain and the interior was just a gaping dark hole. Alex approached the entry first, turned on his flashlight and looked around. Joshua joined him with his flashlight.

"These are massive slabs of shale in here," Alex marveled. "It's amazing."

They started to walk further in, and Jane and I

followed. We walked back for about thirty feet and then the chamber turned to the right. We had to duck as we entered that side room because there was another huge lintel stone over the opening to that area. This chamber was a little shorter, about twenty feet long. At the far end up against the back wall, there was a whitish colored large rectangular slab of stone that was set up on two other smaller rectangular stones; it looked almost like a low table or a wide bench. It was kind of eerie because it was almost luminescent in the blackness of the cave.

"I'm starting to feel a little woozy," Joshua groaned, "I have to get out of here."

We turned and made a quick retreat out of there. Joshua was very pale when we got outside and he sat down on the ground.

"I thought I was going to pass out," he said. "It came on so suddenly."

"That bench was bizarre." Alex mused. "I think it was limestone. You were okay up until we reached that bench, weren't you?" he asked Joshua.

"Yes, it was at the point that I started to look at it that it seemed to almost dance or float before my eyes, and I got somewhat disoriented and felt faint."

"Well, as I said, that is no root cellar. I have heard that there are megalithic sites in Vermont, but have never seen them. However, I know I just saw one now."

The color was returning to Joshua's face. "Where were you girls when you woke up? Were you here near the entrance to the cave?" he asked.

"No," Jane answered. "We were just about directly in the middle of this clearing."

"Right, and the last thing that we remembered before we woke up was that we were standing directly in front of the opening to the cave saying that we had to bring you guys to see it," I added.

"Let's go walk the perimeter of the clearing," Alex suggested to Joshua.

"We'll go sit down on that big rock over there while you explore," I said.

The guys took off, and Jane and I sat down to rest.

"You know, we were lucky there wasn't any wild animal in there," Jane remarked.

"That crossed my mind, too."

"You don't by chance know anything about portals to other dimensions, do you," Jane asked.

"Ah…no, should I?"

"This cave might be a portal to another dimension."

"Have you been watching the Sci Fi Channel again?"

"I'm serious! You're making fun of portals to other dimensions just like some people would make fun of extraterrestrials and UFO's."

"I'm sorry. You're absolutely right."

"It's just something to consider," Jane insisted.

We sat there in silence watching the guys make their way around the property. They stopped for a while over on the opposite side looking at some trees, and finally made their way back to us.

"What were you looking at over on the other side?" I asked.

"There's a yellow birch over there with some branches that looked singed," Alex advised. "Let's head back."

We were almost back to our house when Joshua said "Do you think it could possibly be some sort of portal to another dimension?"

I turned and looked at Jane, and she raised her eyebrows and shrugged, like that was a perfectly sensible question.

To my surprise, Alex agreed, "It could well be. I'm going to search megaliths in Vermont and see if that gives us any clues. I'll also do a search on vortexes and ley lines and while I'm at it, I'll look up portals to other dimensions."

We reached the house, and Alex and Joshua went immediately to the computer.

I put on the kettle for some tea.

"I want to apologize again for making fun of that portal to another dimension suggestion," I said. "I usually have a very open mind; I don't know what got into me."

"And I'm not usually that sensitive," Jane remarked. "Maybe our hormones are out of whack."

"Could well be. Maybe the extraterrestrials made some adjustments to them yesterday."

"Right, we were laughing uncontrollably yesterday, and today we're picking fights with each other."

"Damn those extraterrestrials!"

We sat down and sipped our tea, and we were back to our old comfortable relationship with each other.

Alex was commenting on some site he had come across about Vermont megaliths being built by the Celts.

"Are you saying the Celts built these megalith sights in Vermont?" I asked.

"That is what I'm seeing. They're calling them the Iberian Celts."

"Do you remember what we uncovered during our research about Rh negative blood?" I asked. "Remember the Hyperboreans? Supposedly they interbred with extraterrestrials and after time produced the Celts, and the Celts spread out producing the Scots, Irish, Basque, Spanish, Scandinavians, Icelanders and the Portuguese. All of these people were of Celtic origin. And all of these nationalities have one common genetic trait, a large percentage of Rh negative blood."

"So there might be a connection with the creators of that cave or chamber with Rh negative blood?" Joshua questioned.

"Could be," Alex responded. "Look, right here in South Woodstock is a fairly well known megalithic site called Calendar II. It says that the chamber is located over an underground water source and an energy ley line power center."

"Look up 'ley lines in Vermont' and see if you find

anything," Joshua suggested.

After several minutes with no luck, Alex changed the search to 'ley lines in New England' and found a site that had a drawing of the lines going across the six New England states.

"That looks to me like there are two intersecting lines right over this area," Joshua noted.

"It does, doesn't it?" Alex responded.

"Okay, let's look up 'inter-dimensional portals' next," Joshua said.

Alex entered the search and as I looked over his shoulder, I was amazed at the amount of results he got.

"This one says that vortexes are found along intersecting ley lines and at times open for inter-dimensional passages. These 'portals' are believed to provide capability to travel between this dimension and other dimensions as well as planetary systems within our dimension, and outside our solar system. It continues that ley lines are straight fault lines in the earth's tectonic plates through which magnetic energy is released."

"So it is possible that there is some sort of portal out back then," Jane theorized.

"If those lines do intersect on this property, it is possible," Alex responded. "I think we should go back out there and take another look."

We had a bite of lunch and headed out again. The sun had now shifted to the west and was providing some natural illumination within the chamber.

"This time I think I should go in with Alex. You two stay outside and we'll call if we need any help," I said.

Joshua started to protest, but Alex said he thought it was a good idea that Joshua not accompany us on our trip back in.

I took Joshua's flashlight and followed Alex into the chamber. We reached the right hand turn and flashed the beams of light at the far wall with the bench positioned in front of it. I have to say it was an eerie sight.

We walked further into the chamber and Alex started to examine the stone from which the bench was constructed.

"This is not limestone," he stated. "This is a pale blue marble. It is incredible, isn't it?"

"Do you think that came from somewhere around here?"

"I don't know."

Alex was carefully going over every inch of the bench, and startled me when he said, "Look, there's something carved on the right support stone. Beam your flashlight down here, will you?"

Sure enough, carved into the side of one of the support stones was a symbol that was composed of three spirals that were interconnected. It looked as if the center portion of two of the spirals was very faint as if they had not been completed. Alex reached into his pocket, took out a piece of paper and a pencil and did a rubbing of the carved area.

"You just happened to have a blank piece of paper and a pencil?" I asked.

"You know I'm an old eagle scout and I'm always prepared," he chuckled.

He continued to look at the rest of the bench, but did not find anything else remarkable. We traced our steps back through the chamber and out into daylight.

"Gee, it got awfully foggy all of a sudden," I commented.

"Where are Jane and Joshua?" Alex asked.

"Over there by the edge of the clearing where we came in," I answered.

"What are they doing over there?" Alex asked, and we headed off in their direction. They seemed to be agitated.

"What's wrong?" Alex asked.

"Turn around and look at the cave," Joshua requested.

We turned and there was a cloud of sorts sitting outside the entrance to the chamber. I guess it was more of a haze than a cloud; we had thought it was fog. The rest of the atmosphere was clear and bright.

"We were waiting for you right outside the opening when we saw this haze start to form in the middle of the field," Jane reported. "We thought it was extremely unusual. It was getting denser and more compact. Then it started moving toward us, toward the cave opening. It scared the hell out of us and we took off toward the edge of the clearing."

"Look, it's starting to dissipate!" Joshua exclaimed.

Sure enough, within a few seconds it was gone.

"Weird," I whispered.

On the way back Alex was telling Jane and Joshua about the blue marble, the carving and the rubbing he had made.

"Could I see the rubbing?" Joshua asked.

Alex pulled the piece of paper out of his pocket and handed it to Joshua.

Joshua looked at it and immediately advised, "It's Celtic. It appears to be a triskele. Did you miss rubbing part of it? There's a section at the center of two of the spirals that's missing."

"No, that's all there was. It is exactly as it appears on the paper. You know, you never cease to amaze me," Alex declared.

"What do you mean?"

"There is so much knowledge inside that head of yours; amazing tidbits of information. I was first impressed that day you were telling us about the petroglyphs in New Mexico and the six fingered giants that chased the buffalo. And now, you look at this rubbing and know it is Celtic and even the name of the symbol."

"Don't be fooled. It's just a veneer of knowledge; it doesn't go too deep," Joshua laughed.

When we got back to the house, Alex did a search on 'triskele'. He found various interpretations of the meaning of the symbol which he read out loud to us.

"This site says that the triskele tells a story of forward

motion in the endeavor to reach understanding of the otherworld, the mortal world and the celestial world. And another site says that it signifies personal growth, human development and spiritual expansion."

"That sounds appropriate for the path that we seemingly are on." I affirmed.

"Now I'm going to do a search on blue marble in Vermont," Alex said.

In no time at all he found a site that said a light blue marble had been mined by the Rutland-Florence Company in Florence, Vermont.

"That's just south of here a bit," Joshua noted.

"It's all very interesting," I interjected, "but I'm not sure what this cave or chamber has to do with anything, other than the fact that we were zapped up by our celestial friends while standing outside the entrance and then deposited back in that clearing."

"Remember that portals are believed to provide the capability to travel from within this dimension and other dimensions as well as within our solar system and without? It is possible that the spaceships that we see in the sky are coming from another dimension. Maybe they are using your chamber out back as a portal from another dimension. Gene and Hilda must have named this place 'Meghalaya' for a good reason, and perhaps that reason was that spaceships did frequent this spot, cloaked in clouds of course."

"I'm sure they didn't want the neighbors complaining about this being a rest stop for spaceships. But if a cloud settled on the property every now and then, no big deal, right?" Alex proposed.

"If that chamber was really constructed by the Celts, then they, as their ancestors before them, had extraterrestrial blood in them. They had Rh negative blood in them, just as you and Jane. They had a reason for travelling to this spot and constructing that chamber here. I can't believe this is just synchronicity at work," Joshua surmised.

"So in all the years that we've lived here, how come we haven't seen spacecraft?" I asked.

"Even you mentioned that you can't see that big open field out back because of the height of the trees in the woods. And if they were cloaked within a cloud, you couldn't see them, could you?" Jane responded. "And why are you so incredulous about all of this anyway? You have a little extraterrestrial baby growing inside you, did you forget?"

That comment got everyone laughing.

Chapter 9 – Home Delivery

We spent the next three months pondering the chamber out back situation, but we experienced no epiphanies.

Jane and I continued to do incredibly well for a couple of old pregnant women and we were both on track for home deliveries. All of our comradettes around the world were also doing well. But we were ready; we were more than ready, to get on with the next phase of this odyssey.

Alex transformed one of the bedrooms into a nursery. We decided on a moon and stars motif, which we thought was extremely appropriate. The bedding and accessories had all colors of blue, pink, yellow and green. We decided to paint the walls a very pale green, which was called "crinoline" and the ceiling a light shade of blue called "misty".

It was no surprise to anyone that Jane decided to go with a cloud theme. Fairly early into her pregnancy she started painting the designated nursery room with clouds, both the walls and ceiling. She located interior paint that was made from plant resins and mineral pigments and completely non-toxic. The paint that we used was from this same manufacturer and the quality was exceptional.

Joshua had located antique rocking cradles for both infants and he had lovingly and beautifully restored them.

Just before Thanksgiving I decorated the house, both inside and out, with all of the Christmas decorations.

My sisters returned on December 19th, two days before the winter solstice. We decided that it would make more sense for them to arrive two days before the anticipated arrival date. That way I would be able to have the pleasure of Anne's company for one night before she headed off to Jane's the following day.

I was watching out the window and saw Alex drive up with my sisters. I opened the front door and stood sideways, so they could get a good profile shot. They hadn't seen me in six months and the physical change in me was dramatic. I looked like I was ready to explode at any moment. Actually, I felt like I could explode at any moment.

"Connie, you've changed!" Anne shouted as they approached.

We all exchanged hugs and kisses and I ushered them into the house and out of the cold. Alex was bringing in their luggage.

I poured them some wine and we sat in front of the fire in the living room.

"Remember when we were here in June and we were enthralled by that singed tree out back?" Mary questioned. "Remember how I said that there was real physical evidence of a spaceship being in your backyard, and how amazing that was? Even though you had been impregnated by extraterrestrials at that point, you didn't look pregnant at the time. I was more impressed by that singed tree than I was by your condition. Now, however, I'm blown away by the reality of what has and is happening to you."

"I wonder what this baby is going to look like," Anne said.

"You mean gray or green?" Alex wondered.

"What I mean is we don't know if Connie is the actual genetic mother of the baby or solely a gestational carrier, do we? They could have stimulated the growth of an ovum within Connie and then fertilized it, or they could have implanted an embryo. I'm just wondering if there will be any of Connie in the child."

"Actually, I did have an amniocentesis test a few

months back. The baby is Rh negative and the major blood group was identified as being A, which is my blood group, so my belief is that I am the genetic mother," I stated.

"But they were unable to identify the minor blood group, so most likely the baby has a rare blood type of some sort," Alex added.

"Actually, all of my fellow comradettes also had amniocentesis and the tests showed that each of the fetuses were Rh negative, with the major blood group corresponding to the mother, and with the minor blood group being unidentifiable. So my guess is that it will be confirmed that these children all have a rare blood type and most likely they will all match with each other."

"Right, unless some galactic federation is involved in these extraterrestrial impregnations, and a representative of different individual member galaxies is the father of each of these children. So you would have 24 different minor blood groups. It would be kind of like a human/ET sampler pack," Alex joked.

"Hmmm, I never thought of that," I conceded.

"I never knew there were minor blood groups," Mary announced. "I thought if your blood type was A or B or O or AB, then that was it. Of course the Rh positive/negative factor would also come in to play."

"I never realized it either. Once we got the results back from the amniocentesis test, we did some searching on the internet on the subject. We found that there are over 200 minor blood groups and these are considered rare. All of these blood groups are minor to one of the four major groups, except for the Bombay blood group," I responded.

"The Bombay blood group is extremely rare," Alex added. "It is estimated only a few thousand people in the entire world have it. I think I read it occurs in only 1 out of 250,000 people. At first they thought it was a minor group to the O major blood group, but upon further testing they found it was not."

"How do these rare blood groups form? What is their origin?" Anne asked.

"Ah, that is the question! I don't think anyone has a good answer to that one," Alex answered. There are a lot of mysteries in life. The origin of Rh negative blood is one of them."

"This might sound like a dumb question, but can they use DNA to do maternity testing," Mary questioned.

"Yes, they can, but I don't think I'll go that route," I responded. "As far as I'm concerned, I'm the mother of this child."

"So do you know the sex of the baby?" Anne asked.

"I decided I didn't want to know. I'd rather be surprised. Call me old fashioned."

"In any case, we don't have too long to wait before we find out," Alex said.

"Does Jennifer know we are here?" Mary asked.

"Yes, actually I was going to keep it a secret and surprise you but what the hell; she's joining us on Christmas Eve. By then she should have a half sister."

"Great! We haven't seen her in a couple of years," Mary exclaimed.

"Right, we visited her in London two years ago at Christmas," Anne said. "We had such a fantastic time with her. She showed us a London that we never saw before."

"Actually, she also showed us a whole lot of England that we never saw before," Mary added.

"Yes, remember driving through that beautiful countryside looking at crop circles? She really was fascinated by them."

"She still is," I affirmed. "Crop circles and megaliths are her passion. She certainly is in the right country to find both. I remember the first time we went to London. It was for the Live Aid concert in 1985. She was only 15 then and crazy about Paul McCartney. I guess she got that from me, as he was my favorite Beatle. What a wonderful time we had. We went back to England several times after that, and I could see her falling in love with the country more and more with each trip. I'm glad she's making a living doing something she enjoys in such a special place."

"How is her graphic design company doing?" Mary asked.

"Great. She's got about a dozen people working for her now, including several really top notch designers, which allows her to take some time off now and then. She was a one woman show back when she started out and she couldn't afford to take holidays. I'm so glad that all of that hard work paid off."

"Not to change the subject, but have your heard anything else from Russell?" Anne asked.

"No, but I couldn't help but think of him when we discovered that chamber out back."

"Why? What do you mean?" Mary asked.

"I have a feeling that he knows the history of the chamber and its secrets," I responded. "I hope you ladies will excuse me; I've got to go put the soup on a low heat. I'll be right back."

"I'll do that, Connie. You sit," Alex directed.

"Thank you. Make sure you put on a low heat; it's very thick."

"What kind of soup is it?" Mary asked.

"Lentil and wild rice with little soy sausage meatballs."

"Where do you come up with these recipes? That sounds wonderful!" Anne exclaimed.

"Oh, I just made it up. I never tried it before, so we'll see how it is."

Alex came back with a glass of pale pink liquid in one hand and the wine bottle in the other hand.

"For you," he said, and handed me the glass.

"What is it?"

"Mineral water with a splash of cranberry juice and a wedge of lime."

"Ooh, how delightful! Thank you."

He refilled Anne and Mary's wine glasses and sat down.

"It was outside the chamber that you and Jane were picked up and deposited for your six month check up, right?" Mary asked.

"Right."

"And you think there is some connection between that chamber and the beings in the spaceship? Like it's a portal that they access to enter into this dimension," Mary speculated.

"There is some connection with this property and the extraterrestrials, and that chamber could be the answer," I responded.

"How do you know they're extraterrestrials?" Mary questioned.

"What do you mean?" Alex asked.

"You're assuming that they are from outside of this planet; that they're from somewhere out there in the cosmos."

"Do you have another suggestion as to their origin?" I asked.

"Did you ever consider that they might be intraterrestrial instead of extraterrestrial?

"What?" Alex asked.

"I've been reading about the hollow earth and Agartha, the city that is said to reside at the earth's core. It was quite a popular theory in the late 1800's and early 1900's."

"I do remember seeing that movie 'Voyage to the Center of the Earth'. I recall it was adapted from the novel by Jules Verne. But I thought that was merely science fiction," I responded.

"There were some who considered it to be real; take Admiral Byrd for instance. He flew over the North Pole in 1926 and recorded that he saw lakes, rivers, vegetation, animal life and found a thriving civilization living there. When he was a much older man, he led an expedition to the South Pole and claims to have penetrated 2,300 miles into the center of the earth! It could be that at least some of the UFO's that we see on the surface of this planet actually originate from within it. In addition to the two openings at the North and South Pole, there are others scattered around the earth. Mount Shasta in California and Mammoth Cave in Kentucky are two of them. Others are located at various locations in South and Central America, India, Italy, the Gobi Desert in Mongolia and of course, no big surprise, at the Great Pyramid of Giza."

"Well, I have to give you credit! You're researching and open to new ideas. Good for you! And you know what? Absolutely anything is possible. I assumed that the beings that are in contact with us are from the celestial realms, but I could be wrong about that. They could be from another dimension and no set place at all. I don't know." I admitted.

"So those openings to the center of the Earth, I guess you could consider them portals, right?" Alex questioned.

"I would think so," Mary answered.

"And you're thinking the chamber out back might be a portal to Agartha?" I asked.

"Makes as much sense as anything else," Alex responded.

"Not to change subjects again, but how's Jane doing?" Anne inquired.

"Good! Actually all 24 of us old pregnant ladies are doing extremely well. But then again, that's not unusual, as a great force is controlling us. That's why I think I'm so relaxed about this entire experience. We asked, we received, and all is going as planned."

We moved into the kitchen and continued to chat while we had soup and homemade bread. We played gin for a short while after dinner, but we were all exhausted and called it an early night. I think we were tired mostly from anticipation of what was to come.

The next morning I awoke early and went downstairs to set up the coffee pot, but Alex had it ready to go.

"Thanks for setting the pot up; you might as well turn

it on as I'm sure they'll be down here in no time."

Alex pushed the "on" switch and almost instantaneously the phone rang.

I answered and it was Joshua. He said that Jane had just gone into labor. The midwife was on her way over. He said he'd keep me advised as to what was happening.

I told him Anne would be there as soon as possible and with that, we said our goodbyes.

Just then Anne and Mary came around the corner. I told them that Jane had gone into labor. Anne poured herself a cup of coffee and said she was ready to head on over to Jane's as soon as she got dressed. She took a couple of sips, and headed upstairs, with coffee cup in hand.

"How do you feel, Connie?" Mary asked.

"Great. I slept wonderfully."

"How about you, Alex?' Mary inquired.

"Oh, I had that dragon dream again, they were zooming out of the sky and people were running and screaming to get away from them."

"This is a reoccurring dream?"

"I've had it before, but I associated it with eating sauerkraut. I haven't had sauerkraut in a while, however."

Anne came back downstairs dressed and ready to go. She refilled her coffee cup and took a few more sips.

"I have a travel mug, why don't you take it with you? Actually, I have two travel mugs, one for you and one for Alex."

I got the mugs out and filled them with coffee. I put two raisin bran muffins in a bag for them to eat en route.

Alex went upstairs and got Anne's bag and together they headed out to Jane's.

No sooner had they left when I went into labor. One minute I was fine and then wham, it began with a vengeance. I called Cheryl, my midwife, who said she'd be right over.

Almost two hours later I could hear Alex return. He ran up the stairs to find me with baby in arms. Mary and

Cheryl were sitting on either side of me.

He stood in the doorway with a look of shock on his face. "How did that happen so fast? Are you okay? Is the baby okay?"

"I went into labor as soon as you left. Everything happened so fast. Cheryl got here just in time. But there was no stopping little Hope from making an appearance."

"Hope?"

"Yes, it's a girl."

Just then the phone rang. Alex answered it and I could hear him say "That's wonderful news, Joshua. What a relief, huh? I've got some news as well, Connie just had a baby girl and they are both doing fine. I'll give you a call later, once I calm down and the reality of this whole thing sinks in a little."

"So Jane had her baby…a boy or a girl?" I asked.

"It's a boy. Seth. Mother and infant are doing just fine."

"It's amazing that we both had such quick and easy deliveries," I marveled.

"Alex, could you please do me a favor and post a notice on my blog to let everyone know that both Jane and I have given birth?" I asked.

"Sure, but could I get a peek at the baby first?"

"Certainly, you can even hold her if you'd like."

"Let me calm down some before I hold her; I'm a little shaky."

He walked over and peered into little Hope's face.

"What a doll. Pink and perfect."

Chapter 10 – Sisters

It was late in the afternoon of Christmas Eve when I posted my first blog since Hope's birth. I had recuperated from the delivery extremely fast and was feeling marvelous. Jane and all of the comradettes were doing well, as were the babies.

My Christmas Eve blog read as follows:

"Ladies, we did it. We had the courage of our convictions, took that leap of faith, we asked and we received. Congratulations to us all.

"This is just the beginning, however. These miraculous little babies now need to be loved and cared for and we have a lot of work ahead. Although we don't know what the future holds for them, as well as for ourselves, I am confident that the unseen force that brought us safely thus far will continue to guide and care for us.

"I note the comments submitted concerning the birth of 12 boys and 12 girls. I have to admit that I also wondered if that even number of each sex had some significance. Are these children to meet as adults, fall in love, and produce children that have a greater percentage of extraterrestrial DNA? Time will tell and we need not interfere, as all will happen as planned.

"I ask that we still continue to communicate through this blog. We are a very small and select group of women who share an exceptional experience. We only have each other to confide in. The secret knowledge that we have must be kept within this group for the safety of the children as well as ourselves and our loved ones. We have discussed this many times before, and I know you understand the importance of this secrecy.

"For lack of a better word, previously I had thought of you as my 'comradettes', however that word is no longer fitting as I now consider you my sisters. Stay well my sisters."

Just as I finished, Mary entered the room and said "Hope is fast asleep now. What a good little baby she is...eats and sleeps. No tantrums, no crying other than a little whimper now and then when she is hungry or needs to be changed. You couldn't ask for a better temperament."

"From the comments on my blog, it appears that all of the babies have similar mellow personalities. Surely Jane's little Seth is that way."

"It will be so good to see Jane and Seth tomorrow, oh, and Joshua as well of course."

Just then we heard the sound of a car driving into the courtyard.

"It must be Alex arriving with Jennifer," I announced and we both ran to the front door. I looked out the sidelight and saw Alex taking Jennifer's luggage out of the back of the wagon.

I opened the door and ran out to hug her.

"It's so good to see you," I beamed.

"It's been a long time," she responded.

We stood there for a few seconds just holding each other. I could feel tears welling up in my eyes and I pulled back and looked at her face and could see the tears in her eyes as well.

"Like mother, like daughter," she said and laughed.

"That's for sure. Remember when you were a teenager we'd cry every time we saw that coffee commercial when the young soldier came home on Christmas Eve and surprised his family?"

"And we'd see that commercial several times a day and

still cry every time we saw it," she responded.

We walked to the front door and Mary grabbed Jennifer in a bear hug.

"Hey, be careful, don't break her!" I exclaimed.

"I'll bring Jennifer's bags upstairs," Alex said and squeezed by us.

"Thanks, Alex!" Jennifer called.

"Let's go into the kitchen. Are you hungry?"

"A little, but I can wait until dinner."

"Let me take your coat," Mary offered.

"Oh, thanks," she responded as she slid out of her jacket.

"Did they feed you on the plane?" I asked.

"Yes, I flew Club class and British Airways does a great job. But then I had to wait for almost two hours at JFK for my connecting flight to Burlington and I didn't eat anything at the airport. I knew you'd have something delectable to feed me, so I didn't want to spoil my appetite!"

"How about a glass of wine?" Mary asked.

"Sounds good," Jennifer replied.

"We're having baked shrimp stuffed with crabmeat dressing, asparagus and Caesar salad," I said.

"Yum! So where's my baby sister?"

Alex came into the kitchen and said "She's sound asleep in her cradle in the living room. Want to see her?"

"Sure do!"

We all walked into the living room and Jennifer peered into the cradle.

"She looks just like a beautiful little doll. She's perfect," Jennifer whispered.

"That's exactly what I said when I first saw her," Alex murmured.

We returned to the kitchen and Alex poured himself a glass of wine and joined the girls at the table.

"I have to say that you both look wonderful," Jennifer said to Alex and me.

"Hey, what about me?" Mary asked.

"You always look wonderful," Jennifer responded. "But my mother and Alex look younger than when I last saw them and that's over two years ago."

"Well, the morning after 'it' happened…"

"You mean the morning after the full moon and the UFO sightings?" Jennifer asked.

"Yes. That next morning I took a sip of coffee and it tasted vile, so that was the end of the caffeine for me. And then later that same day, I made myself a martini and it tasted like turpentine, so that was the end of alcohol during my pregnancy. And Alex gave up drinking beer, out of sympathy for me, I guess."

"Actually I felt guilty drinking beer when she couldn't have her beloved martinis, so I stopped drinking," Alex added.

"And we started eating healthier. Lots of whole grains, fruits and vegetables. We felt better, had lots more energy and looked better. Jane and Joshua did the same. However I'm not breast feeding Hope. Actually none of the women produced enough milk to breast feed. Must be the age factor, I guess. So I plan on having a glass of wine tomorrow!"

"I'm going to meet Jane and Joshua and little Seth tomorrow, right?" Jennifer asked.

"Yes, they'll be over for dinner. I haven't seen them since Seth was born and I can't wait to see him," I responded.

I put the oven on and poured myself a glass of cider and sat down at the table. Jennifer looked so good. Here she was a successful, self-sufficient, beautiful woman in her late thirties. Where did the time go? She didn't really look much different than she did when she was a teenager. She wore little makeup, had no wrinkles and her skin glowed. Her dark brown hair had beautiful reddish highlights with no gray yet. She wore it shoulder length in a pageboy of sorts. The style suited her perfectly.

"So, Mom, do you have any idea what lies ahead for these children?"

"Not a clue. We'll just have to wait and see."

"Remember when they gave you your six month checkup?" Mary asked. "Do you think maybe they'll checkup on the babies as well?"

"What do you mean 'six month checkup'?" Jennifer asked.

"Your mother and Jane disappeared for 4 hours; they were abducted," Mary replied.

"What!" Jennifer exclaimed.

"Oh, it was really nothing. Jane and I were exploring the property and found this stone chamber in the hillside and the next thing we knew we were laying flat on our backs in the field in front of the chamber and 4 hours had passed by. We figured we had just been given our six month checkup. No big deal."

"For the two of you to go traipsing off into the woods when you were six months pregnant was just plan foolish," Alex muttered.

"Well, it's all over now so there's no point in discussing it," I retorted.

"So what's with the stone chamber? Did you ever go back to check it out?" Jennifer asked.

"Yes, your mother, Jane, Joshua and I went to look at it the following day," Alex responded. "There is a large stone lintel and two large supporting stones around approximately an 8 foot by 8 foot opening. The first chamber is about 30 feet long and is lined with stone. There is a ninety degree turn at the far right side and there is another chamber which is about 20 feet long."

"Wow, it sounds amazing! I'd love to see it," Jennifer said.

"And at the far end of the smaller chamber is a blue marble table or bench of sorts. It has an engraving on one of the legs. I'll show it to you…" Alex remarked and walked over to the computer desk. He came back with paper in hand and showed it to Jennifer.

"A triskele!" Jennifer exclaimed.

"Right, but how do you know that?" Alex asked.

"It's a well known Celtic pattern. There have been crop circles in this pattern; I've seen them! But it almost looks like this symbol wasn't completed; the center of two of the swirls is missing."

"Yes, Joshua mentioned that as well, but that is exactly how they were carved into the bench," Alex said.

"Okay, I've got to see this. How about tomorrow morning you take me out there?" Jennifer asked Alex.

"Tomorrow morning it is. We're in luck that there is no snow on the ground."

"Be careful. Remember what happened to Joshua," I said to Alex.

"What happened to Joshua?" Jennifer asked.

"He got dizzy when we approached the bench and almost passed out in there. He made it outside just in time," Alex advised.

"I think I hear Hope stirring," Mary murmured. "I'll go take a look."

"I'd better put the shrimp in the oven and clean the asparagus," I said. "Alex, could you please make the Caesar salad dressing?"

"Sure thing," Alex replied.

Mary walked in with Hope just them.

"Oh, can I hold her?" Jennifer asked.

"Of course!" Mary responded and carefully handed the baby to Jennifer.

"I'm going to take a picture of the two sisters together for the first time," Mary announced and went to get her digital camera.

"Truth is stranger than fiction, isn't it Mom?"

"It certainly is."

Chapter 11 – Triskele Metamorphosis

I awoke the next morning to the smell of coffee. I looked at the clock and it was 5:33. Who was making coffee at this hour of the morning and why? I got up and walked over to the bassinet and looked in. Hope was awake and I swear she smiled at me. I didn't think she could really even see yet, but it looked like she recognized me and smiled at me. Must be gas, I thought.

I put on my robe and slippers, picked up Hope and walked downstairs. Jennifer and Alex were sipping coffee at the kitchen table.

"What are you two doing?" I inquired. "It's not even dawn yet!"

"The time change has me all screwed up," Jennifer said. "I thought I heard a noise downstairs, so I came down to investigate, and there was Alex watching television. We put on coffee and here we are!"

"Is that decaffeinated coffee?"

"Yup."

"Oh good, I'll get a cup for myself and put Hope's bottle on to warm."

"Let me hold her while you do that," Jennifer volunteered.

"Thanks. Actually, I should put the oven on and get the turkey out of the refrigerator. I was planning on getting up early to get dinner going, just not quite this early. But this actually works out better."

A few minutes later I had Hope's bottle ready.

"Let me feed her," Jennifer offered.

"Are you sure?"

"I've already had most of my coffee and am raring to go but it's still too dark to go looking at that chamber, so hand me the bottle."

I gave her the bottle and she started to feed Hope.

I put the turkey in the oven and sat down at the table with my coffee.

It was so nice to look over to see my daughter with her baby sister in her arms. I wondered if Jennifer would ever have a child. It was getting late in life for her but anything was possible, as I well knew. There were several men that she had dated over the years who I thought might be "the" one, but it was not to be. She was beautiful, successful and, as far as I could tell, happy. What more could a mother want for her daughter?

"Boy, Hope is really sucking up this formula," Jennifer remarked.

"She's got a very healthy appetite, that's for sure," I said.

"What time do you think we'll be heading out to the chamber?" Jennifer asked Alex.

"There's no great hurry. The sun comes up on the other side of the mountain, so the chamber will be pitch dark. I know you can't wait to see it, but I would think we should wait until 10 a.m. or so. What time are Jane and family arriving?" Alex asked.

"About noon. I'm planning on serving dinner no later than 1:30."

"So maybe we should leave around 9:30 then," Alex said. "It will take us no more than a quarter hour to reach the chamber and another quarter hour to return. I can't imagine it would take more than a half hour to search the cave, and that will give us enough time to clean up when we get home. Okay?"

"Okay! I can't wait to see this," Jennifer declared.

The sound of the pitter patter of little feet preceded Mary's entrance into the kitchen.

"Everyone is up already, even Hope!" she exclaimed.

"Hope is almost finished with her breakfast and the turkey is already in the oven," I laughed.

"But it's only 6:15! I thought I'd beat everyone downstairs this morning but here you all are."

"Better grab your coffee while you can. There are bagels in the bread drawer. Jennifer, want a bagel?"

"I'll get one for myself in a little while, thanks," she responded.

Mary poured her coffee and joined us. "Did everyone sleep well?" she asked.

"I had difficulty falling asleep, but when I fell asleep it was a sound sleep for several hours. I was wide awake around 5 a.m.," Jennifer said.

"I slept fairly well," I replied. "Hope only woke up once during the night for a feeding. Just before I woke up this morning, however, I was in a deep sleep dreaming about Russell"

"Who's Russell?" Jennifer asked.

"You don't know who Russell is?" Mary asked. "He's is the most charismatic person I have ever met. He's quite a handsome man in an untraditional sort of way."

"And Russell is who?"

"Russell is the son of Gene and Hilda, the couple who built this house," Alex advised.

"And how and when did you meet him?" she asked.

"It was in June of this year, just the day before the summer solstice," I responded. "Mary and Anne were up for a visit and we were out for a walk. I met one of our neighbors also out for a walk and he mentioned that Russell was back in town for a visit. I didn't know Russell existed and I was a little unnerved by the news. Later that same afternoon, he shows up at our house and introduces himself."

"We all had lunch at Jane's that afternoon," Alex continued. "Your mother and sisters made a shopping detour on the way back, so I got here first. Russell was here when I arrived. I took an immediate liking to him."

"You talk about a magnetic personality, well he's got it," Mary added.

"He left this area after high school and never returned," I said. "And get this; he is currently living in Meghalaya, India."

"Meghalaya, India! I didn't know there was such a place. Is that weird or what?" Jennifer exclaimed.

"Definitely weird," Mary chimed in.

"And he didn't drive here. I have no idea how he got to the house. As he was leaving, he called across the courtyard 'Do you know what Meghalaya means?' And I answered 'Yes, Abode of the Clouds'. He said 'Correct you are. 'Clouds' being the operative word.' And with that he disappeared down the driveway."

"Then the next morning, I found a note that he had left in the mailbox which said ''of' being the other operative word'," Alex added.

"So what was that supposed to mean?" Jennifer asked.

"We came to the conclusion that 'abode of the clouds' means this property is where the spaceships sojourn," I said, "and not house in the clouds."

"How did you reach that conclusion?" Jennifer asked.

"When Russell said that 'clouds' was the operative word we started discussing it and Anne actually was the one who made the connection between spaceships and clouds. The spaceships are cloaked within clouds," Alex replied.

"Right, and the preposition 'of' indicates possession or belonging. The preposition 'in' is associated with location, so when Russell wrote 'of is the other operative word', it kind of all clicked together," I said.

"We also looked up 'abode' in the dictionary and one of the definitions was 'temporary stay, sojourn' and that's how we came to our conclusion about the meaning of the phrase. It all makes perfect sense," Alex explained.

"Russell's parents named this spot 'Meghalaya'…are you saying they knew the real meaning of the word as you believe it relates to this property?" Jennifer asked.

"Yes, we do," I responded.

"And obviously Russell understands as well," Jennifer murmured.

"Correct."

"Hope has fallen asleep," Mary noted. "Let me take her and I'll put her in the cradle."

Jennifer seemed lost in thought, and then realized Mary was standing there waiting to take Hope from her. "Oh sorry, I guess I was daydreaming. Here you go," and she handed the baby to Mary.

"Okay, I'm going to toast a bagel for myself. Anyone want a bagel?" I asked.

"I'll have one," Alex said.

"Me, too!" Jennifer exclaimed.

Mary returned just as I was putting the first bagel in the toaster. "Bagel, Mary?"

"Sounds good, thanks."

I put a variety of cream cheese and jam on the table and in no time we were munching away on our bagels.

"What kind of bagel is this?" Jennifer asked.

"Sunflower seed," I answered.

"This is the best bagel I've ever had; even the cream cheese is outstanding."

"We're fortunate to have one of the best bagel bakeries relatively close by," I answered.

We ate in silence for a bit, and then Jennifer asked, "Do you think you'll ever see Russell again?"

"Yes. He said he'd be back in a year or so," I responded.

"What does he look like?" she asked.

"Tall, I'd say 6 foot or a little taller, slim, shoulder

length brown hair with a little grey, a longish brown beard also with a little grey mixed in and the most amazing wide set brown eyes," I answered.

Pursuing her line of questioning, Jennifer asked "How old would you say he is?"

"Well, based on what the neighbor told me, I'd estimate he's around 46."

"Come back at the end of June and maybe you'll get a chance to meet him," Mary teased.

"I think I might just do that," Jennifer laughed.

She tried to make light of it, but I could tell she was really intrigued, both about Russell and this whole Meghalaya situation.

"I'm thinking of buying a cottage on the Isle of Arran," Jennifer announced.

"Where is that?" Mary asked.

"Off the west coast of Scotland. You can reach it by ferry just south of Glasgow. The island has a lot of history to it and it's beautiful. One of the guys who works with me told me about it. It was his uncle's cottage. His uncle passed on and the estate is looking to sell. I was seriously considering buying it, but now I'm thinking I'd rather spend more time here with you."

"How long does it take to get from London to Glasgow," Mary asked.

"Well, if you drive it takes about seven hours, but there is rail service now that only takes four hours, so it's not bad at all. And there is direct rail service from Glasgow to the little town where you catch the ferry over to the isle. It's very convenient."

"Have you seen the cottage?" Alex asked.

"Yes, it's lovely. Actually, I can access some pictures on the internet. Want to see?" she asked.

"You bet!" I exclaimed.

In no time at all she had the pictures of the property on the screen. We all huddled around her to look.

"Holy crow, you call that a cottage?" I asked.

"Well, that's what they call it, but it does have 4 bedrooms and there's a separate 1 bedroom cottage on the property. It's in a little village called Lamlash Bay. It's on a half acre, has enclosed perennial gardens out back and it has incredible views of Holy Isle. There are some pictures of the grounds and the views as well. Just bear with me as I click through them all."

"When was the house built?" Mary asked.

"About one hundred years ago. But as you can see, it has been completely modernized."

"Look at that view!" I gasped.

"Yes, that's Holy Isle. The front of the house faces the sea and that is the view from the living room, dining room and master bedroom windows. There is a ferry that goes over to Holy Isle. I think it runs every hour during the summer. Tibetan monks have a monastery there."

"The living room is huge; front to back with lots of light and a nice big fireplace," I commented.

"Yes, and out in front of that big bay window is a brick patio with wrought iron furniture. All of the furniture stays with the house. It's completely turnkey."

"Is it a good deal, financially speaking?" I asked.

"Excellent. The family hasn't listed this house with a realtor yet and they're offering it at an extremely attractive price."

"Have you had an inspection of the property?" Alex inquired.

"Yes, and all is in good condition. I thought I'd mull this over during my visit with you, and now I don't know what to do."

"You're hesitating because you're thinking you'd like to spend more time with us here in Vermont?" I asked.

"Yes."

"Well, realistically, how often would you come over, twice a year tops, I'm thinking."

"That sounds right."

"And this beautiful spot in Scotland is only a four hour train ride away. You can spend many long weekends there throughout the year. It sounds like it is an excellent investment, and I don't think there is any way you could lose out in the transaction."

"You're right about that."

"Plus, it looks like you've got enough room there for us to travel over and see you once a year," I noted.

"Would you?"

"I don't see why not," Alex said. "I've always wanted to go to Scotland."

"You can count on me to visit," Mary piped up.

"That's it! I'm buying it! I'm so excited!"

"Well, I'm glad we've got that all settled," I said.

"Thank you all for talking me through that. It does make perfect sense to buy it. I'm going to email Richard right now and tell him I'll buy it and sign the papers when I get back."

"Good idea," Alex agreed.

Mary and I started slicing, dicing and cooking the side dishes for our turkey dinner. A short while later Jennifer joined us.

"Did you send the email?" I asked.

"Yes, and he's already responded. He's delighted."

We continued to cook and chat about Scotland and England and before we knew it, Alex was standing there saying it was time to head out to the chamber.

Jennifer grabbed her coat from the mudroom and joined Alex at the back door.

"You've got everything you need? Flashlights, rope, knife?" I asked.

"You know me..."

"Right, old eagle scout. Okay, good luck. Be careful!"

"We will!" Jennifer exclaimed and off they went.

"What are we having for dessert?" Mary asked.

"Anne made a buttermilk pie and a pecan pie."

"That sounds good."

"Is that kielbasa you have there?" Mary questioned.

"Yes, fresh not smoked kielbasa. I'm going to make stuffing with it. You've heard of sausage stuffing? Well, this fresh kielbasa stuffing is in memory of our Christmases back home when we were kids. We always had fresh kielbasa."

"Sounds great, what are you going to put in it?"

"Herb seasoned stuffing mix, wild rice, celery, onions, diced apples and dried cranberries along with the kielbasa."

"I think I hear Hope," I noted. "I've got to get her cleaned up and dressed in her first little Christmas outfit."

"Want me to do it?" Mary asked.

"No, it's okay, I'll do it. But could you sauté the kielbasa that I've sliced up with the chopped apple, onion and celery? I've got the rice cooked, so all I'll have to do is combine it with the breadcrumbs and bake it for about a half an hour just before we eat. And could you also do me a favor and set the dining room table?"

"Sure, now how many of us are there?"

"Seven adults and two children, but I think the children will skip the turkey this year."

A short while later I came down with Hope all spiffed up in her white Christmas dress. No one would really see it as she would be wrapped in a blanket, but what the heck, a girl needs to be decked out for the holidays.

Mary went up to dress, and I sat down to feed Hope. As she took her bottle, I wondered about Jennifer. Would she get to meet Russell? What would happen if they met? Would sparks fly? Hope had finished her bottled and dozed off in my arms. I was lost in my reverie when the back door opened and Jennifer and Alex came in.

"You won't believe it," Alex blurted.

Mary just entered the room and heard Alex say, "The triskele changed. The center of one of the other two spirals has been completed. I made another rubbing."

He took a piece of paper out of his pocket and handed it to me. Sure enough, the first and second spirals had now been completed.

"I could feel energy in that chamber," Jennifer claimed. "It was similar to the energy that I've felt in walking some of the crop circles. It was awesome. And here it is, in your own backyard!"

"Do you have any theories on how or why the triskele changed?" I asked of no one in particular.

"I do," Jennifer replied.

"What?" I asked.

"Alex took the first rubbing before the babies were born. I think the birth of those children fulfilled the second spiral and it was completed. If I'm right, then there is one other event that needs to happen."

"I think you might be on to something there," I agreed.

"I wonder what event completed the first spiral," Jennifer mused.

Chapter 12 – First Christmas

"I'm going to light fires in both fireplaces," Alex announced.

"Great, thanks," I replied.

It was almost noon and our guests were due to arrive at any moment. The lights were on the Christmas trees, including Alex's wonderful tree that crept across the ceiling in the living room. I put the accent lights on over Jane's painting and 'The Baptism of Christ'. It was a grey day but there was no snow or rain in the forecast.

"Here they are," Alex said.

I looked out the window and saw the red and white Volvo 445 drive into the courtyard. Anne and Jane got out and Joshua was getting Seth out of the baby seat. I opened the front door as they approached.

"I'm so glad to see you!" I exclaimed to Jane and gave her a big hug.

"Sometimes I almost feel like I'm in a dream," she responded. "It is truly incredible, isn't it?"

"Yes, incredible and wonderful. How does it feel to be a mother?"

"I can't even begin to describe it," she answered. "I am so happy I was chosen."

Anne came up and gave me a hug. "How's it going, Anne? Is it like riding a bicycle? Did everything come back to you?"

"Amazingly, it did," she responded.

"I don't know what I would have done without your sister's help," Jane remarked. "It was such a relief to have someone with me who knew what she was doing."

"Let's move on inside," I said.

Joshua followed with Seth, and Alex followed with the two pies.

Mary took everyone's coats, and we moved into the living room.

Seth was sound asleep as was Hope. Joshua walked toward Hope's cradle to put Seth in his carrier next to her. As he put the carrier on the floor, both babies fluttered their eyelids.

"Did you see that?" I asked.

"Yes, it's almost as if they acknowledged each other's presence," Jane noted.

"I swear Hope smiled at me this morning."

"Do you think we're reading a little too much into their facial expressions and movements?"

"Could be. But they are beautiful babies, aren't they?"

"We did good…with a little help from our friends."

Jennifer entered the room just then, and Alex introduced her to Joshua. She then gave Anne a big hug and kiss, after which she walked over to Jane.

"Me Jane."

"Me Jennifer."

They bother laughed and hugged each other.

"I feel like I've known you all my life," Jennifer admitted to Jane. "My mother has told me so much about you, but still there is something else, like something clicked when I looked in your eyes."

"It's weird, when your mother and I first met, I asked her 'haven't we met before?' And she responded, 'Funny, I was thinking the same thing, but I don't think it was in this lifetime.' I think you must have been with us back in that other lifetime."

"I think you're right," Jennifer commented.

"Okay, folks, I'm taking drink orders. We have Grgich Hills chardonnay and cabernet as well as mixed drinks and beer. Who wants what?" Alex asked.

Everyone ordered wine, and Alex went to fetch it.

"You know, I haven't really had time to take in how beautiful this room is," Jennifer murmured. "I've only been in here a couple of times since I arrived yesterday and I was looking at Hope on both occasions. You've changed some things since the last time I visited, I see. The tree in the corner that branches across the ceiling is incredible."

"One of Alex's projects," I responded.

"What an imagination that man has. He is amazing."

"Isn't he though?"

"Talking about me?" Alex chuckled as he returned with two bottles of wine and glasses.

"Yes, I love the tree you created."

"Pshaw, it was nothing. But thank you."

Alex poured out the wine and handed each of us our glass. "Let me make a toast. To the ladies: Congratulations on a job well done. You are truly remarkable!"

"I'll add another toast which my mother was found of," I proclaimed, "'Here's to us, and those like us, damn few!'"

We took a sip of our wine, and all of a sudden Jennifer gasped "The Baptism of Christ by Aert de Gelder".

"What about it?" I asked.

"I never noticed it when I came into the room before. I took a sip of wine and my eyes went to the picture and it startled me. I've seen the original at the Fitzwilliam Museum."

My heart seemed to skip a beat. I said "That is exactly what Russell said when he saw the picture hanging there on the wall."

I could see the blood drain out of Jennifer's face, and Alex quickly made his way over to her and put his arm around her. "Are you alright?" he asked.

"For some reason, it was almost surreal seeing that picture here. I was so drawn to it when I saw the original. And then when you said that Russell had responded with the exact same words, the room started to spin."

"Let's sit down," I suggested.

"Wait, what's the other painting in the far corner?" Jennifer asked, and walked toward it with Alex right behind her, as if he were ready to catch her at any moment.

"That's one of Jane's paintings," I answered.

"There's a spaceship in that cloud. What a masterful job you've done with this, Jane. If someone didn't know, they'd just think it was a picture of the lake, mountains and a cloud. But look at the glint of metal shining from within that cloud. You managed to capture energy and mystery on canvas."

"Thanks, Jennifer. I was obsessed with painting cloud pictures back then. Some of them came out pretty good if I do say so myself."

I sat down by the fire, as did Anne and Mary. Soon every one sitting and chatting away.

"Well, I've got some news," Alex announced. "Jennifer wanted to see the chamber out back, so we took a walk out there this morning. I was showing her the triskele carved into the side of the leg of the bench, and was astonished to see that it had changed since I last saw it."

"What!" Joshua exclaimed. "Changed how?"

"I took another rubbing. See for yourself." Alex pulled the paper out of his pocket and handed it to Joshua."

"Another one of the spirals has been completed," Joshua murmured in amazement.

He handed the paper over to Anne who stared at it for several seconds and then Anne gave it to Jane.

"What do you think it means?" Jane asked.

"Jennifer's got a theory," Alex said.

All eyes turned to Jennifer. "The first time Alex made a rubbing of the triskele it was before the babies were born. I think the birth of those babies completed a step or phase which was signified by the second spiral in the triskele. The spiral could now be completed because that phase has been completed. Just a guess on my part, of course."

"That seems to make sense to me," Jane agreed. "So then there is one other event that will need to take place in order for the other spiral to be completed, right? And we have no idea what event completed the first spiral."

"That's what I think might be the case," Jennifer responded, "and you're right, we don't know why the first spiral was completed."

"That chamber is at or very close to the intersection of two ley lines," Joshua noted.

"Well that makes sense," Jennifer said. "I felt tremendous energy standing in front of that bench. The English countryside is dotted with megaliths that are built over intersecting ley lines. There is special power at these spots, they are called energy vortexes, I believe."

"We thought it might be a portal to another dimension," Jane advised and gave me a sidewise look. I was certain she wanted to see if I was rolling my eyes or making some kind of face.

I nodded and asked Jennifer if she knew anything about such portals.

"A little bit. We live in a three dimensional world consisting of length, width, and height. Time might be considered the fourth dimension. If 'something' intersects these dimensions, it would create a boundary between the spatial dimensions. If this 'boundary' were to get thin in spots, and a 'hole' formed, it would create a portal which would allow travel between the dimensions. Psychics report feelings of intense energy at such spots, just as I felt incredible energy out back in the chamber. These portals are located in many locations around the world. I believe an interdimensional portal exists in Glastonbury, England where the Michael and Mary ley lines intersect. Another supposedly exists at Mount Shasta, California."

"I had been reading about Admiral Byrd and his belief

that the earth was hollow," Mary related. "One of the supposed portals to Agartha, which is said to be the city at the core of the earth, is at Mt. Shasta."

"Yes, from what I've read, Mount Shasta has a very powerful energy field. Supposedly the Lemurians live in an underground city called 'Telos' which is about a mile beneath Mount Shasta. And you are correct, as I understand it, Agartha is below Telos in the center of the earth. There's a very interesting story about a fellow named J. C. Brown who claims to have found a Lemurian village within the mountain. This happened back in 1904. He was supposed to lead an expedition back into the mountain, but disappeared just before they were to start off on their trek."

"How did you learn all this?" I asked, surprised by her knowledge.

"I read quite a bit about crop circles and megaliths and this interest in portals, vortexes and ley lines naturally grew from that."

"Hey," Mary broke in, "look at Hope and Seth."

We all looked and they were both wide awake and seemed to be listening to our conversation.

"I thinks it's time to feed them," Anne advised and she got up to warm the bottles.

Jane and I picked up the infants and were holding them while waiting for the bottles, and Joshua said, "I'd swear they are looking at each other."

The rest of us looked and it certainly did appear that way.

"But they can't really even see yet, can they?" Alex asked.

"I don't think a normal 4 day old baby can see very clearly, but these aren't your average children," Jane declared. "Maybe they are sensing each other more than seeing each other, I don't know."

After Seth and Hope were fed, we had our dinner and during dinner Jennifer mentioned that she was buying a cottage on Arran Isle.

"I've been to Holy Isle for a retreat once," Joshua said. "Isn't it right across from Arran Isle?

"Yes, you have to take a ferry from Arran Isle to get to Holy Isle," Jennifer responded.

"What an incredibly beautiful and mystical place that is," Joshua commented.

"If you're looking for company, we'd love to accommodate," Jane declared. "Although Joshua has been to Scotland, I haven't."

"Wonderful, I'm so glad I don't have to worry about being lonely out there. I want to spend more time with you all, but now I see that it doesn't necessarily mean here in Vermont."

Chapter 13 – And So It Begins

A little over a week later my sisters were gone, Jennifer was gone, and Jane and I were left with the awesome responsibility of taking care of these children. The good thing was that we were in daily communication with the other 22 women around the globe who were sharing in this experience. If any one of us had a question or concern, someone was always there with an answer. What a support group!

Alex and Joshua were amazing. They helped with cleaning, shopping and cooking to some extent. I even heard Alex reading a recipe to Joshua over the phone. Who says you can't teach old dogs new tricks?

Hope smiled at me every morning since the time she was four days old. It wasn't gas, I was sure. I'd walk up to her cradle, say "Good morning, Hope," she'd look at me and smile. She had the sweetest temperament; she very seldom cried. Comments on the blog indicated this was true of all the children.

All of the infants were way ahead of the curve as far as motor skill development went. They could all roll over by age two months and they were all trying to make sounds. When I spoke to Hope, she would intently watch my mouth form words. She would then try to move her mouth in a similar fashion.

Jane and I would get together with the children as often as possible. We'd put them in a playpen with each other and watch them interact. They spent periods of time when they would just gaze at one another. We felt that they were communicating somehow, perhaps telepathically. They both were extremely fond of a little soft-sided stuffed star that Jennifer had sent to me. She said she had found it at a new age shop in London and thought it would be perfect for Hope to have a star as one of her first toys. Hope latched on to it immediately. She played with it, slept with it, and loved it. But when Seth was over, she would hand it to him, and he would hold it for a while and then hand it back to her. They were doing this when they were just a little over two months old.

They loved to be read to. They would listen with rapt attention to every word and look at the pictures when we held the pages in front of them. Their favorite book seemed to be 'The Moon Shines Down' by Margaret Wise Brown, the author who also wrote "Goodnight Moon'. The very first time I read this book to Hope, she was entranced. The story basically is that God shines the moon and blesses the children all around the world. The illustrations by Linda Bleck seemed to mesmerize the child. If I turned the page too quickly, she would whimper. This book received the exact same reaction from Seth.

I mentioned the book in one of my blogs, and many of the mothers reported that this was their child's favorite book.

Hope and Seth were growing and changing and I swear I actually saw a difference in them from day to day. Jane saw it as well.

Mary and Anne called frequently to see how we were doing, and on one of their calls in March they asked if it would be okay if they came up for Easter, which fell late this year in mid April. I was delighted!

Now that we were into the month of March, Alex was out at different job sites several days a week. He arrived home late in the afternoon shortly after I got off the phone with Anne and Mary. I had just put Hope down for a nap as he was walking into the kitchen. He had pink roses in one hand and a bag of groceries in the other.

"Flowers! How nice! How come?"

"Happy anniversary," he beamed.

"Anniversary, what anniversary?"

"This is the spring equinox. It was a year ago that you thought there was a full moon and little Hope was conceived. I guess you could say it's the first anniversary of the immaculate conception."

I laughed, but my eyes welled up with tears and I kissed his cheek.

"You are a dear, I didn't even remember. Thank you."

"And I have lobster tails stuffed with crabmeat dressing for dinner. I'll get the oven on."

As I arranged the roses in a vase, I told him that my sisters were coming up for Easter.

"Great! How long before Easter?" he asked.

"It's April 19th this year."

"So we've got about a month. Hope and Seth will be just about four months old. I wonder what tricks they'll be doing by then."

"I'm sure my sisters will be amazed by their progress. Hey, I'm going to call Jane and wish her happy anniversary and invite them over for Easter at the same time."

"Okay. I'm going to get a Caesar salad going."

I phoned Jane and Joshua answered.

"Hi, Joshua. How's it going?" I asked.

"Connie, happy anniversary!" he bellowed.

"You remembered too!"

"Sure, how can you forget something as momentous as that? Actually, I have to admit that Alex did remind me a couple of days ago. Here's Jane, she's ripping the phone out of my hand...bye Connie."

"Happy anniversary!" Jane exclaimed.

"And a very happy anniversary to you as well," I responded.

"Did you remember or did Alex surprise you?" she

asked.

"I forgot all about it. He walked into the kitchen with flowers in one hand and stuffed lobster tails in the other and then reminded me it was a year ago that Hope was conceived by the light of the full moon."

"I forgot too."

"So listen, Anne and Mary are coming up for Easter. I'm formally inviting you and Joshua and Seth for Easter brunch on April 19th."

"Wonderful, I can't wait to see them. I will mark it on my social calendar," she joked.

"Great. So I'd better be going and help Alex make dinner. I'll see you tomorrow, okay?"

"Okay, you have a good night."

"Thanks, you too."

Alex was cleaning the romaine lettuce and the lobster tails were already in the oven.

"Is there something I can help you with?" I asked.

"No, all is under control, but thanks."

"Then I'm going to get on my blog and wish everyone a happy anniversary," I said.

"Good idea."

I went over to the computer and saw that I had a new email message. It was from Jennifer.

"You won't believe this, but Jennifer sent an email wishing me happy anniversary. How did she remember? And she goes on to say that she feels a very strong urge to be here for Easter and wants to know if it's okay?"

"You'd better respond right away," Alex urged.

I typed 'Well, talk about synchronicity, I was speaking with Anne and Mary today and they asked if it would be okay if they came up for Easter. And I just got off the phone with Jane and invited them over for Easter. Then I open my email and here's this message from you. Yes! Yes! Please come for Easter! Can't wait! Oh, and thanks for remembering the anniversary. I didn't, but Alex did and he's making me dinner right now. Love you.'

The following month flew by. Hope and Seth were able to sit up by themselves just before Easter and they were crawling as well. Joshua had completed refinishing a pair of antique highchairs for them. They would actually be able to sit at the dining room table at Easter, that is, if they weren't taking naps.

Mary and Anne flew in on Good Friday. Alex collected them at the airport and when they arrived, I swear they almost ran into the house. I got a brief hug and kiss and then they asked to see Hope.

"She's in the living room; go see her."

They walked into the living room and they both let out something akin to a shriek. I hoped they weren't frightening Hope. I came up behind them and looked around them toward the playpen. There was Hope, sitting up, holding her toy star and smiling at them.

"She is gorgeous! Look at that sweet face and blond hair and blue eyes," Mary gushed.

"And she's sitting up all by herself. I've never known a child to do that at four months. It's absolutely amazing," Anne marveled.

I went around them and picked up Hope.

"Hope, this is your Aunt Anne."

"Hello, Hope. You probably don't remember me. The last time I saw you, you were just a tiny little baby," Anne beamed.

Hope was studying Anne's face and after a few seconds she broke out into a big grin.

"And this is your Aunt Mary."

Mary reached out, took Hope's little hand and said "Hellooo!"

Hope began to giggle. I never heard her giggle before, but the noise she was making sure sounded like a giggle.

"Oh, so you think I'm funny, do you?" Mary laughed.

And Hope continued to giggle. I guess she found Mary

quite amusing.

"Can I hold her?" Mary asked.

"Sure, here you go," I said as I handed her over to Mary.

"Can I get you ladies some wine?" I asked.

"I'll get it, I know where it is," Anne replied. "Can I get one for you, Mary?"

"That would be delightful," Mary responded.

Alex walked into the room and saw Mary holding Hope.

"Ah, you two have bonded already, huh?"

"You bet. How are Jane, Joshua and Seth?"

"Great," I declared. "All of the children are doing well and pretty much on course with each other."

Anne walked into the room with two glasses of wine and put one down in front of Mary.

"Let me take Hope from you," I said and took her from Mary's arms.

"Actually, all of the children are for the most part several months ahead of the norm as far as motor skills go. I swear Hope and Seth communicate telepathically. They are truly exceptional children."

"Do all of the children look similar?" Anne asked.

"No, it appears that the children have taken the general physical characteristics of the mother."

We continued to chat away as Hope fell asleep in my arms.

"When will Jennifer arrive?" Anne asked.

"Mid-morning tomorrow," I answered.

"I'm surprised she's back so soon. She must be busy with her new cottage in Scotland."

"Since the closing she has been there several times. She said that the house was in perfect order, she loved the furnishings that came with it, and there was really very little to do but go and pretty much veg out."

"We were thinking of visiting her later this year,"

Mary advised. "We'll discuss it with her when we see her."

"Yes, Alex and I were talking about taking the trip over, too. We'll have to see what works for her."

"Alex, could you please put the oven on at 375°?" I asked.

"Sure, be right back."

"Dare I ask what's for dinner? Mary inquired.

"Lobster mac and cheese."

"Wow, never had that before," Anne proclaimed. "It sounds wonderful."

"Another good company dish. You can make it ahead and then pop it in the oven when needed. That and salad vinaigrette and you've got a good meal."

"Does Hope sleep through the night yet," Anne queried.

"She takes her last bottle around 10 p.m. and she's in for the night. Wakes up around 6 o'clock each morning."

"You are blest, do you know that?" Anne asked.

"You bet I do."

Chapter 14 – Come Fly With Me

When I came down to the kitchen with Hope the next morning, my sisters were already there sipping coffee with Alex.

"What's going on? Why is everyone up already?" I asked.

"I don't know. I fell asleep as soon as my head hit the pillow and the next thing I knew it was 5:30," Mary said. "Anne was just getting up, so I got up too. When we got down here, Alex already had the coffee made."

"Here, let me take Hope," Anne offered.

"Thanks, I'll get her cereal ready."

"Good morning, Hope. How are you today?" Anne asked.

Hope smiled, nodded and tried to talk, but it came out as gibberish.

"She will be talking in no time," Mary remarked.

"I swear I've heard her say something close to 'hello' several times," Alex divulged.

My sisters started repeating 'hello, hello, hello' to Hope who was looking at them like 'Why are you saying that over and over? What's wrong with you people?'

Mercifully, Alex stopped them by saying "It is going to be a spectacular day weather wise. It's predicted to be mid-60's today and maybe even hit 70 tomorrow."

"Great, I'm glad Jennifer has good weather for her flight in," I responded.

"I'll leave around 9 o'clock to pick her up," Alex said.

"So what's on the agenda today?" Mary inquired. "What are we cooking and baking?"

"Well, tomorrow's menu consists of Easter meatloaf, dilled shrimp and rice salad, baked ham, asparagus vinaigrette, smoked kielbasa, three bean salad, hard boiled eggs, paska, ricotta pie and pineapple parfait pie."

"Pineapple parfait pie, isn't that what Grandma used to make?" Mary asked.

"That's right, she loved this recipe."

"How do you make it?"

"Easy. Drain the juice from a small can of crushed pineapple, add water to the juice to make one cup and bring it to a boil. Stir the boiling liquid into a package of lemon Jello and then add a pint of vanilla ice cream by spoonfuls to the hot Jello mixture until completed melted. Add the drained crushed pineapple, put the mixture into a baked pie crust and refrigerate. Simple and delicious.

"Okay, Hope's cereal is ready. Could you please put her in the highchair, Anne?"

"Can I feed her?" Mary asked.

"Sure, let me put the bib on her first."

"That's a beautiful highchair; where did you get it?" Anne asked.

"Joshua found it at some estate sale and he refinished it for us."

Hope must have been very hungry as she was gobbling up every spoonful that Mary gave her.

"Are you making the paska?" Anne asked.

"No, I seldom have success with making any yeast breads, but Jane has the knack. She's making the paska and the ricotta pie. Okay, anyone want some cranberry maple walnut granola? It is absolutely delicious and made right here in Vermont."

"Sounds great," Anne said.

"I'll have some," Mary chimed in.

"I'll pass," Alex said. "Think I'll pick up a bagel on

the way to the airport."

"Oh, if you're going to stop at the bagel bakery, could you pick up a couple dozen assorted?" Anne asked.

"A couple dozen?'

"I can put some out for brunch tomorrow, plus they refrigerate well."

"Hey, here's Itzy!" Anne exclaimed.

Itzy went right up to Anne and rubbed against her leg.

"She's my little buddy. She slept with me again last night," Anne said.

"I used to be her favorite. I don't know why she prefers you now," Mary muttered.

"She goes in cycles. Sometimes all she wants to eat is chopped liver and then other times all she wants is shrimp," I joked.

"Hmmm, so maybe I'm chopped liver," Mary muttered. "Look, Hope has finished all of her cereal!"

I put some of Hope's warmed formula in a sippy cup and handed it to her. She picked it up with two hands and took a drink.

"She can drink from a cup already!" Anne exclaimed.

"Yes, that's a relatively new development. But she still likes a bottle before bedtime."

I started cleaning and chopping the parsley for the Easter meatloaf.

"That meatloaf is called 'polinina' in Slovak, right?" Mary asked.

"Right. I still have the recipe that Mother wrote, and that is what she called it. I also have the round aluminum pan that she baked it in. See, it's on the counter over there by the stove."

I put the oven on to preheat, and then mixed the ground pork, egg, breadcrumb, garlic and parsley mixture.

"How many eggs did you put in that?" Anne asked.

"A dozen, but I think I need one more. Mother always said the mixture should be a little 'loose', not stiff. Could you please grab me one more egg, my hands are covered with this stuff."

Anne broke one more egg into the mixture and that did the trick. It was perfect. I put it into the round pan and placed it in the oven.

"So the only other things you need to prepare are the dilled shrimp and rice salad, the three bean salad, asparagus vinaigrette and the pie, right? Anne asked.

"Right. I'll put the ham in to bake when the meatloaf comes out. This is a pretty easy holiday to cook for. And what's great is that everything is served cold tomorrow. No juggling around trying to get everything warm at the same time. It's just a nice cold smorgasbord type brunch."

"So you wouldn't mind if I went with Alex to pick up Jennifer? I'd like to see that bagel bakery," Anne remarked.

"Sure, go for the ride. How about you, Mary? Why don't you go too?"

"Okay, I'd like that," she said.

Both girls left to get dressed and in no time they were back down and ready to go. Alex pulled the wagon into the courtyard, they got in, and off they went.

After I gave Hope her bath and got her dressed, I put her in the playpen and then wheeled it into the kitchen. She grabbed her star and hugged it.

I put a on a Mozart CD. Hope seemed to be very fond of Mozart. She swayed to the music at times.

I watched as she put her star down and went for the felt blocks. She picked one up and shook it, listening for the bell jingling inside. Then she picked up another and did the same thing. She looked up at me and smiled. I smiled back and waved at her. She surprised me by waving back! Her first wave!

The meatloaf was finished baking, so I took it out and put the ham in the oven. I then got 12 small bowls for coloring the Easter eggs. I had 6 colors of egg dye and I planned on doing marble effects, so I needed a double amount of little bowls. I got 2 dozen eggs out of the refrigerator which I had already hard boiled. This would be ready for the girls when they returned.

I had finished making the bean salad and dilled rice and shrimp salad when I heard Alex returning.

Jennifer was coming through the front door before I reached it. She grabbed me in a bear hug and gave me a big kiss and asked "Okay, where is she?"

"In the kitchen."

"You've put her to work already?" she asked and took off in the direction of the kitchen.

Anne, Mary and Alex followed, with Alex carrying a large bag from the bagel bakery.

"Twenty-four assorted bagels, as you requested, madam."

"Merci beaucoup," I responded.

"Il n'y a pas de quoi!

"Oh, I just love it when you speak French to me!"

We walked into the kitchen, and there was Jennifer holding Hope who was hanging on to her star.

"She is amazing! I walked into the kitchen and she waved at me! She was holding on to her star with one hand, and waving with the other."

"We saw her waving,' Mary affirmed, in support of Jennifer's statement as if it were too incredible to believe.

"I picked her up and kissed her cheek and she puckered up her lips as if she wanted to kiss me back."

"Yup, she's quite the kid," Alex declared.

"Well I guess so!" Jennifer exclaimed.

"What are all these little bowls out for?" Mary asked.

"We have to color eggs, and we're going to marbleize them, so we need double the number of little bowls."

"I haven't colored eggs in decades," Anne stated, sounding please.

"Okay, then I'll put the 6 colors in one set of bowls, and then I'll put a smaller amount of the same 6 colors in another set of bowls, but these will have vegetable oil added to the color. You put the egg in the water dye mixture first, let the egg dry a bit and then you put it in the oil and water mixture second."

"Okay, Hope, you're going to have to sit this one out," Jennifer said, and put Hope back in the playpen.

"Jennifer, want some coffee, granola, bagel or anything else?" I asked.

"A glass of water would be perfect, thanks. Alex bought an extra bagel for me and I ate it on the drive here."

"That's beautiful music, what is that?" Anne asked.

"Mozart, it's Hope's favorite," Alex answered.

"Oh, a classical buff, eh?" Jennifer chuckled.

"She's got impeccable taste," I responded.

The girls had a great time coloring the eggs. Even Alex did a couple. They were unique, and for the most part gorgeous.

"Can I help you do anything?" Anne asked.

"The only thing that I have left to do today is make the pie. I'll steam the asparagus tomorrow morning. So I'm all set. But thanks for asking."

"Would you ladies like to walk out to the chamber?" Jennifer asked.

Anne and Mary both said 'yes' simultaneously.

"Okay, let's go!" Jennifer proclaimed.

Alex interrupted and said he'd better go with them, and he would get his gear together before they headed out. A few minutes later I watched as they walked off into the backyard.

The pie crust went in to bake when the ham came out, and a few minutes later it was nice and brown and cooling on the counter.

"Okay, Hope, let's go outside for a while."

I bundled her in a couple of blankets, put her in her stroller and wheeled her out the door onto the patio. What a treat it was to have such a warm day this early in spring. I wondered if I had overdone it with the blankets, but Hope looked perfectly comfortable. She was intently gazing across the lake.

I was lost in thought, just staring at the cloudless blue sky, when I heard the gang returning.

"How'd it go?" I asked.

"You won't believe it," Alex groaned.

"What?"

"Mary accessed the portal," he responded.

"What!"

"Tell her what happened, Mary," Anne urged.

"Well, we went into the chamber and walked up to the bench, and I don't know why I did it, but I hopped up on the bench, lay down and closed my eyes. I was just kidding around. A split second later it seemed like I was up on the ceiling, looking down at my body laying there. I saw everyone looking at me in shock, and then off I went."

"Off you went where?"

"I was soaring through the sky. Everything was so beautiful, the blues and greens were so vivid, so incredibly clear. I wasn't afraid. I flew over the Green Mountains, over the Connecticut River, over New Hampshire and I had just passed the Maine coastline when I came back."

"She was right; we were standing there in shock. I couldn't believe she jumped up on the bench. And then when we couldn't wake her, I was frightened. It looked to me as if she was getting fuzzy around the edges," Alex related.

"Fuzzy around the edges, what does that mean?" I asked.

"At first I thought she was clowning around, but it looked like her body was changing. It seemed to me that it was getting a little transparent," Anne added.

"I thought she was going to dematerialize right in front of our eyes!" Jennifer exclaimed. "Alex grabbed her off the bench and carried her out of the chamber. He put her down on the ground when he got outside and it took several seconds for her to come to."

"I felt a little disoriented at first," Mary admitted. "Within a few minutes I was fine though. What an incredible experience. I would do it again, that's for sure. I wonder where I was headed."

"Did you ever wonder how you would get back?" Alex asked sounding a little irritated. "Do you know you scared the hell out of me? How could I come back here and tell Connie that you dematerialized in the cave? Huh?"

Anne started to chuckle and Alex gave her a piercing look. Then Jennifer started to laugh, and before you knew it, we were all laughing, including Alex. I looked down at Hope and she was sound asleep.

Mary's excellent adventure was pretty much the topic of discussion for the remainder of the day. She said that she remembered having flying dreams when she was a child. Now she was thinking maybe they weren't dreams.

I told them about my out of body experience when I was a child; how I was looking down at myself standing there with my cousins but 'I' wasn't in that body.

We had an early dinner, as everyone seemed ravenous. I found an old recipe that I had written out when I was a teenager for 'Flounder a' la Gypsy' and vaguely remembered that everyone liked it all of those decades ago, so what the heck, I'd try it again. It had a sauce that consisted of sautéed onions and mushrooms combined with sour cream and paprika in which the flounder fillets were baked. It was similar to chicken paprikash, only with fish instead of chicken. I served it on buttered spinach noodles and it was a hit.

Chapter 15 – Kismet

We were all up bright and early Easter morning. It was as if we couldn't wait to begin the day.

Jennifer fed Hope her cereal and we all sat around the table, sipping our coffee and watching.

"So what can we do for you this morning?" Anne asked.

"The ham needs to be cut up in cubes as does the polinina. The kielbasa needs to be sliced. There are a dozen hardboiled eggs that we didn't color that need to be shelled and sliced. I've got to steam the asparagus and make the vinaigrette. The dining room table needs to be set. Hope needs to be bathed and dressed. Tulips, daffodils and narcissus need to be cut and arranged. I know I'm forgetting something else."

"I'm exhausted just listening to that list," Alex muttered.

"So how did you sleep last night, Mary, after your flight yesterday?" I asked.

"I slept wonderfully. I can't begin to tell you what an incredible experience that was. When I got in bed last night and closed my eyes I envisioned that flight again. I think I might have been heading to Scotland to check out Jennifer's cottage."

"How is your cottage?" Anne asked. "Are you happy with it?"

"Very. I've been up there for several long weekends. It was spotless when I arrived and the furniture is very comfortable and in good condition. I just had to stock some supplies, and that was it. There is a little general store close by. I actually bought a used bicycle that has a little wire basket on it, so I can ride the bike to the store and around the village. It is all so quaint. I kind of think of myself as the Maureen O'Hara character in 'The Quiet Man'."

"Right, she biked all over the Irish countryside, didn't she?" Anne recalled. "I love that movie."

"So, Mary, if you do happen to 'show up' at my cottage, there is a spare key under the flower pot on the wrought iron table out front."

"Thanks, that info might come in handy," Mary responded.

"If you don't mind, I'm going to take a shower and get dressed before I start doing anything else," I said.

"And I'll get the ham out and start cutting it up," Anne volunteered.

"Thanks. Just put it in one of those large food storage bags when you get through. We can arrange all of the meat and eggs on a large platter just before we sit down to eat."

When I came back down to the kitchen, Anne was slicing the polinina, and everyone was tasting it.

"I finished with the ham, so I figured I'd do the polinina next," Anne said.

"And does it pass the taste test?" I asked no one in particular.

"It is out of this world!" Alex exclaimed. "How come we only have this once a year?"

"Because you appreciate it more that way," I answered.

"Okay, I'm going to take a shower next and get dressed," Jennifer announced. "Then I'll cut the flowers and arrange them for you."

"Great, thank you!"

I cleaned the asparagus and put them on the stove to steam.

"I'll make the vinaigrette," Alex offered.

"Wonderful, we're moving right along."

"I'll set the dining room table," Mary chimed in. "Seven adults and two children, right?"

"Right. We'll put Hope's highchair at the table. Joshua is bringing Seth's highchair as well, so we will all be sitting together at the dining room table for the first time."

Anne was now working on slicing the kielbasa, and Alex was sneaking a piece every now and then.

"Are we having wine with brunch?" Alex asked.

"Yes, we Merry Edwards Sauvignon Blanc," I responded.

"Oh, that sounds perfect for brunch," Mary remarked as she finished setting the table.

Jennifer walked into the kitchen just then and everyone commented on how beautiful she looked. She had on a very pale aqua colored dress that was just stunning. It had a fitted waist and a full skirt with a scoop neck and three-quarter length sleeves.

"I got this in a little shop in Belgravia," she related. "I saw it in the window and fell in love with it."

"My turn to hit the shower," Anne announced and headed up the stairs.

"You know there is another shower in the bathroom down here," I reminded Mary, "you don't have to wait for Anne to get through."

"Hey, good idea!" she agreed and headed off to get her change of clothes and take a shower.

"Would you like me to bathe and dress Hope?" Jennifer asked.

"I've got plenty of time to do that myself, but thanks," I said.

"You want a flower arrangement for the dining room table, right?" Jennifer asked.

"Yes, and one for the cocktail table in the living room, and another one for the table here in the den. There are lots of flowers out on the other side of the courtyard, just as the woods meet the driveway."

"I'll go check out the vases in the cupboard in the mudroom to see which ones I want to use."

A few minutes later she came back with her selection of vases and put them on the counter. "Okay with you?" she asked.

"Perfect. The snips and a basket are out there under the counter," I advised.

A few seconds later she announced, "Okay, I'm off to pick flowers!"

Alex had finished making the vinaigrette and was out on the patio, sipping coffee and enjoying the beautiful day. All of a sudden I heard him almost running toward the kitchen. I looked up, startled, and asked "What's wrong?"

"Someone is walking down the driveway. I think it's Russell!"

Mary was just entering the kitchen from the other side, and heard what he said. Anne was coming down the stairs toward the front hall. We all ran into the living room and looked out the front window. We could see Jennifer standing there, staring down the drive with basket and flowers in hand. At this point we could see that it was definitely Russell. She slowly started to walk toward him, and he extended his hand. He was saying something; most likely he was introducing himself.

She took his hand and they stood there hand in hand talking.

"Are they actually shaking hands or just holding hands?" Mary asked.

"I think it might have started out as a shake, but it looks like they're holding hands now. Oh, they just let go."

I could see Jennifer looking up at him and smiling as he talked.

He had his duffel bag slung over his shoulder, but apparently offered to hold her basket while she picked more flowers, as she handed the basket to him.

"I'd better get Hope washed and dressed," I said, and hurried off. I don't even think Anne, Mary or Alex heard me; they were so engrossed looking out the window.

I got Hope ready in record time, and as I came downstairs I could hear Mary say "They're coming toward the house, let's go into the kitchen."

I just made it into the kitchen when I heard the front door open. I could hear the footsteps coming down the hall and then I heard Jennifer say "Look who I found!"

We all looked up supposedly in complete surprise, except for Hope, who was already smiling and looking at Russell like she had been waiting for him.

"Russell," I exclaimed, and walked over to him with Hope in my arms. "How good it is to see you! I'd like to give you a hug, but I've got my hands full."

"It's good to see you, too, Connie. I understand this is Hope. Let me give you both hugs." And he put his arms around the both of us and gave us such a loving hug. Then he reached over and took Hope's little hand in his, and she gazed at him almost tenderly.

"Anne, it's wonderful to see you again," Russell said.

"I've got to have a hug, too!" she proclaimed and they embraced.

"And Mary, I'm delighted to see you!" he declared and hugged her.

"I'm glad to see you, Russell," Alex commented, "but please, don't hug me."

"Alex, you're a lucky fellow; you've got a house full of beautiful women."

"They certainly keep me hopping, that's for sure," Alex responded.

I looked at Jennifer and she had a look of pure joy on her face as she gazed at Russell.

"So you've met my daughter, Jennifer?" I asked.

"Yes, I introduced myself outside and I guess my reputation preceded me, as I felt she knew who I was before I made it all the way down the driveway."

"Will you have a cup of coffee?" I asked him.

"A glass of water would be great," he replied.

"Come sit down," Alex urged.

Russell joined Alex at the table, followed by Anne and Mary.

"I've got to get these flowers arranged," Jennifer said and headed toward the vases she had selected earlier.

I put Hope in the playpen and got a glass of water for Russell. As I handed him the water I said, "We're having brunch in a little while. Jane, the woman whose cloud painting you commented on will be here as well as her friend Joshua and her son Seth. I hope you will join us?" Out of the corner of my eye I could see Jennifer look up at Russell as I asked this.

"Connie, I'd love to join you. Thank you."

"A lot has happened since we saw you last," Alex advised. "So much, in fact, that I don't even know where to begin. And we have so much to ask you."

"Why don't we wait for Jane, Joshua and Seth to arrive," I suggested, "as they are very much a part of the story."

"You're right, good idea," Alex responded.

"That flower arrangement is beautiful, Jennifer," Russell remarked.

"Why thank you!" Jennifer said as she placed it on the table in front of the group. She finished arranging the other two, brought them into the living room and dining room, and then went over to the playpen and picked up Hope.

"Maybe Hope would like to go outside on the patio for a little while," she suggested.

"I'm sure she would. She loved being out there yesterday, and it's even warmer today. Just wrap one blanket around her, okay?" I asked.

"Can I help?" Russell asked.

"Yes, would you please get the stroller over there in the corner?"

Jennifer wrapped Hope in her blanket and put her in the stroller.

"Do you mind if I accompany them out on the patio?" Russell asked me.

"I think that would be nice," I responded.

We watched as the three of them made their way through the living room and out the patio door.

"Well, what do you make of that?" Mary said.

"I think the man of her dreams just walked into Jennifer's life," I answered.

Chapter 16 – The Story Begins

"I'll set another place at the table," Mary announced, and hurried off into the dining room.

"I can't wait to see Jane and Joshua's reaction when they meet Russell." Alex remarked. "What a surprise they have in store for them."

If I stood in just the right spot near the kitchen table, I could see all the way through the living room and out the French doors to the patio. Russell was wearing faded tan pants and a white shirt, unbuttoned at the neck with sleeves rolled up. He and Jennifer were sitting and chatting like they were old friends. Their body language indicated they were extremely comfortable with each other. I looked over at Hope, and she was sound asleep. Good, she needed a little nap.

"Are you peeking?" Alex asked.

"Caught me. They look perfect together. Jennifer said she had a very strong urge that she needed to be here at Easter. Russell was the reason. Remember that great force that is controlling my life? Well it's controlling all of our lives, even Jennifer's."

"Funny, I was thinking he'd be back here on the summer solstice," Anne commented. "I was shocked to see him walking down the driveway just now."

"Everything happens for a reason," I said and went to get the bagels to slice them.

"Is there anything else I can do?" Mary asked.

"No, I think we are all set now. All we need is for Jane and family to arrive."

We sat around the table, sipping coffee and taking turns every so often to get up and peek out at the patio.

"I think I hear a car approaching," Alex proclaimed and headed toward the front door.

"It's them!"

Anne, Mary and I followed him to the front door and out into the courtyard.

Hugs and kisses were exchanged and we headed back into the house. Anne carried Seth. Mary carried the ricotta pie. Jane carried the paska. Joshua carried the highchair. And Alex and I just sauntered in behind them carrying nothing.

Joshua placed the highchair by the dining room table and then joined us in the kitchen.

"Where's Jennifer and Hope?" Jane asked.

"Outside. Why don't we walk out to the patio and join them," I suggested.

We all headed through the living room toward the patio and I could hear Jane whisper "Is that who I think it is?"

Once outside I introduced Russell to Jane, Joshua and Seth.

Russell shook Jane's hand and said, "Jane, I admired your painting the last time I was here. I'm very pleased to meet you."

"What a surprise!" Jane exclaimed. "I had no idea you'd be here. It is so wonderful to meet you."

Russell shook Joshua's hand and then went over to Anne who was still holding Seth, and shook Seth's little hand. Seth smiled and seemed to nod.

"The day is so gorgeous, why don't we have a little wine out here on the patio before we go in for brunch," I suggested.

"Sounds like an excellent idea to me, I'll get the wine," Alex volunteered and headed for the door.

"Could you please wheel out the playpen first? Hope is wide awake now and it's warm enough for the children to be in the playpen here outside."

"I'll get the playpen," Joshua offered.

"Okay, thanks," Alex responded, and the two of them headed into the house.

"Jennifer, that dress is gorgeous. That color is great on you," Jane remarked.

"Why thank you very much."

Joshua wheeled the playpen out onto the patio, and took Seth from Anne and put him in it. Then he took Hope from her stroller and deposited her next to Seth. They looked at each other, smiled, and Hope handed Seth her star.

"They both love that star, Jennifer. You certainly picked out the right gift," I noted.

"How about those felt sided blocks, do they play with them?" she asked.

"They are their second favorite toy. They'll get around to the blocks next, just watch."

Joshua jumped up and opened the door for Alex who was approaching with the wine. Alex put the tray down on the table and handed a glass to each of us.

"I'd like to make a toast," he said and everyone raised their glass.

"This is the first time we have all been assembled together and I feel there is much adventure ahead for us individually as well as a group. Here's to us and to the future!"

"To us and to the future!" we chorused.

I gazed over toward Jennifer and Russell and they had eyes only for each other as the toast was said.

"So Russell, what do you do for a living?" Joshua asked.

"I'm a teacher," he responded.

"Where do you teach?" Alex asked.

"I'm based out of Meghalaya, India, but I have students all around the world."

"What subjects do you teach?" Anne inquired.

"Various subjects. My students are gifted students, and the curriculum varies from student to student."

"What ages are your students?" Mary asked.

"Well, you might find this hard to believe, but my students range in age from infants to young men and women in their early 20's. I've taught some individuals for over two decades, starting when they were just Hope and Seth's age."

"Where did you go to school, Russell?" Joshua queried.

"After graduating from high school here in Vermont, I spent several years studying in India. After that, I studied several more years in England; Cambridge to be exact. But I'm still learning everyday from what life has to teach. What do they say, 'experience is the best teacher'?"

"So it was when you were at Cambridge that you saw the original of 'The Baptism of Christ' at the Fitzwilliam Museum?" I asked.

"Yes, that's correct."

"Do you know that Jennifer also saw the original at the Fitzwilliam Museum?" I continued.

"Yes, I mentioned that to him as we passed it on our way out here to the patio," Jennifer said.

"Oh, look! Seth placed a block on top of the block that Hope just positioned in front of them, and now Hope is trying to place another block on top of that!" Mary exclaimed.

"She did it! "Good girl, Hope," Alex cheered.

We watched with amazement as Seth picked up another block. He looked up at us and gave us a broad smile. Then he very carefully placed the block on top of the other three. He actually did it! We all broke out into applause. Hope was intently watching us clap our hands, and she started clapping. Then Seth started to clap and the vibration made the little tower of blocks fall. At first he looked startled, and it appeared that he might cry. We were all laughing and still clapping. A big grin spread across his face. Hope picked up one of the blocks and positioned it in front of them, and the whole thing started all over again.

"Russell, we were wondering why your parents named

this spot 'Meghalaya'. Do you know why?" Anne asked.

"Actually, I think there were a couple reasons. When they were first married, they chose to build on this land because of the incredible view. What could be better than looking down at Lake Champlain and across at the Adirondacks? The sunsets here are some of the best seen anywhere. They actually camped out on the property as the house was being built. You know that stone foundation out back? Well, it used to be a barn, an old rickety barn, but it did provide shelter. My parents put up a large tent inside the barn and lived there. I remember my mother speaking very fondly of that time. She said they would lie outside on summer nights and watch the stars. Sometimes they seemed so close, she thought she could reach up and touch them. The house began construction in spring of 1936 and was completed in late autumn of that same year. They moved into the house just before the first snow fall.

"They lived here very happily, with the only disappointment being that they learned that my mother was unable to have children. They spent the war years working on this house and yard, pouring all of their love into their work and this house. My father dismantled the barn out back and used all of the salvageable wood to build the barn in front by the courtyard. He did the majority of that construction himself with my mother's help. Once the new barn was complete, they bought two horses named 'Satin' and 'Silk' and they would ride most days up and down the dirt roads that dot this hillside. When World War II was over, they decided it was time to travel.

"I hate to interrupt you, Russell, but perhaps this might be a good time to move our conversation into the dining room. I can't be the only one who's starving out here!" I said.

"Good idea, I'm famished," Jane agreed.

We picked up and moved inside and a short while later we were all seated around the dining room table with our smorgasbord in front of us. I sat at the head of the table with

Hope in her highchair next to me, and Jane sat at the other end with Seth. Russell sat to my right, with Jennifer next to him and Joshua on the other side of her. Alex was to my left with Mary and Anne next to him.

"What a feast this is!" exclaimed Russell.

"I hope you enjoy it," I responded. "It's a variation of the Slovak Easter breakfast we used to have when I was a child. Everyone, please help yourselves."

After a good bit of passing platters, bowls and baskets, we settled down to eat. Things got quiet for a several minutes as we ate.

"Jane, the paska is wonderful," I commented, breaking the silence.

"Thanks, I never made it before so I wasn't sure how it would turn out, but I'm very pleased with it. I made several of them. I froze a few and Joshua and I had some for breakfast this morning, so I knew it turned out well."

Seth and Hope had little dishes of diced bananas. They'd reach into it, pick up a tiny little piece, and then chew it to nothing. They both loved bananas. It was good for them, and it kept them busy.

As the feeding frenzy quieted down, Jennifer said "Russell, you said you're parents started to travel soon after World War II. Where did they go?"

"The first place they went was Europe. Neither one of them had been there before, and it was the first place they wanted to see."

"They didn't happen to go to Czechoslovakia, did they? I asked.

"Yes, they did. Why do you ask?"

"We found a smallish green stone out by the foundation of the barn. It was almost luminescent and slightly transparent. The structure was unusual as the exterior almost appeared to have little feathers extruding from the sides," I stated. "I think it is Moldavite."

"Yes, my mother found that in the Moldau River

Valley in Czechoslovakia. She felt that it was a beacon for the higher realms."

"Do you have any idea why it was out back at the old barn foundation? Alex asked.

"Yes, when my cousin reached me and told me my mother had died, he asked if there was anything he could do for me. I asked him to locate the green stone that my mother had carried and place it somewhere within the stone foundation of the barn. I asked that because my mother had mentioned to me that she was happiest camping out in the foundation of that old barn when she was first married. My father was still alive at the time my mother died, but not well. I told my cousin that if he couldn't locate the stone, to ask my father. I was sure he would know. Sure enough, my father had the stone in his possession. When my cousin told him what I had asked, my father agreed that it was the perfect spot for the stone. My father took the stone out of a box that he had stashed away in his bureau drawer and gave it to my cousin to put in the stone foundation."

"Alex was recently working out there by that foundation and found the stone. I recognized it as Moldavite, but I couldn't imagine how it got to that spot. Thank you so much for resolving those questions for me," I said.

"It's back out there sitting on that foundation now," Alex added. "Jane and Connie decided that it should go back where I found it."

"Thank you. That stone meant a great deal to my mother. She carried it with her at all times until the day she died and I'm sure that is where she would have wanted it placed."

"In addition to Europe, where else did they travel?" Jennifer asked.

"After Europe they traveled to South America, Africa, the Orient and Asia, in addition to Canada and various spots around North America."

"Did they travel to Meghalaya, India?" Jennifer asked.

"Yes, they did."

"Excuse me for asking this question, but you had mentioned that your mother was not able to bear children. How did you 'happen' along then?" Alex inquired.

"The same way that Hope and Seth 'happened'.

There was stunned silence. I don't know why, as I had anticipated this answer somehow. But actually hearing it in words was a real shocker.

"So your mother was impregnated by extraterrestrials, just as Jane and I were?" I asked.

"Yes."

"And we truly are all meant to be together. There is a reason for this?"

"Yes, there is," Russell affirmed.

Chapter 17 – The Story Continues

"We all have free will," Russell continued. "You and Alex could have decided this house wasn't right for you, but you didn't. And you could have ignored the true message of the bible, but you didn't. You could have stopped right there, but you didn't. You kept searching. You wanted to share your knowledge. And there were others who were receptive to your words. You had the courage to ask, and to receive."

"How do you know that we found the true message of the bible?" Alex asked.

"My parents found the truth in the bible. When I saw the books on your table and 'The Baptism of Christ' hanging on your wall, I knew that you had found truth as well."

"You had mentioned that you believe there were two reasons why your parents called this spot 'Meghalaya'," Jane said. "One was due to their experience from visiting Meghalaya, India, I would assume."

"Yes."

"And the other would be what?"

"I know you have now figured out the true meaning of 'Abode of the Clouds'; is that correct?"

"Yes, we believe it means 'temporary sojourn of the spaceships' or something similar; right?" I asked.

"Right. Remember I had mentioned that my parents would gaze at the stars on summer nights? Sometimes the stars seemed so close, my mother thought she could reach out and touch them? Well, stars aren't the only things my parents saw in the sky. They also saw spaceships in the night sky. At times they saw spaceships during the day, enveloped in a cloud, just as you depicted in your painting, Jane."

"These clouds would 'settle' over the field out back in front of the chamber. My parents would watch them come and go. At that point they never made a connection between the chamber and the spaceships."

"They could see the field from the house?" Jane asked.

"Yes, you have to remember it was over 50 years ago; the trees out back were not so high back then."

"And there is a connection between the chamber and the spaceships?" Jennifer asked.

"Yes, there is a portal located within the chamber."

Jane gave me this look like 'I told you so' and smiled.

"Russell, I know I interrupted you before," I noted, "and I do apologize, but I'm going to have to do it again. Why don't you folks stretch your legs a bit while I clean the table and put this food away?"

"I'll help you, Mom," Jennifer offered.

"Me too," Jane added.

"Why don't you fellows take Hope and Seth back out to the playpen. It looks like they're ready to doze off, so they'll probably lay right down. When they do, cover them with a blanket. Okay?"

"Are you sure I can't help you in the kitchen?" Anne asked.

"Thanks, but the three of us can handle it in no time. You and Mary have been working all morning; take a break for a change."

They took the children and went outside and Jane and Jennifer and I started putting the food away and cleaning up the kitchen.

"You have to admit, we have some interesting conversations, don't we?" I asked.

"Amazing, truly amazing," Jane marveled.

"What do you think of Russell?" I asked Jennifer.

"I was immediately drawn to him. I was standing there and I saw this man walking down the driveway toward me, and my heart skipped a beat. I knew it was him. And just like you, Mom, when his hand touched mine I felt a slight shock, like an electric current had passed between us."

"I had no inkling that he was of extraterrestrial parentage. That really surprised me," Jane confided.

"Somehow I kind of expected it" I replied. "When he said that his mother was unable to have children, the thought popped into my head. It's all starting to make perfect sense now."

"Do you think Russell's 'father' is the same as Hope's and Seth's?"

"I don't know. I wonder if Russell actually knows," I answered. "I guess that's something we're going to have to ask him."

"And what do you think about the portal out back?" Jane asked.

"I know I shall never doubt you again." I said jokingly.

Everything was in order in the kitchen. I put the coffee on and we joined the rest of them on the patio. Hope and Seth were sound asleep in the playpen.

"Coffee is on and we'll have dessert in a little while," I announced. "Russell, you were just starting to tell us about the portal out back."

"Yes. Through that portal you can connect with other portals located around the globe. Beings from other worlds, both from within and from without our solar system, can access that portal to travel here. As I understand it, entities from other dimensions can also use that portal for travel."

"So the beings in the spaceships can access that portal to travel to this spot?"

"Yes, this location and many other locations around the world."

"I had a personal experience with that portal," Mary confessed.

"What happened?" Russell asked.

Mary told him the whole story about how she was kidding around, jumped on the bench, had an out of body experience, and went zooming across New England in her astral state. If anyone else had heard this story, they would be fitting Mary for a straight-jacket. Thankfully, she was with a bunch of people who believed every word she said.

"Please, promise me that you won't do that again until you've received instruction on how to use that portal. Okay?" Russell asked.

"Receive instruction? Who is going to instruct me?"

"I am," Russell said.

You could actually hear a group gasp at that response.

"You are going to teach Mary how to use the portal?" Jennifer asked.

"I'm going to teach each and every one of you how to use the portal," Russell answered.

"Have you used the portal?" Jennifer asked.

"Ever since I was a child."

"Is that how you got here today?" Jennifer asked, continuing her line of questioning.

"Yes. Whenever I travel here, I use the portal."

"Sounds almost like a commercial 'whenever I travel, I use the portal'," Jane joked.

"Can't beat the price," Alex laughed.

"So how come you walked down the driveway instead of coming through the backyard?" Anne asked.

"I had to gradually explain to you that there was a portal on your property, so I walked up through the woods to the road and then down the driveway. Remember the last time I was here? If I had walked across your backyard instead of leaving via the driveway, wouldn't you have asked where I was going? And if I said I was going to hitch a ride on the interdimensional portal out back, wouldn't you think I was a lunatic?"

"Not us! We're a very broad minded group!" I

exclaimed and everyone laughed, including Russell.

"I think the coffee is ready," I advised. "Everyone stay here and I'll get it."

Russell got up and said, "I insist on helping."

"Since you put it that way, okay!" I responded.

When we reached the kitchen, Russell commented, "I know you are already aware of this, but you have a wonderful family and friends."

"Thank you."

"Jennifer is an especially beautiful woman. She made me feel so welcome and comfortable when we first met this morning."

"I'm very proud of her. She is extraordinary and a constant source of joy for me."

"She is what you have made her; how could she be otherwise?"

I poured the coffee into a carafe and put it on a tray along with mugs, dessert plates and utensils.

"I'll take these out and I'll be right back to help with the dessert."

"Oh, I hope those two get together," I thought to myself as Russell left the room. "He is perfect, and part extraterrestrial to boot!"

A minute later he returned and I handed him Jane's ricotta pie. I took the pineapple parfait pie in hand, and we walked out to the patio together.

"Ah, dessert!" Joshua proclaimed.

"They both look wonderful, I don't know which to have," Mary said.

"Have a little bit of both," I urged.

"Or you can have a lot of both, whatever!" Anne chimed in.

As it turned out, everyone had a little bit of both and Jane and I received rave reviews on each.

"So, Russell, how does this portal thing work?" Mary asked. "I was on my way to somewhere, but I don't know where."

"See that's the problem; you need to know where you are going. You have to connect with a portal on the other end. So if you don't know where the portal is at the other location, you'll just be flying around aimlessly."

"And what would have happened to me?" Mary asked.

"At some point your etheric cord would return you to your physical body located at the portal from which you left."

"I thought she was going to dematerialize," Jennifer claimed. "Alex described it as if she were getting fuzzy and Anne thought she was a little transparent."

"Oh, so you think I'm a little transparent, do you?" Mary kidded Anne.

"If Alex didn't remove her from the chamber when he did, she would have remained in a semi-transparent state. The body doesn't dematerialize until the etheric or astral body has successfully reached the portal on the other end. When he brought her out of the chamber, it jolted her astral body back into her physical body."

"How do you know where the portals are? You said they are located all around the world, right?" Anne inquired.

"You learn over time. Plus we have resources at the Center to help locate portals for us in whatever location to which we need to travel."

"Sort of like a portal travel agent?" Jane asked.

"Something like that."

"I have a cottage in Scotland. It's on Arran Isle in Lamlash Bay across from Holy Isle. Is there a portal near there?" Jennifer asked.

"There is a portal on Arran Isle, but it is at the other end of the island from Lamlash Bay. This is a good example of what I was trying to explain. You could project yourself to that portal on Arran Isle, and then what would you do? You'd either have to walk to the nearest transportation, or walk all the way to your destination. It does take some planning."

"So how would you recommend I get to Lamlash

Bay?" Jennifer asked.

"There is a portal in Glasgow. It's down an alley not far from the train station. Once you materialize at that portal, then you could walk to the train station, take the train that brings you to the ferry, and there you have it!

"There is also a portal on Holy Isle. It would be closer for you, but you would have to be aware of the ferry schedule, as, if I recall correctly, that ferry does not run frequently other than during the summer months. Another issue is that the portal is located in a rather secluded spot in a rock outcropping, so it is not all that easy to climb out of there and access the ferry."

"How did you learn all this?" Jennifer marveled.

"I had a teacher."

"Where did you find this teacher?" Jennifer asked.

"He was assigned to me."

"Assigned to you by whom?"

"By the Center."

"And why would the Center assign a teacher to you?"

"Because of my heritage."

"Meaning your extraterrestrial heritage?"

"Yes."

"Does that mean Hope and Seth will be assigned a teacher?" Jennifer continued to ask.

"They have already been assigned a teacher."

"And is that teacher you?" Jennifer asked.

"Yes, that is correct."

"You have been assigned as teacher to Hope and Seth?" Jane asked.

"Yes."

"Well, I for one couldn't be happier," Jane confessed.

"Me, too," I added.

"When does this teaching begin?" Alex asked.

"It has already begun," Russell responded.

"I have a zillion questions to ask you, and I know there are a zillion more I haven't even thought of yet. You won't be leaving any time soon, will you?" I asked.

"No, I was hoping to stay here for several days to explain everything to you. Is that alright?"

"It's perfect," I answered.

"You've provided us with so much information today, that I think my mind is in overload right now," Jane said. "How about we resume this discussion tomorrow morning?"

"Yes, that would be good. There is only so much that can be assimilated at one time," Russell responded.

"How about we take a walk?' Jennifer asked Russell.

"Great idea," he murmured and with that they got up and took off toward the 'Meghalaya' bench and the lake.

"So what do you think?" I asked.

"He is part of that grand design. He was meant to be Hope and Seth's teacher. Actually, he was meant to be teacher to us all. I am perfectly happy and have complete confidence in him," Jane declared.

"We'll see what happens tomorrow," Alex added.

Hope and Seth woke up shortly after Jennifer and Russell left. Jane and I fed them their dinner, and soon after that Jane, Joshua and Seth left for home. Jane said they would be back the next morning.

Every now and then, I would look out at Jennifer and Russell, walking the property, sitting at times, and talking. They looked like they belonged together. They looked so happy.

It was shortly after dark that they came back into the house.

"Russell, I don't have any spare bedrooms. Would you mind sleeping on the couch in the living room? There is a bathroom down on this level. Alex can tell you the couch is comfortable; he's slept on it enough."

"That would be great, Connie. Thank you."

"I'll put some sheets, blankets and pillows on the couch for you."

"Again, thank you so much for your hospitality," he

responded.

"After that, I'll be going up. I'm exhausted!" I exclaimed.

"I'll see you tomorrow morning then. I hope you sleep well."

Jennifer came to give me a hug and said "Thanks so much for a marvelous day. I am so glad that I'm your daughter!"

Mary and Anne were already upstairs and I could hear them talking as I approached the open door to their room.

"Hey, ladies, it's been quite a day, hasn't it?"

"Unbelievable," Anne admitted.

"I can't wait to see what tomorrow brings," Mary added.

"Me neither," I replied and headed to bed.

Chapter 18 – Teacher

Anne, Mary, Jennifer and Alex were sitting around the kitchen table, sipping coffee and listening to Russell when I came down the next morning.

"Good morning, Mom!" Jennifer piped and got up to take Hope from me. She seemed to be very chipper this morning.

"If you get her cereal ready, I'll feed her."

Russell came over and gave me a hug, which surprised me. "How'd you sleep, Connie?"

"Great. How about you? Was the couch comfortable?'

"It was. I went out like a light and I don't think I moved all night."

I poured myself a cup of coffee and made Hope's cereal. Jennifer put Hope in her highchair and started to feed her.

I began toasting a variety of bagels and Anne got the cream cheese and jam out of the refrigerator. In no time at all, we were munching away.

"So what's on the agenda for today?" Mary asked Russell.

"I thought we'd start experimenting with the portal," Russell suggested.

"Experimenting how?" Alex asked.

"I'll take you somewhere."

"You'll use the portal to take us somewhere?" Anne asked.

"Yes. I'll do this one by one with each of you. I will accompany each of you on the trip."

"Couldn't that be dangerous?" Alex asked.

"Not at all. Believe me, it is the safest form of travel!"

"Can I go first?" Jennifer asked.

"If you'd like," Russell answered. "How about we travel to Glasgow?"

"Great! Can we go to my house on Arran Isle?"

"Not today, that will take too long. Once we reach Glasgow, then we'd have to take the train, and then the ferry and come back that same way. Although travelling to Glasgow would be almost instantaneous, the remainder of the trip would be in real time. I think your mother would be most anxious to make sure you were alright on your first portal trip; you wouldn't want her waiting for hours, would you?"

"Oh, I didn't consider that. You're right. But can we travel to Arran Isle some other time?"

"Certainly. We'll have to leave very early in the morning. You have to consider the time difference between here and Scotland. So although it will be morning here when we leave, it will already be afternoon there."

"Can I go somewhere in Greece?" Anne asked.

"No problem," Russell affirmed.

"I think Jane and Joshua just pulled up," Alex said and went to the front door.

"They're earlier than I expected them," I noted. "They probably couldn't wait to get started either."

After some coffee and a little more discussion, the plan was that Jennifer would be the first to try the portal. I would go out to the chamber with her as well as Alex, Mary, Joshua and of course, Russell. Anne and Jane would stay behind at the house with Hope and Seth.

The grass and the woods were still thick with dew and bathed in shadow cast from the mountain. As we reached the chamber Alex mentioned that Joshua had almost fainted the last time he approached the blue marble bench.

Russell said that there was a vortex of swirling energy at the sight, and it was not unusual for that type of reaction. He asked Joshua to signal by raising his left hand if he was feeling uncomfortable in any way.

Russell continued to explain that he would lay down on the bench first and Jennifer should follow. He said he would put his right arm around Jennifer's shoulder. She should then reach up with her right hand and hold his hand as it draped over her shoulder. She should then hold his left hand with her left hand. He would give her left hand a squeeze, as a signal to close her eyes. As soon as that happened, they would be off.

I asked if there were any chance that they could be separated. He said as long as they held hands as he explained, that would not happen. I then asked if Jennifer should be given the exact location of the portal in Glasgow, so that if she were somehow separated from Russell, she could reach it on her own. He said that if two people traveling by this method both had the exact location in their minds somehow one of them might misunderstand the coordinates of the location, and then they could possibly be separated. There was less chance of failure if only one of the two had the coordinates of the destination portal in mind.

We all walked into the chamber. It was extremely dark, only poorly lit by the several flashlights which we carried with us. Russell climbed onto the bench. He advised it would most likely take several minutes for Jennifer and him to travel to Glasgow and return. He asked that we not be anxious and told us to leave the chamber and wait for their return outside. He then asked Jennifer to lie on the bench next to him. He put his right arm around her shoulder and she reached up with her right hand and held his right hand. Then he reached over with his left hand and took her left hand in his. He instructed, "Okay, Jennifer, when I squeeze your hand close your eyes and try not to think of anything. Try to keep your mind blank."

He squeezed her hand and they both closed their eyes. Almost immediately I could see a difference in their physical bodies. They were getting somewhat transparent. Seconds later they had dematerialized. I felt frantic, but I tried to remain calm. As a group we turned and left the chamber.

"How do you feel, Joshua?" Alex asked.

"A little shaky, but not as bad as I did the first time."

"And how are you, Connie?" Alex inquired.

"Nervous."

"That's understandable. It's not every day that you see your daughter traveling through an interdimensional portal."

"Who is going next after Jennifer?" Mary asked.

We all looked at each other in silence.

"Well, if nobody minds, then I'd like to go next," Mary said. "I already have a feel for what is going to happen and I'm looking forward to it."

"Okay, you go next," I replied.

"Where are you going to go?" Alex asked.

"I'd like to go to Machu Picchu in Peru. I don't know if there is a portal there, but I'll ask Russell when he returns."

Minutes passed by. It seemed like it was taking too long; at least it seemed that way to me. It should have been an almost instantaneous thing…there and back. Why had several minutes passed? Had something gone wrong? Had they been separated?

There was tense silence, and then we heard voices and looked toward the chamber opening and there appeared Jennifer and Russell walking toward us deep in conversation.

"What took you so long?" I questioned.

"Your daughter insisted that we buy a newspaper to prove that we had been to Glasgow, so we had to walk around the corner to the newsstand. I'm very sorry if it made you anxious, Connie."

Jennifer held up today's edition of the 'Daily Record', one of Scotland's daily newspapers. She had a big grin on her face.

"What an incredible experience! I loved it. There is absolutely nothing to fear. Like Mary mentioned, we zoomed across New England, then the Atlantic and finally zeroed in on our portal in Glasgow. It was only a matter of seconds and we were there."

"And how do you feel now?" I asked.

"Perfectly fine. No different than when I left."

I felt so relieved. Words cannot begin to tell how relieved I felt.

"Okay, so who's next?" Russell asked.

"I am," Mary advised. "Can you take me to Machu Picchu?"

"Sure can. There's a portal there that is very convenient to the ruins. We might be there for a few minutes, so please don't get nervous if we don't return immediately, okay? After travelling all that way, Mary should at least see a little bit of the scenery."

With that, the two of them headed off into the chamber opening.

I looked at Jennifer and she was absolutely aglow.

"It was really that good, huh?" I asked.

"I just can't describe it in words. And the thing of it is, the entire world is pretty much open to us. There are portals all over England, which I would love to visit for a start. And to think I almost didn't buy the cottage in Lamlash Bay. I can travel from here to there, or at least very close to there, in a blink of an eye pretty much."

"So who's going next after Mary?" Alex asked.

"If you don't mind, I'd like to," Joshua blurted. "I just want to get it over with."

"Do you know where you'd like to go?" Joshua asked.

"Sedona. I would think there'd be quite a few portals out there."

Several minutes later Mary and Russell appeared at the chamber entrance.

"How was it, Mary?" Alex asked.

"Incredible. I know for sure I definitely want to spend some time visiting Machu Picchu. We followed the East Coast southward, crossed the Caribbean and on into South America and Peru. It was an amazing trip!"

"Why don't you and Jennifer head back to the house and take over the babysitting role and let Jane and Anne come out here?" I suggested.

"Okay, sounds good," Jennifer said and took off with Mary toward the house.

"And who's next?" Russell asked.

"I am," Joshua advised. "Know any good portals in Sedona?"

"Do I! Follow me..." Russell remarked and they disappeared within the chamber.

"Are you nervous?" Alex asked me.

"You have no idea how nervous I am."

"I think I do."

"You're nervous too?"

"Incredibly so. But, hey, if Joshua can do it, so can I."

"Do you want to go next?" I asked.

"Yes. Like Joshua said, 'I just want to get it over with.'"

"Have you decided where you would like to go?"

"Somewhere on the Orkney Islands. I think I remember reading that some of the oldest and best preserved Neolithic sites in the world are located there. I'm sure there must be a portal."

A couple of minutes later we heard Joshua's voice and turned around to see him emerge from the chamber with Russell.

"There is absolutely nothing to be afraid of," Joshua reassured. "It was a piece of cake. What an adventure. Russell took me to Boynton Canyon in Sedona. It was early morning and the sun was just coming up over those beautiful red rock cliffs. Everything was so still and then all of a sudden a pack of deer ran by very close to where we were standing. What an experience."

"Let me guess," Russell speculated, "Alex is next."

"How'd you know?"

"Just had a feeling."

With that they took off toward the chamber and I could hear Russell ask, "Okay, where are we headed?"

Joshua couldn't stop talking about his experience. He seemed euphoric. "There's a resort in that canyon. You could hike to it from the portal. Just pack a duffel bag like Russell does, travel to that portal, hike to the resort and stay for a few days. No airfare involved. Isn't it amazing?"

"I guess this is just one of the perks of having an extraterrestrial child," I stated with just a touch of sarcasm.

"Ha, that's very funny, Connie. But don't you see? This is opening a whole new world for us."

"Yes, you're right. I guess I'm still a little nervous about this whole thing."

No sooner had I said that when Alex walked out of the chamber with Russell.

"Connie, I don't know if you've decided where you want to go, but I would strongly recommend the portal that Russell just took me to. He took me to the Neolithic village of Skara Brae on the Orkney Islands. Russell said he believed it was first inhabited about 3000 BC. Can you imagine?"

Just then Anne and Jane appeared at the edge of the clearing and approached us.

"So how's it going?" Jane asked. "Have you all taken your trips?"

"Alex and I have, but not Connie." Joshua said. "I went to Boynton Canyon in Sedona. What a trip."

Joshua continued to talk about his trip and his plans on staying at that resort in the future.

"Connie, are you next?" Russell asked.

"Yep, I guess I am."

"Where do you want to go?"

"Could you please take me to the same portal in Glasgow that you took Jennifer? I'd like to see how to get from there to the train station, just in case I want to take a trip over in the future."

"Are you sure? There are many other exciting places in the world to visit. We can take that trip anytime."

"I'm sure."

"Let's go!" Russell exclaimed. I waved goodbye to everyone and followed Russell into the chamber. His flashlight dimly lit the way for us as we approached the marble bench.

"Okay, I'm going to lay down first, Connie. You slide on after me. Don't close your eyes until I squeeze your left hand."

We positioned ourselves on the bench and then Russell put his right arm around my shoulder and I reached up with my right hand to hold his hand. Then he took my left hand with his left hand.

"Do not move and do not let go. Are you ready?"

"Yes."

"When I squeeze your left hand, close your eyes."

As instructed, I closed my eyes when he squeezed my hand and had a brief view of our bodies lying next to each other on the bench. Then it was up, up and away. I could see the mountains, rivers and lakes below us. We approached the coastline, crossed over what I assume was Nova Scotia and then the Atlantic. I could see land ahead of us and then all of a sudden I felt like I was standing on good old terra firma. I could still feel Russell's arm around my shoulder and we continued to hold hands."

"You can open your eyes," Russell instructed as he removed his arm from my shoulder.

We were standing in a recessed opening in an old stone wall. There was an iron gate behind us and a courtyard beyond that. In front of us was a narrow cobblestone alley. To the right there was a dead end.

"How do you feel?" Russell asked.

"Wonderful. I don't really feel any different from when I left Vermont, except that I'm a lot less nervous now."

"Good. Shall we head over to the train station?"

"Let's go," I replied.

We turned left and reached the main street. Then we made a right and another right and the station was two blocks up on the left side.

"This is Glasgow Central Station. The train you need to catch is the Ardrossan train which will bring you directly to the ferry to reach Arran Isle. So it's a left out of the portal, then a right and another right. Simple, huh?" Russell asked.

"Very. Do you mind if I grab one of those timetables over there?" I asked.

"Good idea. They do change the schedules every now and then, but this will at least give you an idea of how the trains run."

I took one of the timetables then Russell and I retraced our steps and returned to the portal. We repositioned ourselves exactly as we had been when we arrived, his arm around my shoulder, holding hands.

"Okay, Connie. Stand very still, don't let go of my hands. When I squeeze your left hand, close your eyes."

Several seconds later I felt the hard cold marble beneath me and I knew I was back.

"Feeling okay?" Russell asked.

"Fine, just fine. That was incredible. Thank you so much."

I sat up on the bench. Russell reached over for his flashlight and we got up and walked out.

"How was it?" Jane asked when we walked into daylight.

"I know how to get to the Glasgow train station to get a connecting train to the ferry for Arran Isle!" I responded. "Look, I already have the train schedule," and I pulled it out of my pocket to show them.

Anne and Jane looked at the train schedule and I could almost see a sense of relief on their faces. I'm sure that they, too, were anxious about the 'trip'. My safe return and that train schedule helped them to relax.

"Ladies, I'm going to head back to the house," I said. "How about when you return from your trips we sit down and eat some of yesterday's leftovers?"

Everyone agreed that it sounded like a good plan. Anne was travelling next and Alex stayed with Jane while she waited for her turn.

I reached the house and immediately Jennifer asked me what had happened? Was I okay? Where did I go?

I pulled out the Glasgow Central Station train schedule out of my pocket and showed it to her.

"You went to Glasgow, too?"

"Yes, Russell showed me how to get to the train that would take me to your cottage."

"Of all the places in the world that you could have gone, you wanted to see how to get to my cottage?"

"I couldn't think of anywhere else I would rather go. It was the short and not winding road that leads to your door."

Jennifer gave me a hug and asked "Do you know I love you very much?"

"I do."

"Let's get yesterday's leftovers out of the refrigerator. We'll just have an informal buffet in the den. So we can put plates and utensils on the kitchen counter along with the food and everyone can help themselves."

A short while later the remainder of the group returned, telling all about their travel adventures.

I had glasses of wine on the counter, and everyone took a glass.

Jane declared, "Here's to our travel guide. Russell, thank you so much!"

Chapter 19 – Questions and Answers

After lunch we sat outside on the patio. Hope and Seth were back in their playpen taking turns building with their blocks.

We sipped coffee and reflected on our portal travels that morning.

"I'd like to thank all of you for trusting me," Russell said.

"Trusting you?" Mary asked.

"Yes, you all trusted me with your lives. You trusted that I would transport you safely through the portal."

"How did you learn to use the portal?" Alex asked.

"My teacher showed me. His name is Joseph. When I was a very young child he would take me to India with him via the portal. As I got older, I would travel to the Center alone."

"How did you meet Joseph?" Anne asked.

"He walked down the driveway one morning when I was several months old and introduced himself to my parents."

"So he traveled from the Center via the portal just as you did?"

"Yes. As I understand it he introduced himself to my parents and explained that, if they so desired, he had been assigned to be my teacher. Please understand that they could have refused his offer; they had free will to accept or reject what was being proposed to them. They welcomed him into their home then and many times thereafter. They accepted that he would be my teacher and allowed him to spend time with me periodically while I was just an infant. As I grew older, he would spend several hours with me over the course of each month, at times taking me with him to the Center via the portal."

"How did your parents learn of the Center?" I asked.

"Joseph told them of its existence and described its mission to them."

"When your parents traveled to Meghalaya they didn't visit the Center?" I queried.

"No. It is not accessible to the public. More than that, it's not even visible to the public. Only those who are chosen can travel there. It is located beneath the mountains of Meghalaya and can be reached via the portal system. Within it is housed an amazing support system for humans of extraterrestrial heritage. There are various components, education and training being the largest."

"Were you told that you were to be a teacher?" Jennifer asked.

"No, we have free will just as a normal human has. We can choose to live a life free from any association whatsoever with the Center. Or, we can choose to use the Center as a resource as we live fairly normal human lives. And then there are others who choose to affiliate with the Center and make it their life's work. I chose to become a teacher at the Center. There are others who have chosen other professions within the Center, such as medicine, science, administration."

"How long has the Center been in operation?" Joshua asked.

"It's been in operation for almost as long as there have been humans with extraterrestrial heritage and that's been occurring for thousands of years."

"I have reached the conclusion that described within the bible are instances of extraterrestrial insemination of women which have produced extraordinary humans," I asserted. "This is described in both the Old and New

Testaments, with the most notable being Jesus Christ. I also came to the conclusion that Jesus had what Alex called 'a double dose of extraterrestrial DNA' in him, as his mother, Mary, was also of extraterrestrial heritage. Am I correct in this assumption? And if I am correct, did Jesus study at the Center."

"Yes you are correct on both accounts. You might recall there were 'the lost years or hidden years' of Jesus. These were the years during the ages of 13 to 29. There is much speculation about what did or what didn't occur during that period of time. I can confirm to you that Jesus did travel to India and he did study at the Center for a period of time. "

"And he travelled via portal as well?" Jane asked

"Yes."

"How did he learn of the portal?" Alex asked.

"He had a teacher who took him to Meghalaya via the portal."

"Jesus also had a teacher?" Jane asked.

"Yes, he was one of the magi, one of the three wise men or three kings who had followed the star to Bethlehem when Jesus was born."

"Before we continue," I interrupted, "the 'star' was not just a star, it was a spaceship, is that correct?"

"Yes, that's right. This was a very important extraterrestrial/human hybrid about to be born. There was more extraterrestrial DNA in Jesus than any other human before him. The spaceship and the magi were there to observe and they were also there as a sign to others of extraterrestrial ancestry who had been awaiting Christ's birth. Through their witness, the word would be spread."

"This is the first time you used the word 'hybrid' in relation to humans with extraterrestrial heritage. Is there a reason you have been avoiding that word 'hybrid'?"

"It has been used so often today, and it means so many different things to different people. I have to admit, I bristle when I hear it used repeatedly by people who have no clue as to what it's really about."

"So the magi actually existed?" Joshua asked.

"Yes.   There were more than three of them that followed the star. They were all of extraterrestrial heritage and affiliated with the Center.   Within a couple years, Jesus exceeded the abilities and knowledge of his teacher. At that point, a group of teachers banded together to work with him, but for the most part they were learning more from him than visa versa.

"I've been told that at this point in his education, he had direct contact with his 'father'."

"Meaning his extraterrestrial father?" Jane asked.

"Yes, there was nothing else for him to learn from his earthly teachers. He was taken up into a lightship and was given direct instruction by his father. The major part of that teaching involved the power of the mind."

"I always believed an important part of his ministry related to the power of belief, the incredible power of the mind," I interjected.

"Yes, it was one of the major subjects of his teaching here on Earth. However, it seems that it has been downplayed for the most part by organized religion which didn't want humankind to learn of the power which each one of us possesses within our mind.

"After his teaching was concluded, Jesus travelled throughout India, Tibet and Nepal teaching. He also travelled elsewhere around the world using the portal system. I believe he travelled around the globe."

"I've got a question that is a little off track with this discussion," I broke in. "It concerns the parentage of those who are of extraterrestrial heritage. Since this 'seeding' has been occurring for years, am I correct in assuming that there are many different 'fathers' involved? And is the use of the word 'seeding' objectionable to you?"

"The word 'seeding' is also used by many in many different ways. However, it does define what has and is happening to some extent, which we will discuss later. The federation involved with the Center includes beings of light representing numerous celestial bodies from within this universe as well as from outside this universe. The most esteemed members of all of these extraterrestrial races have contributed to this 'seeding' over these thousands of years."

"So are you saying that Hope and Seth do not have the same 'father'?" Jane asked.

"I don't believe so, but I am not privy to that information. Their blood type should be the same major group as the mother; the minor sub group will be that of the father. If they have different sub groups, then that will confirm that they have different fathers."

"Do you have Rh negative blood?" I asked Russell.

"Yes."

"Are you aware that Jane and I, as well as the other twenty-two women who had their babies at the same time, have Rh negative blood?"

"It is not surprising."

"And you have a rare minor blood type?" Jane asked.

"Yes."

"What type is it?" she asked.

"So rare that it hasn't been named."

"What happens if you need a transfusion?"

"We periodically donate blood and plasma for our own use which our Center's health unit stores for us."

"How long does the stored blood last?" Mary asked.

"Red blood cells can be frozen for up to ten years. Fresh frozen plasma can be kept up to one year," he responded.

"Do you have medical doctors and a hospital at the Center?" I asked.

"We have both doctors and a hospital; however, they function differently than the average medical professionals here on earth. The goal of the 'doctors' at the Center is to keep you healthy. Their primary objective is not to treat you once you have already become 'dis-eased' as is the goal of doctors here on Earth, but to keep you well. They monitor any deficiencies within your system and supply you with vitamins, minerals and enzymes that you are lacking. If herbal products are determined to be of benefit, they are prescribed. Proper diet consisting of fresh fruit, vegetables, whole grains, seeds and nuts is the most important aspect of health, and these doctors monitor your diet to assure optimum well-being."

"I have a question," Mary said. "You referred to beings of light within the federation, which I would assume are benevolent beings. Are there beings of darkness?"

"Did you read about the temptations of Jesus in the gospels?" Russell asked.

"Yes, a very long time ago, but I did read it. It was during the period that Jesus was fasting forty days and forty nights in the desert. The devil appeared and tempted Christ to prove his divinity by demonstrating supernatural powers in various ways. Like 'turn this rock into a loaf of bread'."

"That's right. The 'devil' as described in this passage of the bible was a being of darkness."

"Do these beings still exist?" Mary asked.

"Yes. There are benevolent extraterrestrials as well as malevolent."

"I'm going to get the bible. I remember there was something about the temptation of Christ passage that I questioned when I read it, but I don't remember what it was," I remarked. I went into the house and returned with both the King James and Douay-Rheims bibles in hand.

I opened the King James Bible and found the passage in Matthew 4:1-11 and read it out loud:

"'Then was Jesus led up of the spirit into the wilderness to be tempted of the devil. And when he had fasted forty days and forty nights, he was afterward hungry. And when the tempter came to him, he said, If thou be the Son of God, command that these stones be made bread. But he answered and said, It is written, Man shall not live by bread alone, but by every word that proceedeth out of the mouth of

God.

"Then the devil taketh him up into the holy city, and setteth him on a pinnacle of the temple, and saith unto him, If thou be the Son of God, cast thyself down: for it is written, He shall give his angels charge concerning thee: and in their hands they shall bear thee up, lest at any time thou dash thy foot against a stone. Jesus said unto him, It is written again, Thou shalt not tempt the Lord thy God.

"Again, the devil taketh him up into an exceeding high mountain, and sheweth him all of the kingdoms of the world, and the glory of them; And saith unto him, All these things will I give thee, if thou wilt fall down and worship me. Then saith Jesus unto him, Get thee hence, Satan: for it is written, Thou shalt worship the Lord thy God, and him only shalt thou serve. Then the devil leaveth him, and behold, angels came and ministered unto him.'"

"The King James bible wording is a little archaic, isn't it? But what I was thinking of was the part where the devil showed Jesus all of the kingdoms of the world and said he would give all this to Jesus if he would worship him. What made the devil think the kingdoms of the world were his to give? Actually, I think there is even a more peculiar wording in one of the others gospels. Let me look."

I flipped over to Mark's gospel, but there was only a very brief reference to the temptation of Christ. I found what I was looking for in Luke, however. I read out loud from Luke 4:5-8:

"And the devil, taking him up into a high mountain, shewed unto him all the kingdoms of the world in a moment of time. And the devil said until him, All this power will I give to thee, and the glory of them: for that is delivered unto me; and to whomsoever I will I give it. If thou therefore wilt worship me, all shall be thine. And Jesus answered and said unto him, Get thee behind me, Satan: for it is written, Thou shalt worship the Lord they God, and him only shalt thou serve."

"It's that phrase 'all this power will I give to thee...for

that is delivered unto me' which intrigues me. It sounds like all the kingdoms of the world were given to the devil, and as such, they were his to give away. And one other thing, in Matthew's gospel he specifically says 'Jesus was led up of the spirit into the wilderness to be tempted by the devil.' You have to remember that this happened right after the baptism of Christ, where the spaceship hovered over Jesus in the River Jordan and said 'thou art my beloved son in whom I am well pleased'. So the father of Jesus is saying he's well pleased with Jesus at one moment, and the next he takes him to the wilderness to be tempted by the devil. What do you make of all this, Russell?" I asked.

"Well, I guess you could say the power and kingdoms of this world do belong to the devil," Russell responded.

That response certainly got everyone's attention.

"Could you please hand me the bible, Connie?" Russell asked.

We watched as he flipped over to the Gospel of John.

"Okay, this is it. John Chapter 8, starting with verse 43. Jesus is speaking to the Jews and this is what he says: 'Why do you not understand what I say? It is because you cannot bear to hear my words. You are of your father the devil, and your will is to do your father's desires. He was a murderer from the beginning, and has nothing to do with the truth, because there is no truth in him. When he lies, he speaks according to his own nature, for he is a liar and the father of lies.' Jesus is calling Yahweh a devil, a murderer and a liar.'"

"So 'God the Father' in the New Testament is not the 'God' of the Old Testament?" Joshua asked.

"Right. The so called Christian churches want you to believe that the Old and New Testament 'gods' are one in the same, but they are not. The Christians even put the New Testament together with the Old Testament and called it 'the bible'. They didn't want the human to start thinking about the possibility of two separate 'god' entities, as it might actually lead to the truth."

"Organized religion doesn't want the human to think period," Alex complained. "Just accept what they tell us 'on faith', that's what they want. And the good little sheep follow."

"You're right about that, Alex," Joshua muttered.

Then Russell turned to Ephesians, and I knew the section he was going to read next.

"This is Ephesians 6, verse 12: 'For our struggle is not against flesh and blood, but against the rulers, against the authorities, against the powers of this dark world and against the spiritual forces of evil in the heavenly realms.' These two selections from the bible pretty much describe the situation with the malevolent extraterrestrials."

"Are you saying that Yahweh, the god of the Old Testament, is a being of darkness?" Anne asked.

"Yes. He is responsible for creating 'this dark world' and belongs to 'the forces of evil in the heavenly realms' as stated in Ephesians. He is the Demiurge, an imperfect being who created this imperfect, material world. The beings of light are working to turn this dark world into a world of light. I am the result of their efforts, as are Hope, Seth and many others."

"I've got a question," Alex uttered. "Are the beings of darkness just going to sit back and watch you do this?"

"They haven't been."

"What do you mean?" Alex asked.

"Have you ever heard the term 'sell your soul to the devil'?"

Chapter 20 – Selling Your Soul

"Sell your soul? Does that have anything to do with extraterrestrials? Doesn't that relate to an individual's spiritual relationship with god and/or the devil?" Jane asked.

"Do you believe in reincarnation?" Russell asked.

"Yes." Jane responded.

We all murmured that we believed in reincarnation.

"And have you heard the term 'seventh heaven'?" Russell asked.

We all nodded our heads.

"What I am about to tell you is my belief. I might be of extraterrestrial heritage but I am still human. I have a slightly broader perspective of the cosmos than you have, that is all. I do not have access to spiritual truth or infinite knowledge, so please keep that in mind when you hear my words.

"When our spirit leaves our body at the time of death, it travels to an astral plane that is commensurate with the evolutionary level of our spirit at death."

"Sorry to interrupt, but before you go any further, I have a question," Jennifer said. "What is the difference between the soul and the spirit? Is there a difference?"

"Good question. And the answer is yes, there is most definitely a difference. Spirit is the spark of life; it is the breath of the Infinite Spirit that animates us. It is our divine connection. The conscience and intuition are part of this spirit. The soul is the seat of the human personality. Intellect, ideals, emotion, love, decision making and such are functions of the soul. The spirit and soul move together as one."

"Okay, now I've got to interrupt you." I piped in. "You said that spirit is the breath of the Infinite Spirit that animates us. It is our divine connection. Yet you also say that this world was created by the Demiurge, the Yahweh of the Old Testament, a malevolent extraterrestrial. If the Demiurge breathed the breath of life into the beings he created, then it wasn't the breath of the Infinite Spirit, it was his own."

"Yahweh was created by the Infinite Spirit. The divine spirit is within him as it is within each of us. It was that same breath of the divine spirit which he breathed into the first humans. Yahweh used his free will to turn to the dark side but the divine spirit is still within him. He and his followers have chosen a very difficult learning path. He could turn again to the light if he so desires. And I do believe that this will happen in time."

"Okay, now I have another question. There are two creation stories in the bible, the first in Genesis Chapter 1 and the second in Chapter 2. Let me turn to the wording so that I have this right," I said as I picked up the bible and turned to Genesis.

"In Chapter 2, verse 7 it says 'And the Lord God formed man of the dust of the ground, and breathed into his nostrils the breath of life; and man became a living soul.' It is describing Yahweh animating man by breathing the breath of life into man. And you just said that the breath that Yahweh breathed into man was the breath of the divine spirit. However, the first creation story in Chapter 1 does not mention Yahweh breathing life into man. Verse 27 simply reads 'So God created man in his own image, in the image of God created he him; male and female created he them'. Does this mean that the beings created in Chapter 1 do not have the divine spirit within them?"

"Correct, they were an experiment which wasn't successful."

"They were told 'to be fruitful and multiply'. Did they do that? Were they still in existence when the second creation took place?"

"Yes, they did multiply and they were very much in existence when the second set of beings were created. That was why Adam and Eve were kept separate in a garden. However, when they left the garden, some of their offspring did mingle with the first creation beings."

"Do you know if some of that bloodline is still on Earth today?" I asked.

"It is possible, but I do not know that for a fact. If that bloodline is still walking this planet, they have no connection with the divine spirit. They have no conscience, just as an animal has no conscience. I would imagine that they are predators who plunder and destroy for their own gain."

"Not only do we have to keep our eyes open for the dark extraterrestrials, we also have to be on the lookout for the empty shells walking around from the first creation!" Joshua exclaimed.

"Okay, Russell, we've rudely interrupted you enough. Please continue," Jane remarked.

"I believe that the spirit within each one of us is seeking to return to its origin, to reunite with the Infinite Spirit and end the cycle of birth and rebirth. As we grow in spirit through reincarnation, hopefully we ascend to higher levels on the astral plane. And we grow in spirit by listening to our conscience and following our intuition, as those are our connections with the Infinite Spirit.

"However, as the beings of light seek to influence the future of this planet, so do the beings of the darkness. The beings of light answered your pleas for help. You, Connie and Jane, as well as your sisters around the world, asked for extraterrestrial intervention to help in the ascension of this planet. Your prayers were answered. However, there are those who seek assistance from the forces of darkness.

"Every time a human disregards what is being told to him by his conscience, every time he ignores his intuition, he is seeking the assistance of the forces of darkness. Every time he does that he is selling his soul to the devil. There are humans on this planet who have extraterrestrial heritage that are of the dark side, not the light. They are here to influence those who are on the brink for whatever reason, humans who are easily influenced. And one by one, these humans make decisions that are opposite to what their conscience is telling them, opposite to what their instincts are telling them. At that point they are starting to walk into the dark side. The more they ignore their conscience and discard their instincts, the deeper and deeper they get into the dark side. They are selling their souls to the devil.

"When these humans die, they too travel to an astral plane that is commensurate with the evolutionary level of their spirit at the time of death. But that level is lower than when they began that life. Instead of growing in spirit, they are regressing. They are sinking to a lower level from which it is harder to escape. When they reincarnate, they reincarnate at a lower level and as they sink lower and lower spiritually, it is more difficult to ascend. These are the souls that the dark forces seek and latch on to. These souls eventually reincarnate into a world which is even darker than this planet Earth. There are many celestial bodies in the cosmos that are controlled by the beings of darkness. Some are darker than others and are pure hell. The spirits that find themselves there put themselves there."

"I hate to interrupt again, but are you saying that the planet Earth is a dark planet and controlled by beings of darkness?" Jennifer asked.

"Yes. The Book of Revelation even speaks of this 'And the great dragon was cast out, that old serpent, called the Devil, and Satan, which deceiveth the whole world; he was cast out unto the Earth, and his angels were cast out with him'."

"And we chose to be here?"

"Correct. When you advance spiritually and you reflect on your progress during the astral plane interval between lives, sometimes you choose to come back in a very difficult situation to expedite your advancement. You could have chosen a very easy existence, but that wouldn't afford you with challenges to be met. What makes it so difficult for advanced spirits on this planet is that they are surrounded by spirits who are in or heading toward the darkness. You specifically choose to come to this hell here on Earth in hopes that it will expedite your ascension.

"Keep in mind that there are beings from many other worlds within this galaxy and from without that currently occupy human bodies on this planet. Just because you are here in human form now does not mean that you have always incarnated on Earth. This might be your first trip here. It might also be your last."

"Yet the benevolent extraterrestrials have seeded this planet for thousands of years and still continue to do so. Why do this if Earth belongs to the dark, malevolent extraterrestrials?" Jennifer persisted.

"Because we see more advanced souls reincarnating on this planet and we feel there is a possibility to reach a critical mass that will swing Earth over to the light. Your mother and Jane recognized this and asked for our intervention. We did not thrust it upon them. Many other women have done likewise. There are many humans on this planet that are of benevolent extraterrestrial heritage. There are also many humans here that are of malevolent extraterrestrial heritage. We feel it is worth trying because it is so close, so very close to tipping the scales toward the light."

"Have there been humans in direct contact with the beings of darkness? You mentioned people ignoring their conscience and discarding their instincts and slowly getting further and further into the darkness. Have there been people who have directly asked for assistance from malevolent extraterrestrials?"

"Yes. If you think of the most evil persons that ever existed in the history of this planet, they were most likely in direct contact with the dark extraterrestrials. They directly sold their souls to the dark side. And there are currently many such people in very high levels of the government, military, the media, industry, technology, science and religious institutions.

"The temptation of Christ in the desert was perhaps the most well-known of the historical conflicts on an individual level between a being of light versus a being of the dark. And there have been wide scale struggles as well; the Inquisition being one of them."

"What about all the wars that have occurred throughout history? Didn't they involve light versus darkness?" Mary asked.

"Some of them did, yes, but not as many as you would think. There were many conflicts that were dark against dark. Those responsible on both sides for making the decision to go to war were not listening to their conscience or their intuition; they were only listening to ego, greed and envy."

"Are we and our children at risk from these dark beings?" Jane asked.

"I don't believe that you are any more at risk than the rest of us."

Alex had been very quiet during all this discourse and seemed to be deep in thought. I asked him what he was thinking.

"When Russell quoted from Revelation, '...the great dragon was cast out...' reminded me of the recurring dreams I've been having of flying dragons. It sent chills down my spine. Are those actually malevolent extraterrestrials that I've been dreaming of?"

Russell had a very pensive look on his face and it appeared he was just about to say something when Jane spoke.

"I hate to be a party pooper, but it's getting late and we really should be heading home," Jane announced. "How about getting together again tomorrow for lunch at our house?"

"Sounds good to me," I replied. "How about everyone else? Okay with you?"

Everyone agreed it sounded like a plan, and with that Jane picked up Seth, Joshua got the highchair and they headed on home.

Russell made us a delicious dinner of brown rice and black beans with salsa made from chopped tomatoes, onions, parsley, garlic and cayenne pepper tossed with olive oil and fresh lemon juice. It was so simple and so very delicious.

Everyone pitched in to help clean up the kitchen, and very soon thereafter Jennifer and Russell headed back to the patio. Was it a match made in heaven?

Chapter 21 – Blood Brothers and Sisters

We headed out for Jane's shortly before noon the next day in two cars. Jennifer, Russell, Anne and Mary were in the convertible and Hope, Alex and I were in the wagon. It was a blustery cold grey day and dramatically different than the past few unusually warm days.

As we drove off the main road down towards Jane's house, I commented on the lively whitecaps speckling the dark surface of the lake. We parked in front of the studio and I noticed that the tulips that Jane had planted around the flagpole were being whipped by the wind; the petals of some of the flowers that might otherwise have lasted for a couple more days were now skipping across the lawn.

I took Hope out of her car seat, bundled her in the blanket and headed toward the front door. Alex was right behind me with the highchair. Jennifer was just pulling up as Jane opened the door.

"What a difference a day makes!" she exclaimed. "Come in from the cold!"

"The cold I can take, it's the wind that almost cuts right through you," I shivered.

Alex headed into the dining room with the highchair while the rest of the group piled into Jane's foyer. Joshua collected everyone's coats and Jane ushered us into the living room. There was a fire burning in the fireplace which was very welcoming.

"Can you imagine we were sitting out on the patio the past couple of days, and today it's so cold we need the fireplace going?" Jane questioned.

"Typical New England," Alex retorted.

"Jane, that is an amazing painting!" Jennifer declared, gazing up at the cloud picture over the mantel.

"Right, this is the first time you've been in the house," Jane said. "I forgot!"

"You captured it perfectly," Russell added. "The flashes of metal shining through the cloud are so realistic. It's magnificent!"

"Thank you. I have quite a few more similar paintings squirreled away in the studio if you'd like to take one home with you. They were painted during my obsessive compulsive period. Thankfully that's over with," Jane chuckled.

"Something smells good," Anne sniffed.

"Oh, thanks for reminding me. I was just about to take the mushroom quiches out of the oven when you pulled up. Why don't you all come into the kitchen with me?" Jane asked.

As we passed by the back hall, Joshua stopped and showed Jennifer and Russell the view out the back door including the patio and steps that Alex had built.

"Do you mind if Jennifer and I go out on the patio and down to the lake edge for a few minutes?" Russell asked Joshua.

"Go right ahead. But let me get your coats before you do."

Joshua came back with their coats in a few seconds, and out they went.

"So do you think there is a mutual attraction going on between those two?" Jane asked me as we settled in around the kitchen table.

"Oh, I hope so!"

I had put Hope in the playpen in the kitchen alongside Seth. He had his own set of building blocks and handed one to her. They started their little construction game, taking turns positioning the blocks.

Jane took two quiches out of the oven and slid a cookie

sheet into the oven.

"What's on that cookie sheet?" Mary asked.

"Little crab cakes," Jane replied.

"Wow, I never made baked crab cakes. I always pan fried them. Can't wait to try them," Anne said.

"Drinks, anyone? Wine, beer, mixed drinks, whatever?" Joshua asked.

"I'll have a glass of white wine," Mary replied.

"That sounds good to me," Anne echoed.

"Do you have any V-8 or tomato juice?" I asked.

"We have V-8," Joshua replied.

"Could I have a glass of that with a little horseradish mixed in?"

"That sounds good to me, too," Alex agreed.

Just then Jennifer and Russell came in the back door.

"What a beautiful piece of property you have," Jennifer declared.

"And the curved patio and steps compliment the Palladian window on the second landing. Really nice touch," Russell added.

"We saw the glint of a UFO in a cloud right there down by the lake last year," Anne mentioned.

"And Joshua and I saw a triangular shaped UFO fly across the lake a couple years before that," Jane added.

"UFO hotbed, is it?" Russell asked.

"Is that because of the close proximity of the portal on Connie's property?" Jane inquired.

"Most likely," Russell answered.

We talked for several minutes about the mass UFO sightings the prior year during the night of the immaculate conception and the lack of any resulting significant changes.

"Do you think there will be more mass sightings like that?" Mary asked.

"I don't know," Russell responded. "There have been more individual sightings, however. And do you know what I attribute that to? More people are actually looking at the sky because of the worldwide sightings! And more people are reporting what they see. There is a tremendous amount of interest out there and the topic is being ignored and not reported by the news media."

"The crab cakes are done, the quiches have cooled sufficiently, so let's go into the dining room," Jane urged.

I picked up Hope and Alex picked up Seth and we put them in their highchairs in the dining room with sippy cups and sliced bananas before them. It was amazing how they never got bored with sliced bananas!

"This is the first time I've been served in your dining room," I mentioned to Jane. "The table is beautifully set with the Indus pattern."

"I rarely use the dining room or the transferware. It's a real treat for me to have you all here."

Joshua got drinks for Jennifer and Russell and then put a large mixed green salad on the table followed by the quiche and crab cakes. Jane brought in some crusty rolls and remoulade sauce.

A few minutes later we were well into devouring lunch.

"Everything is delicious, Jane," Anne declared. "The crab cakes are especially good. I'd love to have this recipe. They are so crispy and full of crab meat. And the seasoning is perfect."

"Thanks, Anne. I think it's the perfect blend of Dijon mustard, cayenne and Old Bay Seasoning that makes it work."

"And the quiche is marvelous," I chimed in. "It has such a fantastic creamy texture."

"It's the heavy cream that makes all the difference. If you use milk or light cream it just doesn't turn out the same. Heavy cream is definitely the key to a successful quiche."

"So what's the story with the Rh negative blood thing?" Jennifer asked Russell a few minutes into lunch. "You have Rh negative blood, and all the women who recently gave birth along with my mother and Jane all have Rh negative blood. I have Rh negative blood. What's with that?"

All eyes turned to Russell.

"It indicates that there is extraterrestrial DNA in your family history. In general we reincarnate within the same family group. This tendency is even stronger for those with the common bond of Rh negative blood. As we pass from lifetime to lifetime, we remember our path during prior incarnations. And we are drawn back to that same path, usually within the same grouping of spirits."

"I have a question," I stated. "In Luke's gospel he goes through a genealogy backward in time listing who begat whom. He ends with '...the son of Seth, the son of Adam, the son of God.' That says to me that Adam was the son of God, and if you are the son of someone, then you would have their DNA. The 'god' that is supposedly the father of Adam is the god of the Old Testament, Yahweh, who was an extraterrestrial. So if all that is true, wouldn't Adam and all his descendants have Rh negative blood?"

"Yes, Adam and his descendants had the DNA of the creator god, Yahweh. The first humans were apes that had been genetically altered with extraterrestrial DNA. That is where the Rh positive factor originated in humans, from monkeys/apes used in the creation process. However, Yahweh's DNA did not alter the Rh factor. An individual's DNA can change over time. The benevolent extraterrestrials' DNA has mutated over millennia to an extremely advanced level. They have on average 8 strands of DNA and use 50% of it. The human has 2 strands and uses approximately 5% of it. Yahweh had considerably fewer strands than 8; I've heard somewhere between 4 and 5. He wanted to be worshipped and obeyed by the humans he created, so he only gave them 2 strands with minimal activation of even that paltry amount of DNA. When the more spiritually evolved benevolent extraterrestrials join in the creation process with humans, the DNA mutates to a higher level and one of the changes that occurs is the elimination of the Rh factor. These humans have

Rh negative blood. Jesus was Rh negative."

We all sat there staring at him. There it was; the answer to so many of our questions.

"Any other questions?" Russell inquired.

"The so-called 'junk DNA' that the scientists call it is actually DNA that has yet to be activated?" Joshua asked.

"Correct. Yahweh disabled many of our code segments including the code segment whereby we could reproduce our cells or duplicate ourselves. We were programmed to make cells that cause our bodies to age, become sick and die. "

"What about Adam and his descendents in the Old Testament who lived hundreds of years? Is their longevity due to the fact that they had a preponderance of extraterrestrial DNA which became diluted over time?" I asked.

"Yes."

"If Adam and Eve had unlocked the secrets to the Tree of Life, they would have unlocked this code?" Jane queried.

"Their descendants would have over time. They would have discovered how to activate and program DNA to slow the aging process. We were not intended to unlock the secrets of the Tree of Knowledge, but we did to some extent. If we had unlocked the secrets of the Tree of Life, the entire puzzle would be ours to solve. Yahweh could not let this happen, and he sent the Cherubim to guard the Tree of Life."

"And what exactly are the Cherubim?" Mary asked. "Are they angels?"

"I guess that depends on how you would define 'angel'," Joshua answered. "They were created by Yahweh to be his eyes and ears. They were strange looking creatures and the exact description is open to speculation. However, it has been said that they had several wings which were completely covered in eyes, signifying they were all seeing. I believe what they saw here on Earth was transmitted to Yahweh in his ship. I don't believe they were spiritual beings; I think they were machines of some sort."

"Oh, I have one other question that I've been meaning to ask," Jennifer said. "There is a triskele carved on the bench in the portal chamber. Are you aware of that?"

"Yes."

"And when Alex took a rubbing of it before Hope and Seth were born, it looked like two of the three spirals were incomplete. Then after they were born, Alex took me out to see the chamber and made another rubbing and only one spiral was incomplete. I think that the birth of Hope, Seth and the other children prompted the completion of the second spiral. Do you have any idea if my supposition is correct?"

"Yes, I believe you are correct. And if you are then going to ask about the first triskele, the answer, I believe, is that it signified my birth. Concerning the third triskele, however, I have no idea what it will mean. I have no knowledge of what is yet to happen. I cannot see into the future."

"When will you begin teaching the children?" Jane asked.

"Actually, I've started my teaching responsibilities with you, the parents and family. You needed to learn about me and my extraterrestrial heritage, about the Center and the portals as well as past history and philosophy which has brought us to this point.

"Tomorrow I'd like to speak with you some more about the power of the mind, as that topic will be the most important subject I teach your children. Tomorrow will be the last day I spend with you right now, but I will return within a few weeks to begin spending time with the children. I hope this is acceptable to you?"

"Yes, although I do hate to see you leave. We've learned so much from you in the past few days," I declared.

"I feel so fortunate that you've been provided as teacher to our children," Jane confessed.

"Okay, I have one problem with your leaving," Jennifer complained.

We all gave her a startled look.

"And what's the problem?" Russell asked.

"I thought you were going to take me to my cottage in Scotland via the portal before you left!"

"Well, if your mother can stand having me as her guest for one additional night, we'll do that the day after tomorrow."

"Great! Mother just said she hated to see you leave, so we've got you for one additional day," Jennifer beamed with a look of pure joy on her face.

It looked to me that Russell was very pleased with Jennifer's request, as he had a big smile on his face.

"Ah, this might be the start of something big," I thought to myself.

Chapter 22 – Mind Over Matter

When Hope and I came downstairs the next morning, Jennifer and Russell were looking at something on the computer, Anne was sipping coffee and Alex had the steel cut oats cooking on the stove.

"Good morning, all!"

I received a round of greetings in reply.

"Here, let me take Hope while you get her breakfast ready," Anne said.

I deposited Hope on Anne's lap and went to prepare her breakfast.

"What are you two looking up on the computer?" I asked.

"Tomorrow's weather forecast for Glasgow," Russell responded.

"It looks good, clear and around 60 degrees," Jennifer added.

"So your trip is a 'go' then?"

"Looks that way," Russell replied. "We'll have to leave early in the morning, like around 6:00 or 6:30 because of the time difference. We should be able to make Lamlash Bay in time for a late lunch."

"That's pretty neat; you can have lunch in Scotland and then be here in Vermont for lunch that same day as well," Alex said.

"There goes the diet," Jennifer chuckled.

"And here comes Mary!" Anne said.

"Helllooo!"

"Good morning! Just in time for some oatmeal," Alex greeted.

"Wonderful, I'm famished for some reason."

"Anne, here's Hope's cereal. I'll get her sippy cup ready."

Jennifer and Russell shut down the computer and sat down at the table. Alex put the butter and maple syrup on the table and started ladling out the oatmeal.

"Do I smell cinnamon in that oatmeal?" Anne asked.

"Just a touch. I also added some dried cranberries," Alex answered.

A couple of minutes later we were savoring the flavor and texture of the oatmeal that Alex had made.

"That little touch of cinnamon combined with the cranberries works so well with the oatmeal," Mary remarked.

"That combination just came to me for some reason. I'm glad you like it; I think it's pretty good myself."

"Do you know when Jane et al will arrive?" Jennifer asked.

"About mid-morning, I think," I responded.

"I had a strange dream last night," Alex said.

"Those dragons zooming out of the clouds again?" I asked.

"No, it was like a flotilla of spaceships that had come slowly from the south over Lake Champlain and just hovered within view of the house," Alex responded.

"A 'flotilla'?" Anne asked.

"There were many of them, and they were 'floating' over the lake. I think 'flotilla' works."

"Do you recall what they looked like? Do you remember their shape?" Russell asked.

"They were cylindrical and I'd estimate that were easily 100 feet wide. They weren't moving like you would see a blimp move, with the narrow end moving forward; they were moving from the wide side. It appeared to be just after sunset and there was enough natural light for me to see that the exterior was like a dark mirror. It reflected the fading light to the west as well as the lake and mountains. I didn't see any lights on the ships or windows. I felt that the exterior shell was transparent, sort of like a two way mirror; that they could see everything from within. They could see me, but I couldn't see inside the craft. In my dream they seemed to be ominous and I became very frightened."

"Was that the end of the dream?" Russell asked.

"No. They were standing still over the lake. I'd say there were 6 of them. And then one by one the end opened up and smaller saucer shaped craft shot out, at least a dozen from each of the larger ships. It was almost as if they were stacked within the cylinder on their sides kind of like checkers. They flew off in all directions, just leaving the 6 larger ships stationary over the lake. At that point I woke up."

"I never heard of cylindrical spaceships before," Anne said.

"Me neither. I have no idea where that idea came into my mind," Alex confessed.

"Do you know anything about them, Russell?" I inquired.

"Yes, they are the ships of the beings of darkness. They are the only ones who use that shape, exactly as Alex described." Russell replied.

"What do you think the dream means?" Alex asked.

"I don't know and I wouldn't want to speculate," Russell answered.

We sat around the table in silence for a while, eating our oatmeal and thinking about those ships. I noticed that Russell especially seemed to be deep in thought.

A couple of hours later Jane 'et al', as Jennifer referred to them earlier, arrived.

It was another cold grey day, and we positioned ourselves around the fire in the living room. Hope and Seth were in the playpen, but it looked like they would be settling down for a nap shortly.

"Well, as promised yesterday, today's main topic is the power of the mind. It was one of the most important of Christ's messages. I've marked the bible so I can read some of the verses to you."

We watched as he opened the first page he had marked, and listened to him read:

"Whatever you ask for in prayer, believe that you have received it, and it will be yours."

He continued with the remander:

"For verily I say unto you, That whosoever shall say unto this mountain, 'Be thou removed, and be thou cast into the sea' and shall not doubt in his heart, but shall believe that those things which he saith shall come to pass; he shall have whatsoever he saith."

"If ye have faith as a grain of mustard seed, ye shall say unto this mountain, 'Remove hence to yonder place' and it shall remove; and nothing shall be impossible unto you."

"Truly I say to you, if you have faith and do not doubt, you will not only do what was done to the fig tree, but even if you say to this mountain, 'Be taken up and cast into the sea,' it will happen."

"All things are possible to him who believes."

The following verse about Jesus walking on water is significant because Jesus is telling Peter that if he had faith in his own abilities and did not doubt, he could walk on water:

"But the ship was now in the midst of the sea, tossed with waves: for the wind was contrary. And in the fourth watch of the night Jesus went unto them, walking on the sea. And when the disciples saw him walking on the sea, they were troubled, saying, 'It is a spirit' and they cried out for fear.

But straightway Jesus spoke unto them, saying, 'Be of good cheer; it is I; be not afraid'. And Peter answered him and said, 'Lord, if it be thou, bid me come unto thee on the water'. And he said, 'Come'. And when Peter was come down out of the ship, he walked on the water, to go to Jesus. But when he saw the wind boisterous, he was afraid; and beginning to sink, he cried, saying, 'Lord, save me'. And immediately Jesus stretched forth his hand, and caught him, and said unto him, 'O thou of little faith, wherefore didst thou doubt?'"

"That first verse, however, bears repeating," Russell continued. 'Whatever you ask for in prayer, believe that you have received it, and it will be yours.' Believe that you have already received it. Believe that is yours now, not some point in the future, but right now.

"I know this is extremely difficult to do. You're asking your subconscious mind to believe that you have something when your conscious mind is telling you that you don't. But it's the subconscious mind that is really in control, not the conscious mind. The subconscious mind keeps our heart beating and our blood flowing. It contains all of our memories. It controls our emotions. Will-power is part of your conscious mind and it's usually a battle to win with will-power because it's fighting your subconscious which is vastly stronger. Your habits are controlled by your subconscious mind.

"Your subconscious mind, however, can be programmed through repetition. Once you consciously do something or say something over and over again, it becomes absorbed by the subconscious. I'm sure you all can relate to driving your car and arriving at your destination only to think to yourself, 'How did I get here? I don't even remember driving I was so lost in thought." Your subconscious mind was doing the driving. You didn't have to consciously think about turning here or turning there, stopping at red lights and so forth because you were on automatic pilot, your subconscious mind. Through driving every day for months and years, that repetition was accepted by the subconscious and you no longer need to have your conscious mind in control at times when you drive. However, if some emergency arose as you were driving, your conscious mind would immediately snap back in control.

"Have you ever experienced something being 'on the tip of your tongue'? For example, the name of an actor in a certain movie? You work and work trying to remember the name, and it just won't come to you. Then you put it out of your mind and several hours later the name pops into your conscious mind. That is your subconscious at work. You aren't even aware that it is working on retrieving the answer, and it provides you with the answer when you are no longer consciously thinking about it.

"What messages are we sending to ourselves, sending to our subconscious mind, day after day year after year? Whatever they are, those messages have created your world.

"Our minds are going continually, even when we sleep. All kinds of thoughts pop in and out. Do we ever think about controlling those thoughts? I know that's not easy. Have you ever tried to meditate? Can you really clear your mind of thought?

"How do we communicate with our subconscious mind?" I asked.

"One way would be through hypnosis or self-hypnosis," Russell responded.

"Hypnosis? Isn't that all just a bunch of hooey?" Joshua asked.

"No, it isn't. Hypnosis is a state of restful alertness during which an individual has a heightened sense of concentration. During our waking hours we are in the beta state, and when we are in a deep sleep we are in the delta state. In between those two states are the alpha and theta and these are the states to which a hypnotist will bring us prior to imparting hypnotic suggestions.

"Just before we fall asleep at night and just before we are fully awake in the morning we are in the alpha state. That is the time when we can speak to our subconscious directly. What we are looking to accomplish, our goals, should be repeated over and over during this relatively short period of time. These goals should be positively stated and phrased in the present tense, as if you already have attained them. For example 'I am vibrantly healthy' instead of 'I will not catch the flu'. As you repeat your goal or goals, visualize what you state. Do this faithfully every morning and every night and you will achieve your goals. And should you wake up during the night, take that opportunity to repeat your goals to yourself then as well.

"The subconscious mind is not a part of your brain, it is actually located in your solar plexus and through your etheric cord it is actually connected to the Universal Mind. Wisdom and power are available to you through your subconscious, and this was an important part of the teaching of Jesus.

"Jesus' message was love and the power of belief. I took the liberty of grabbing the dictionary before I came out here, as I wanted to read the definition of 'belief' to you. I have it marked."

Russell opened the dictionary to the marked page and read:

"Belief: 'A state or habit of mind in which confidence or trust is placed in some person or thing; a conviction of the truth of some statement or the reality of some being or phenomenon'. It's the 'state or habit of mind' that I wanted to bring to your attention. Jesus wasn't talking about belief in himself or his 'father'. He was talking about belief in ourselves. He was talking about the incredible power of our minds. He wanted us to believe that anything was possible. He didn't want us to fear.

"Fear is the tool of the beings of darkness. It produces nothing but negative energy. Thoughts are energies. They can vibrate on both high and low levels. What we send out comes back to us on the same vibrational level. The fear that we feel and the negative thoughts that accompany it produce more of the same.

"If we worry about something and think about it constantly, then we are drawing it to ourselves and it will eventually manifest. Our thoughts are waves of energy and they vibrate at a certain energy level. Once released, they link with other similar energy waves and come back to us reinforced. It's similar to a radio frequency. If we set our radio to a certain frequency, it is impossible to receive at another frequency. We attract vibrations at the same energy level that we send out.

"Negative thoughts or energies are dense and are difficult for the body to process and release. They can become blocked and the stagnant negative energy can produce a harmful effect, such as 'dis-ease'.

"On the other hand, if we are thinking positive thoughts and believe that we have received what we have asked for, those thoughts vibrate at a higher level or frequency and also return to us in a positive manner.

"Take a moment to think about what we see on television for the most part. If you're watching the news, it's usually bad news being reported. If it's drama, it's usually blood and gore or greed that are the major topics. If it's comedy, it's usually mindless drivel. Even if it's the weather, it seems like they're trying to frighten us by blowing many impending storms way out of proportion.

"And while I'm on the topic of television, I'm going to ask you one thing. Don't let your children watch television. In addition to teaching the children fear, which is not inherently within them, they are also indoctrinated on how to think. They are taught a materialistic mindset. They are also taught what kind of behavior is acceptable and how to judge."

"What about educational programs? Aren't the children allowed to watch them?" Jane asked.

"No. There are subliminal messages programmed into even the supposedly most benign, informative shows. The media is controlled by the beings of darkness. Television is their mouthpiece and the great majority of the world's population has access to television."

"Does that mean that we adults shouldn't be watching television?" Jane asked.

"Don't watch it when the children can see or hear it, and when you do watch it, be very selective about what you watch."

"I still remember that morning we turned on the TV to hear the news that UFOs were reported to have been seen around the world overnight. How thrilling that was."

"Yes, I'm sure it was. But that was a very rare occurrence, was it not?" Russell asked.

"It was probably the only thing of value that I've seen on that TV set in decades," Alex muttered. "And what Russell said about television being the mouthpiece of the beings of darkness really rings true with me. How ingenious of them; we welcome the devil, the father of all lies, into our homes with open arms."

"Not to change the subject," Jennifer interjected, "but do you know how to hypnotize people?" she asked Russell.

"Yes. Why? Do you want to be hypnotized?"

"I do!" I shouted.

"Me, too!" echoed Jane.

It was quickly evident that we all wanted to be hypnotized, and Russell said he would conduct a guided imagery group hypnosis.

"Before I start, however, I want to explain the importance of deep breathing. The majority of people breathe with their chest muscles instead of their abdomen. I'm going to put my hands on my stomach and take a deep breath. Watch my hands."

We watched as he slowly inhaled and we watched his hands move as his abdomen expanded out. We continued to watch as his abdomen moved back in as he slowly exhaled.

"That's called 'belly breathing'. Your lungs have five lobes and they go much further down than just your chest. Most people only breathe using the top two lobes of their lungs."

"I swear sometimes I hardly breathe at all!" Jane exclaimed.

"And you're probably right; your breathing could be very shallow at times, and it's extremely harmful to your well being! Okay, let's all try this together. Put your hands on your abdomen. Just breathe in deeply yet comfortably; then slowly exhale. Your exhalation should take about twice as long as your inhalation. Every one is different. Just do what feels comfortable to you."

We all took our first belly breaths and looked at each other with amazement.

"I never ever took a breath like that. It felt strange, unnatural in a way, yet so wonderful!" Jennifer marveled.

"You used your diaphragm to take that breath. That kind of deep breathing oxygenates the blood, nourishes every cell of the body and promotes relaxation. Slow deep breaths change our vibrations, by increasing the molecular activity of our cells. I mentioned earlier that the solar plexus is the seat of the subconscious mind. Deep breathing massages the diaphragm and increases the flow of blood to the solar plexus.

"What I'm going to do now is conduct a progressive relaxation exercise which will relieve stress. Position yourself comfortably in your chair, take a couple of deep calming breaths, close your eyes and just listen to me."

A while later I opened my eyes at the count of five, feeling very relaxed and yet alert.

"That was hypnosis?" Joshua asked.

"Yes," Russell replied.

"But I heard everything you said. I wasn't in some sort of trance or asleep."

"Right, you were in a very relaxed state which allowed me to speak to your subconscious mind."

"I still can't believe I was hypnotized," Joshua persisted.

"Take a look at the back of your right hand. Do you see the impression I made with my fingernails when I pinched you?" Russell asked.

"I see the mark. You pinched me?" Joshua asked.

"I pinched each of you, and I pinched you hard enough that the mark is still there. Do you remember when I touched your hand and told you that you would feel a little pressure? No discomfort, only a little pressure? That was when I pinched you. Before I did that, I told you that your hand was numb; as if you had it immersed in a bucket of ice water or was given a shot of Novocain. I was speaking to your subconscious mind and gave it the suggestion that you had no feeling in your hand at all, and then I pinched you to prove it. Before I brought you out of hypnosis, I told you that all normal feeling was returned to your hand."

"The entire experience was so relaxing," Jane murmured. "I feel marvelous!"

"And it's all simply mind over matter," I remarked.

Chapter 23 – Grab a Wing Darling

As we sat and discussed our thoughts on our recent hypnosis experience, Hope awoke from her nap. I watched as she quietly laid there in her playpen looking over at Seth. She just kept staring at him for a minute or two at which point he slowly opened his eyes, looked over at her and smiled. It was almost as if she had telepathically told him to 'wake up'! I looked around to see if anyone else had noticed, but they were all very intent on their conversation about hypnosis and it didn't appear that anyone had seen what I had.

"How about we have some lunch?" I asked. "Hope and Seth are awake now and I'm sure they're hungry."

"Good idea," Alex agreed.

"How does everyone feel about liverwurst?" I asked.

"Liverwurst, liverwurst! I hate liverwurst!" Anne exclaimed as she carried Hope into the kitchen, followed by everyone else.

"You really hate liverwurst?" I inquired.

"Don't you remember that 'I hate liverwurst story'? Anne laughed.

"It seems familiar to me, but I can't recall what it is."

"Remember when you were babysitting the kids for a couple of weeks while I was off in Europe? I told you that the boys liked ham, turkey or roast beef sandwiches, except for Jimmy who was extremely fond of liverwurst. I said that you could pack liverwurst sandwiches for Jimmy every day and he'd be happy. So while the other boys were having roast beef one day, turkey the next and ham the following day, Jimmy was having liverwurst sandwiches each day. At the very end of the two week period, you told me that Jimmy was heading out the door with his lunch bag in hand. He asked you 'What kind of sandwich do I have today?' And you answered, 'Liverwurst,' surprised that he had asked. He exploded with 'Liverwurst, liverwurst! All I ever get is liverwurst! I hate liverwurst!'."

"Ah, yes, I remember it now!"

"But I do like liverwurst," Anne chuckled.

Everyone else indicated they liked liverwurst as well, so liverwurst it was. Alex got the plates and utensils out while I took out the liverwurst, mustard, pumpernickel bread, pickles and chips. Jane was feeding Seth and Mary was feeding Hope.

In no time we were all munching our sandwiches and the conversation went back to hypnosis. Jennifer asked Russell if there were certain people who couldn't be hypnotized.

"If you don't have a willing client who trusts your abilities, it is almost impossible to successfully hypnotize the individual. A good hypnotist will work toward establishing rapport with the client which should help to build confidence and trust in his or her abilities. The hypnotist as well has to believe in his or her own abilities, so there is an important element of faith that needs to be present on both sides."

"Do you think Jesus used hypnosis when he healed people?" Mary asked.

"I think it is entirely possible that he made use of the power of suggestion and the subconscious mind to bring about some of his miracles. So I guess my answer would be 'yes', I do think he used a form of hypnosis in some of his healings. You might recall that he couldn't perform miracles in his home town."

"Why was that?" Jane asked.

"Let me read something to you," he said as he reached over to the counter where he had deposited the bible just before he sat down to lunch.

"And Jesus went out from there, and He came into His home town; and His disciples followed Him. And when the Sabbath had come, He began to teach in the synagogue; and the many listeners were astonished, saying 'Where did this man get these things, and what is this wisdom given to Him, and such miracles as these performed by His hands? Is not this the carpenter, the son of Mary, and brother of James, and Joses, and Judas and Simon? Are not His sisters here with us?' And they took offense at Him. And Jesus said to them, 'A prophet is not without honor except in his home town and among his own relatives and in his own household.' And He could do no miracle there except that He laid His hands upon a few sick people and healed them. And He wondered at their unbelief.'

"That was Mark 6:1-6. Note that it doesn't say he 'wouldn't work miracles there', it says 'couldn't work miracles there'. He did not have a willing and trusting audience, and as a result he could not perform miracles.

"I recall that he specifically asked certain people if they believed that he could heal them before he healed them. Let me find one example for you," Russell said as he flipped through the pages of the New Testament.

"Ah, here's an example. This is Matthew 9:27-31: 'And when Jesus departed thence, two blind men followed him, crying and saying, Thou son of David, have mercy on us. And when he was come into the house, the blind men came to him: and Jesus saith unto them, Believe ye that I am able to do this? They said unto him, Yea, Lord. Then touched he their eyes, saying, According to your faith be it unto you. And their eyes were opened; and Jesus straightly charged them, saying, See that no man know it. But they, when they were departed, spread abroad his fame in all that country'."

"But you're not saying that all of his miracles were the result of hypnosis, are you?" Mary asked.

"No. His powers were way beyond that. I would venture to guess that he had more than two strands of DNA, with a considerable amount of activation in those strands."

We nibbled on some homemade orange shortbread cookies as we sipped tea.

"You said you'd be back in a few weeks, right?" Jane asked Russell.

"Yes, I would expect I'd be back in about three week's time," he responded.

"And at that time you'll actually begin teaching the children?" I asked.

"Yes, I'll spend several hours a day with them. We'll work on a wide variety of topics such as music, art, reading, languages, math, science, geography, biofeedback…"

"Biofeedback!" Anne exclaimed.

"Yes, they'll learn to voluntarily control bodily functions that normally occur involuntarily. Not right off the bat, of course! And they will learn about the power of the subconscious mind which is linked to biofeedback."

"Hey, can I take your course?" Alex chuckled.

"I'd like to take it, too," Anne agreed. "Why do you think it is that they don't teach you about your subconscious mind in school?"

"I think it's because they really don't want you to know how powerful your mind really is," Alex surmised.

"Right, if you realize that you can keep yourself healthy by using your mind, then the doctors and drug companies would be out of business," Joshua declared.

"Never mind all of those health insurance companies down the tubes," Alex added.

"Well, I'd have to agree with you that 'they' don't want us to know how powerful our minds are. And I think it's primarily the malevolent extraterrestrials who are controlling this. As I said before, look at what you see on television. The primary purpose of what is on television is to either keep you mindlessly entertained or sell you something. What you hear on the news and read in the papers is all controlled by the powers of darkness. It kind of gives a new meaning to being 'in the dark', doesn't it?"

After Jane, Joshua and Seth left later that afternoon, the remainder of us had a quiet evening playing Scrabble. Jennifer and Russell were planning on leaving early the next morning, so they made sure to call it an early night.

I awoke around 5:30 the next day. Hope was still asleep in her crib, but I could smell the coffee wafting up the stairs. I went down and Russell and Alex were sitting at the table with coffee mugs in hand. I poured myself a cup of coffee and joined them.

"What time do you think you'll be back here?" I asked?

"Just like a mother to worry about what time her daughter will be back home," Alex joked.

"I would think we'd be back here no later than 1:00 to 2:00 in the afternoon," Russell replied. "Don't worry, Connie. I'll take very good care of her."

"I know you will and I'm not worried."

Just then Jennifer walked into the kitchen all dressed and ready to go.

"Did I hear you say 'you're not worried'?" Jennifer asked.

"That's right. I know you couldn't be in better hands."

Russell took a final sip of his coffee and off they went.

Mary and Anne left later that same morning. As always, I hated to see them go. Alex took them to the airport as he had some job estimates to do in the area.

I kept myself busy with laundry and cleaning. After that Hope and I took a trip to the grocery store. We got back just after noon. I kept my eye on the clock, watching the minutes slowly ticking by. After Hope and I had lunch, we sat down at her little keyboard and we were in the midst of playing 'Twinkle Twinkle Little Star" when I heard the back door open. I looked up and saw Jennifer and Russell walk into the living room.

"How did it go?" I asked.

"Wonderful, Mom. We had a marvelous lunch at a little pub not far from my cottage. The weather was great; a little cool, but clear and crisp. I took Russell over to the cottage after lunch. He loved it. Didn't you?"

"I was expecting a small 'cottage' as you describe it. But it is so much more than that. It's a lovely home and the location and the views are incredible."

"And the train connections went well?"

"Couldn't have timed it better. And there was hardly any wait to connect with the ferry either," Jennifer noted. She had a glow about her. She looked so happy and I was happy for her.

"I'd better collect my belongings and be off," Russell stated.

"I'll help," Jennifer said and the two of them headed toward the laundry room. Within a few minutes Russell appeared with duffel bag in hand.

"Connie, thank you so much for your warm hospitality. I feel like a member of the family."

"The next time you come back, you'll be able to get off the couch and sleep in a bedroom! So we'll see you in a few weeks then, right?"

"Right." With that he gave me a kiss and a hug and he and Jennifer headed back out the back door.

A while later Jennifer returned alone. I thought she might be sad about his departure, but she looked euphoric.

"So what really happened on that trip to Scotland?" I asked.

"We are so comfortable with each other. It's like we've known one another forever. We're never at a loss for words. It's just wonderful being with him. On our way back to the train station in Glasgow he extended his arm and said to me 'Grab a wing, darling.' Isn't that just divine? 'Grab a wing, darling.' He said he'd drop in and visit me in a couple of days in London. I think this is it, Mom. I think he's the one I've been waiting for."

I could feel my eyes tearing up and I reached out and hugged her.

"And I couldn't be happier. I think he's the one for you as well."

Jennifer left the following day via British Airways. She already had her round trip ticket and she had considerable luggage, so there was no point in trying to 'portal' it alone. Besides that, Russell had told us not to attempt to try to do that without consulting him.

So off she went and we waited for Russell's return.

Chapter 24 – Dream Becomes Reality

Spring was exceptionally lovely that year. There were no hard frosts after the flowers and trees were in bloom and everything was lush outdoors. It was now the first week in May and I expected Russell to return at any time.

Early one evening I was in the living room, reading to Hope, when Alex ran to the patio door and shouted "Come out here!"

From the tone of his voice, I knew not to question and to just 'get out there'. I picked up Hope and out we went.

Alex was standing far out in the lawn close the 'Meghalaya' bench. He was looking up and toward the south. I walked to where he was and looked in the same direction. To my amazement, I saw six cylindrical shaped UFOs flying slowly northward over Lake Champlain. I recalled they seemed to be similar to the ones that Alex had dreamt about. Their exterior appeared to be a dark glass-like surface and reflected the mountains, lake and sky.

I could hear the phone ringing in the distance. I handed Hope to Alex and ran toward the house. I knew it had to be Jane. I picked up the receiver and didn't have a chance to say hello. I heard Jane say "Do you see them?"

"Yes. They're just as in Alex's dream."

"And Russell said ships in that shape belonged to the beings of darkness."

"Yes, I remember."

"No, I can't believe it!" Jane exclaimed.

"What?"

"They opened up on the end and smaller disk shaped craft are zooming out. Again, just as Alex described."

"I'll call you back. I've got to see this."

I ran outside and saw some of the smaller craft zooming north over the lake.

Hope was watching them as well. She had a very pensive look on her face.

We stood there and watched until all the ships, both large and small, were out of sight.

"I guess this is a special occasion," Alex announced.

"Special occasion?" I asked.

"Yes. I think we should turn the television on."

We got inside and Alex turned the TV on. There were special reports on every channel. Craft similar to what we had just seen had been spotted around the globe.

"I'm going to get Hope ready for bed and put her in for the night."

The idea came to mind that she should not be seeing or listening to this. She still seemed to be lost in thought, and she put up no struggle at all as I put her in her crib.

I joined Alex on the sofa as he clicked from channel to channel each reporting the UFO sightings.

I picked up the phone and dialed Jane.

"This isn't good," she said as she answered the phone. She didn't need to say 'hello' or wait to see who it was, as she knew it was I.

"I took a quick look on the blog and it's on fire with comments. Everyone is alarmed…and they don't even know about Alex's dream and Russell's remarks about these shaped ships belonging to the beings of darkness. It seems they all sense a foreboding."

Just then a special report came on the TV. The President was going to make an announcement the following morning at 8 a.m.

"Do you mind if we come over to your place in time

for the President's announcement?" Jane asked.

"That would be great. Actually, you can come over right now because I don't think I'll be getting any sleep tonight."

"Seth is already in his crib and I don't want to disturb him. We'll head over first thing in the morning. See you then."

Alex and I sat transfixed in front of the TV for several hours. These same cylindrical shaped ships had been seen around the world. Smaller disc shaped ships were seen to depart from the larger.

"I've never had a precognitive dream before," Alex remarked. "I have a very uneasy feeling about this whole thing."

I slept fitfully and was thankful when the first light of day appeared through my window. I took a quick shower. Hope was just waking as I was finishing getting dressed.

When we reached the kitchen Alex said "Here, give Hope to me."

"Have you been up all night?" I asked.

"Just about. I don't know why I've been glued to the TV. They haven't said anything new."

I got Hope's sippy cup ready for her and started to make her cereal. I was thankful that Alex had the coffee made and as I poured myself a cup, something caught my attention out the back door. It seemed that something was moving across the lawn in the morning fog. My heart skipped a beat. What could that be?

"What's the matter, Connie?" Alex asked.

"Something is coming across the lawn," I whispered.

I saw the look of alarm on his face a split second before I could make out the forms of Jennifer and Russell as they made their way to the back door. I ran over and opened the door.

"You have no idea how happy I am to see you both!" I exclaimed. I gave them both big hugs and told them to sit down. I put the coffee carafe on the table and handed them mugs.

"We both felt we needed to be here with you right now," Jennifer advised.

"I felt uneasy when Alex recounted his dream about these ships. I felt it was a premonition of things to come," Russell said. "And it was."

"I'm not too happy with developing precognitive skills this late in life either!" Alex mumbled.

"Jane, Joshua and Seth will be here shortly. They wanted to listen to the President's speech with us."

Hope's cereal was ready and Jennifer started to feed her. While she was doing that, I made some cornmeal muffin batter, poured them into the cast iron muffin pan and placed them in the oven to bake.

The television had been on nonstop since last night. The pundits were all speculating on what the President was about the say, but of course none of them had a clue.

"It is okay with you if we watch TV, right?" Alex asked Russell.

"Yes. After all, this is history in the making," Russell responded.

"Did you see the ships yesterday?" I asked Jennifer.

"Yes, they flew up the Thames and across the City of London. Everyone was out in the street staring at the sky. They seemed to exude evil; their exterior had that reflective darkness and they moved so slowly, almost as if they were looking down at each and every one of us," Jennifer replied.

"And you, Russell? Did you see them?"

"Yes, I was working in a little town along the coast of Portugal and we saw them fly slowly northward over the beach. I saw the smaller disc shaped craft shoot out and they all appeared to head in westerly directions."

Just then the phone rang. I picked it up on the first ring and it was my sister, Mary.

"Are you watching TV?" she asked.

"Yes, we've been watching since this all started last evening."

"Did you actually see them?" she asked.

"Alex spotted them flying slowly northward over the lake. He called me; Hope and I both saw them. Jennifer and Russell just arrived via the portal this morning and Jane et al are due to arrive any minute to watch the President's speech with us. Is Anne with you?"

"Yes, she came back to my house last night. We had dinner over in Harbor Town and we saw them heading north over Calibogue Sound. They were ominous looking things. We knew they were exactly the same as Alex saw in his dream, ships of the beings of darkness. So listen, I know you're busy. I'll call you later, okay? It's going to be interesting to hear what the President has to say."

"It sure will. Talk to you later."

I could smell that the corn muffins were ready and I took them out of the oven just as Jane and Joshua were pulling into the courtyard.

"I'll get the door," Russell volunteered.

I could hear the surprise in Jane's voice as she greeted Russell. I reached the door in time to see her hugging him, followed by Joshua.

"Here let me take Seth," Russell said. He reached out, took Seth from Jane's arms and headed toward the kitchen.

"Did Seth have breakfast?" I asked.

"Yes. As soon as he finished eating we headed out the door. He watched the ships fly by yesterday. His eyes had an almost piercing look to them, as if he knew exactly who they were."

"I think he probably did."

Hope had finished her breakfast and she accompanied Seth in the playpen.

I put the corn muffins, butter and jam on the table and put another pot of coffee on.

"You have no idea how surprised and delighted I am to

see you both here," Jane declared.

"So, Russell, what do you think this means? Is this the beginning of the battle for the planet Earth?" Joshua asked.

"I think it could very well be. I had mentioned previously that the scales were so very close to tipping over to the light on this planet. It appears the dark ones are not just going to sit back and watch that happen."

"And what does that mean for Seth and Hope and the other children?" I inquired.

"Most likely it means that they will have to use all of the power, knowledge and goodness within them to win out."

"The President is about to speak," Jennifer announced.

I filled the carafe with fresh coffee and sat down to watch as 'Special Report' faded from the TV screen, replaced by the President's face.

"Good morning. As your President, the well-being and security of you, the citizens of the United States of America, is of paramount importance to me. Yesterday's mass UFO sightings have spawned fear among some of you and, at the very least, concern among others of you. You want answers and you need the truth. The time has come for the truth to be told.

"This planet has been visited by extraterrestrials for a very long time. Exactly how long, I don't think anyone knows. I can now tell you that a UFO did crash at Roswell, New Mexico. Bodies were recovered, both dead and alive. There have been other crashes and other beings recovered as well. Up until today this information had only been shared with certain individuals on a need to know basis. In light of yesterday's sightings, the decision was made to disclose this information to the general populace for your welfare.

"The U.S. government has been in communication with several extraterrestrial communities over the decades. We have built positive working relationships with these benevolent beings. There is absolutely nothing to fear from the groups with whom we communicate.

"However, we have come to learn that not all extraterrestrial races are benevolent. The ships that appeared in the skies yesterday are unknown to us. Whose ships they are and what their motives might be in visiting this planet have yet to be determined. You can rest assured that this government, in collaboration with other governments worldwide and in conjunction with the United Nations, is diligently working on identification of these ships. Our goal is communication. Only through communication can there be understanding.

"I have asked the Vice President to assemble a scientific task force to research further and coordinate information as it becomes available. If anyone has information that they believe might be helpful to us, please call the toll free number at the bottom of the screen. All information will be kept strictly confidential.

"Please rest assured that your government is working to protect you. There is no cause for alarm. I will be providing periodic updates on developments. Peace to you all."

Alex hit the 'mute' button on the remote control and we sat there in silence for a few seconds, just staring at each other. Joshua was the one to break the silence.

"The last thing they wanted was a sequel to the prior sighting. But guess what? They got it. They got the sequel. And they were prepared for it."

Chapter 25 – Far From the Truth

"I never thought I would hear a President admit that we have been in communication with extraterrestrials. However that 'speech' if you could call it a 'speech' was pathetic. What about the prior mass UFO sighting? Did the government know who they were and therefore didn't feel the need to make a statement or even comment on it then or now?" I asked.

"If they weren't these cylindrical shaped ships, but were instead the same triangular shaped ships of the 'immaculate conception' from last year, would he have made an announcement at all?" Jane queried.

"And what about the groups the President says the government has been in communication with? Who are they? What have we been working on with them?" Alex asked.

"I don't believe for a minute that they don't know whose ships those were. I know the origin of those ships as do others. They come from the planet Ketu," Russell uttered.

I had never heard Russell speak other than in a calm and controlled manner. However now I could hear something akin to annoyance and exasperation in his voice.

"Ketu? I never heard of Ketu," Alex said. "Is it outside of this solar system?"

"No, it's within this solar system. There are only a certain few who know of its existence. For some reason the scientific community has kept its existence under wraps. It could be because it is known to be a malevolent planet and they don't want to cause alarm."

"How do they know it's a malevolent planet?" Jennifer asked.

"The galactic federation with whom we work has provided us with that information. And if we know who they are, I'm sure the government knows who they are."

"And what do you think their little 'outing' in the skies of planet Earth was all about?" Joshua queried.

"I suspect it was for the same purpose as the federation's 'outing' last year," Russell answered.

"Are you saying that you think they impregnated Earth women during their little trip?" Alex questioned.

"That would be my guess."

"So our children will have flesh and blood adversaries?" Jane asked.

"It appears they will," Russell replied.

We sat there in silence for a few seconds, digesting what we had just learned.

"Do you know if the malevolent extraterrestrials have a center on this planet similar to the one the beings of light have in Meghalaya?" I asked.

"I don't believe they do," Russell said. "At least not yet."

"Do you think the women involved volunteered?" Jennifer asked.

"I sincerely doubt it."

"So nine months from now women around the world will be giving birth to malevolent hybrids?" Jennifer asked incredulously.

"I could be all wrong about this," Russell acknowledged.

"But if you're not, then several months from now these women are going to discover they're pregnant. If that is a physical impossibility for whatever reason, don't you think that would start off some alarms within the heads of these women? Like 'how on God's green Earth did that happen?'"

"I would think so, but we'll just have to wait for this to

play out," Russell replied.

"If the world leaders knew what has happened, or at least what we suspect may have happened, wouldn't you think they would demand the fetuses be aborted?" Jane asked.

"First of all, how would you even go about identifying those women?" Alex inquired.

"Oh, I don't know. How about worldwide public service announcements like 'If you think you were impregnated by extraterrestrials the night of the mass UFO sighting three months ago, please contact us at the number below…' or something like that?" Jane retorted.

"I would think that forced abortion of the fetuses would definitely be a violation of civil rights," Jennifer argued.

"Even if it means saving the planet from domination by malevolent extraterrestrial beings?" Jane shot back.

"Ladies, ladies, calm down now," Joshua urged.

"Okay, I just had a thought. This planet already belongs to the malevolent extraterrestrials. Russell said Earth is a dark planet. I'm sure the majority of those in power on this planet are already in cahoots with the malevolent ones, and they'd probably welcome those little evil hybrid babies with open arms!" Alex exclaimed.

"So if that is the case, then why would the President make the announcement he just made?" Jane asked.

"He had no choice. He had to say something. This was the second mass UFO sighting in a little over a year. Politically he couldn't afford to ignore it. But think about it. What did he really say? He didn't say much of anything, did he? Oh, sure, he threw in that Roswell reference to appear to be sincere and truthful. But the whole 'speech' was much ado about nothing," Russell complained.

"So then there will be a battle for the planet Earth," Jennifer stated.

"It looks that way. However, we do have one major advantage," Russell replied.

"What's that?" I asked.

"Remember I mentioned that when the more spiritually evolved benevolent extraterrestrials join in the creation process with humans, the DNA mutates to a higher level? That is a distinctive advantage which our adversaries do not have."

"That is encouraging," I responded. "Actually, if we use our subconscious minds to envision and believe that we are victorious in our endeavors, and do not doubt, it will happen. We need to use the amazing power of our minds. That's all there is. Am I correct, Russell?"

"I wouldn't say that is all there is, but it is a major component."

"Could you put the volume back on the TV, please?" Jennifer asked Alex. "I want to hear what that woman is saying."

Alex clicked the button and we listened as the woman on the screen was talking about a close encounter she had with extraterrestrials the night before. "...I awoke from a sound sleep and there was a strange light streaming through the bedroom window. I wanted to see what time it was, but realized that I couldn't move my head. I could move my eyes but not my head. Then I realized that I couldn't move any other part of my body. I was in a panic. I didn't know what was happening to me. Why was I suddenly paralyzed? And then I moved my eyes over to the other side of the bed and that's when I saw them. There were three figures standing there looking down at me. I couldn't make out their features as there seemed to be a haze around them. And that's all I remember. The next thing I knew it was morning and I felt fine, just like normal. I thought the episode was just a dream, a very vivid dream. Then I turned on the television and realized that it could possibly have actually happened. I didn't have the TV on the night before as I was studying for a test. I had no idea about the UFO sightings..."

"So, Russell, it appears you are correct; there will be evil hybrids working against us," Joshua surmised.

"I wonder what's going to happen to this woman,"

Russell murmured.

"What do you mean?" Jennifer asked.

"They can't let her continue to speak in public like this as it's going to freak out a lot of people, right?" Joshua questioned.

"Right. I'm sure they set up that toll free number in hopes of getting these people before they make public statements. I don't think we'll see much more of her and I'm sure they'll make up a good excuse for her disappearance from public view," Russell responded.

"Do you think there will be any more mass UFO sightings in the near future?" Jane asked Russell.

"I wouldn't think so. It appears that they've accomplished what they set out to accomplish. Now we just have to sit and wait for the next generation. At least that would be my guess."

We sat and talked well into the afternoon. Jennifer and Russell said they'd stay overnight and leave the next morning. Actually, Russell would take Jennifer back to London via the portal and then he'd return later tomorrow to begin working with Hope and Seth. Jane et al left just around 4 p.m.

Alex had a craving for pizza, so he and Russell headed out to the pizza place to pick up a couple pies. Their pizzas were assembled with all your favorite toppings but you had the option of buying them unbaked. This way you could have them hot out of your own oven. They were wonderful that way.

I was happy to have a few minutes alone with Jennifer as I was hoping she'd tell me what was going on between her and Russell. I promised myself I wouldn't ask. If she wanted me to know, she'd tell me.

I didn't have to wait too long. No sooner had Alex and Russell driven away when she said, "He's the one, Mom."

I was going to pretend that I didn't know what she was talking about but she knew me too well for that.

"Russell is the one you've been waiting for?"

"Yes."

"Does he feel the same way?"

"Yes, he does."

"So do you have plans for the future?"

"You mean like getting married?"

"Possibly, but not necessarily," I replied feeling that I was fumbling for the right words now.

"We have talked about the future and we have discussed marriage and we've both decided that we don't need the government or the church to sanction or legitimize our commitment to each other."

"Wow, I'm impressed…impressed that you've had that discussion and impressed by your decision."

"Look who I have for a role model, Mom. You and Alex have been together for years and I couldn't imagine any couple being more committed to each other. For heaven's sake, he even went along with you when you said you wanted to have an extraterrestrial's baby!"

My eyes had started to fill with tears when she mentioned the role model thing but I had to laugh when she brought it around to having an extraterrestrial's baby. And she was right!

"So," she continued, "we were thinking that we'd like to have a little gathering to celebrate our commitment to each other. I'd invite Anne and Mary and a few old friends and a couple of co-workers. And we'd like to have it here maybe in a month or so…how does that sound?"

"Wonderful, absolutely wonderful," I responded, crying unabashedly now. She put her arms around me and we just stood there hugging and crying.

"Okay, let's get a grip and call Mary," I said.

"Great idea! I'll call her," Jennifer responded.

"Wait, let's look at a calendar first," I suggested and walked over to my appointment book by the phone. "Okay, the first Saturday in June is the 6th. How does that sound?"

"Sounds good to me. I'll double check with Russell to

make sure it works for him. So I'll tell Mary the tentative date is June 6th. Okay?"

"Okay, make that phone call!"

A few seconds later she was chatting away with Mary. I could hear them talking about the UFOs and the President's speech. Then Jennifer moved into the real purpose of the call. I could actually hear something like a squeal come over the phone. They continued talking for a while and then Jennifer handed the phone to me.

"Great news, huh?" I asked.

"I couldn't be happier for them both. I was hoping they'd get together. I just wasn't expecting it this soon. What a surprise! I told her I'd be there whatever the date. Just let me know once the date is confirmed and I'll make reservations. Actually Anne is still here and she heard the whole thing on speaker phone. She also said to count her in no matter the date."

I had just hung up the phone when I could hear the car pull into the garage. I quickly turned on the oven to preheat it for the pizza.

Russell walked in carrying two pizzas. He put them down on the counter and I could hear him quietly say to Jennifer "I told Alex about us."

I could see Jennifer smile and say "And I told my mother as well as Mary and Anne!"

Alex came in with a bottle of Valpolicella wine in hand.

"We have something to celebrate," I exclaimed.

"Jennifer told you?" Alex asked.

"She sure did, and I couldn't be happier. Come here and let me give you a hug, Russell."

He came over and put his arms around me, and then Jennifer joined, followed by Alex. Nothing like a group hug before dinner!

It was wonderful to have good news and something to look forward to. We emphasized only the positive that night.

We didn't watch television and we didn't discuss the latest extraterrestrial activities. It was an opportunity to marvel at the wonders of kismet.

Chapter 26 – Carefully Taught

Russell escorted Jennifer back to London the next morning and he returned later that afternoon. He settled into his boyhood bedroom and a short while later we discussed what the 'routine' was to be. We agreed that it wasn't fair to have Jane and/or Joshua drive up to our house every day for Seth's lessons. We thought it would make more sense for us to rotate weeks. The first week would be at our house, and the second at Jane's, etc. The schedule would be four days a week from 9 a.m. to 4 p.m. This would continue until June 6th, which was now confirmed as the date for Jennifer and Russell's celebration. They would then take two weeks off and travel wherever they wanted. It must be nice to have a portal travel agent and go wherever you wanted at no cost.

I called Jane and explained what Russell and I had discussed and asked if it was acceptable. She agreed and said she'd be here at 9 a.m. tomorrow morning.

Russell insisted on making dinner for us that night. He surveyed what I had in the pantry and refrigerator and concocted a wonderful shrimp and asparagus risotto. His imaginative culinary skills only added to the pleasure I felt in having him with us. The turn of events that brought us together were amazing. But then, there was a great force controlling our lives.

When I arrived in the kitchen with Hope the next morning, Alex and Russell were sipping coffee and looking at an old atlas.

"Good morning!" Russell proclaimed as he got up to take Hope from my arms.

"Good morning to you. How'd you sleep your first night back in your old bedroom?"

"Wonderfully. When I awoke this morning and opened my eyes I could see the tops of the Adirondacks in the distance, just as I had when I was a boy. I was thinking to myself, 'I'm home, I'm really home,' but it just wasn't the physicality of it all. I was here with you and Alex and Hope; where I was meant to be. Jennifer has joined my life and we are all entwined into one family now; I am truly home."

Ah, nothing like getting all teary eyed first thing in the morning. I gave him a hug and changed the subject to avoid becoming a sobbing fool.

"So what are you looking at in the atlas?"

"Russell was showing me the area of India where Meghalaya is located," Alex answered. "This atlas was printed back in the 1930's, which was before the state was formed."

"Right, Meghalaya was formed in 1972 from Assam. Shillong is the capital where the highest peak in the state is located. The locals call that peak 'abode of the gods'."

"Well that's interesting, 'abode of the gods' not 'clouds'. Those terms are pretty much interchangeable, at least as far as we've determined," I commented.

"The peak called 'abode of the gods' is located in the state whose name means 'abode of the clouds'. And here we are living in another Meghalaya on the opposite side of the world," Russell observed.

Shortly before 9 a.m. a large wooden trunk was delivered to Russell. Alex helped him carry it up to Russell's room. They were up there for a few minutes when Alex returned to the kitchen and said "There are some really amazing things in that box. There's a globe that illuminates from within, a planetarium of sorts, only it contains some planets and constellations with which we are unfamiliar. And there are rock samples, some that have a glow about them and vibrate. He's got an old phonograph and records of classical music, an amazing collection. There's an abacus. Books full of art. There was much more, but I couldn't see it all. The only things he really had time to at least partially show me were that planetarium and the rock collection."

Jane and Seth had just arrived. Russell went out to greet them in the courtyard and carried Seth into the house.

"We'll conduct classes for the most part in my bedroom; however, if the weather is good we might work outside on the patio. Jane, why don't you come upstairs with me and Seth? Connie, could you please bring Hope to my room?"

"I'll get Hope," Alex said.

I followed them upstairs with Alex and Hope trailing behind me. Russell had a nice thick quilt on the floor on which he placed Seth. Alex positioned Hope on the quilt next to Seth.

"Don't worry about them, they'll be fine. If they get sleepy, they can take a nap. If you come up around noon, we'll break for lunch then. Any questions?"

Jane looked at me and I looked at Jane and we both shook our heads.

"Their first day of school; somehow I envisioned putting Seth on a yellow bus five years from now," Jane murmured.

We turned and slowly walked downstairs. I felt sad for some unknown reason. Maybe it was because my little baby wasn't just my little baby anymore. She was commencing her training for greatness, for the mission that lay ahead.

The three of us silently sat around the kitchen table sipping coffee. Alex left for the current job site several minutes later. Jane and I sat there staring at each other.

"Hey, I almost forgot!" I exclaimed.

"Forgot what?"

I told Jane all about Jennifer and Russell and the celebration that was to take place on June 6th.

"You are available to attend, aren't you?" I questioned.

"I wouldn't miss it for the world. I am so happy for them I could just burst!"

"Well, don't do it in my kitchen; I don't feel like mopping up."

"So now what? What are we going to do with the hours we'll be spending together?" Jane asked.

"You don't have to stay here. You could go run errands, or go home. I could drive Seth back at the end of the day, or you could come back and pick him up. "

"Ah, so you don't want me around, huh?"

"No, that's not what I'm saying. But this is the start of a long process and we need an arrangement that is workable for both of us."

"I know what you mean. Let's just get through this first day and see what happens. So you're stuck with me today at least. Is there some project I can help you with?"

"Well, I have been meaning to get my recipes organized and nicely typed. My sisters have been asking me for copies of many of them. You could help me with that."

"Great idea. You could write a cookbook, 'Connie's Cookbook'. Has a nice ring to it, don't you think?"

"You know, you're right! There are websites devoted to producing cookbooks. It would be so much better than emailing a bunch of recipes to them. It would look professional and be a nice gift. I'd want it spiral bound so it could lay flat on the counter."

"Now you're cooking!"

"Ha, very funny!"

I pulled out my index cards with recipes, folders with recipes, cookbooks with handwritten recipes stuck between the pages, all the recipes that I could find. And we started going through them one by one, identifying which ones were worthy of inclusion in the book.

Time flies when you're having fun and it was almost noon now. We quietly walked up the stairs towards Russell's room. I could faintly hear music playing; it sounded like Mozart. Jane knocked on the door and we heard Russell say "Come in."

Jane opened the door and there was Russell sitting in between Hope and Seth on the quilt. He had an art book open on his lap and both children were looking very intently at a painting on the open page. It was hard to believe they were only five months old!

"How's it going?" I asked.

All three of them looked up and gave us big smiles.

"Hope, is that your mama?" Russell asked and pointed toward me.

Still smiling, Hope nodded her head.

"Seth, is that your mama?" Russell asked and pointed toward Jane.

Seth nodded.

"Very good, children. That's right. I think it's time to go have lunch now," Russell advised.

We picked up the children and headed downstairs for lunch.

"I was amazed that they understood your question and responded by nodding their heads," Jane remarked as we sat at the table.

"With children this young, many times parents talk around them and not directly to them, or perhaps they talk baby talk or gibberish. You'd be surprised what children can understand even at this young age if they are only given the chance," Russell responded.

"Makes sense," Jane remarked.

"Jane and I were talking earlier about our schedules while the children are in class with you. Would it be okay with you if, for example, Jane dropped Seth off in the morning and picked him up in the afternoon?" I asked.

"Sure, that's fine," Russell answered. "Actually, if you let me borrow your car, I could drive him home. I do have an international driver's license, so I can legally drive."

"You wouldn't mind doing that?" Jane asked.

"Actually, I'd enjoy it. I haven't driven around these parts in a long time."

"Well, it might not be every day, but I certainly will take you up on that offer," Jane replied. "Thank you!"

"So I hear you and Jennifer are officially a couple. Congratulations! I'm so very happy for you both," Jane continued.

A big smile broke out on Russell's face, "Thanks very much. I knew the moment I first saw her that she was the one. Plus I get great perks."

"Great perks?" I asked.

"Sure, I inherit a wonderful extended family and friends. Not to change the subject, but what is that pile of paper on the counter?"

"Recipes! At first we thought we'd be spending days together while the children were in class, and Connie thought it might be a good idea to compile a cookbook of recipes for Anne and Mary," Jane responded.

"I thought I'd have free labor for a while, but now Jane knows she doesn't have to stay here while the children are in class so that thought is out the window. I'm going to continue with it, however. It's something I've been meaning to do."

"Dedicate the book to me, and I'll help as much as I can," Jane teased.

"Deal."

After lunch Russell and the children went back upstairs to continue their lessons. Jane and I continued to sift through a pile of recipes and made considerable headway.

The following day Jane dropped off Seth in the morning and Russell drove him home late that afternoon. Jane called me right after Russell left.

"You won't believe it," she said.

"What?"

"When Russell and Seth arrived, Russell said to Seth, 'Who's that waiting for you at the door, Seth?' And Seth said 'Mama.' He said 'Mama'; can you believe it? I just burst into tears. My little boy called me 'Mama'."

I could hear her voice breaking now as she described it.

"After two days with Russell, Seth is calling me 'Mama'.

Later that night as I was putting Hope to bed, Russell came in and asked Hope "Who's this lady?" and pointed to me.

Hope looked at me with loving eyes and said "Mama".

I looked at Hope and said "Mama loves you, Hope."

By the end of the week, Hope was calling Alex 'Papa'. The first time she did, it was quite an event, I must say. It was the end of the fourth day of the first week. Alex had come home early and walked in while we were having lunch. Hope looked up as he walked into the kitchen and said "Papa!"

Alex stopped in his tracks and replied, "Yes, it's Papa, Hope. How's my little girl?"

She gave him a big smile and he went over and kissed her cheek.

Later that afternoon Alex admitted that he intentionally never had children as he didn't feel it was the responsible thing to do for a multitude of reasons. But when Hope called him 'Papa' he said he was overcome with emotion, which astonished him.

"Thank you, Connie. It's because of you that I'm experiencing something I never thought I'd want to experience. And I love it."

Chapter 27 – Celebration

The intervening weeks passed like a flash and here it was Thursday, June 4th. Russell had just completed the day's lessons when Alex arrived from the airport with my sisters. Jane was with me, still helping me review my recipes. I think she was really enjoying going through all those dog-eared faded pieces of paper. She was making copies of the ones that appealed to her, so that must have been her ulterior motive.

I heard Mary's distinctive "Hellooo!" at the front door and I jumped up to greet her and Anne.

"So good to see you both!" I exclaimed as I gave them hugs. "Come on to the kitchen, Jane is here."

"What are you doing?" Anne asked when she saw Jane sitting at the table with a mound of paper in front of her.

"Connie put me to work."

"Doing what?"

"Mary, remember you said that if I had any free time maybe I could put together some of my recipes for you? Well, it just so happens that I do have some free time right now, so does Jane."

"How wonderful! I had no idea you had such a stash of recipes. I don't want you to go through a lot of work on my behalf, though."

"We're both enjoying it for some odd reason. It's almost like a trip down memory lane for me and Jane is along for a vicarious ride. I've got some of Grandma's and Mother's recipes and even a couple of Father's bread recipes."

"Where are Russell and the children?" Anne asked.

"Out on the patio," Jane said.

"Well, I've got to go and see them!" Anne replied and headed off with Mary right behind her.

I turned to Jane and suggested, "Why don't you call Joshua and see if he can come over for dinner? We could grill some veggie burgers and make-believe hot dogs. It would be fun, don't you think?"

"Make-believe hot dogs?"

"You know, tofu or soy hotdogs, whatever. They're really very good. And I still have some sauerkraut from Champlain Orchards to put on the dogs."

The sauerkraut must have done the trick, as she walked over to the phone and dialed. It didn't take any arm twisting; Joshua said he'd be right over.

Alex walked into the kitchen after depositing my sisters' luggage up in their bedroom.

"We're having a cook-out!" I proclaimed.

"When?"

"Now. Everyone is here except for Joshua, so Jane just called him and invited him over. We're having hotdogs and hamburgers on the grill."

"Real hamburgers and hotdogs?" he asked.

"No, but we do have real sauerkraut," I joked and watched him grimace.

"I'd better get some wine for your sisters and light the grill," Alex remarked. "You girls want some wine?"

"Don't mind if I do," Jane nodded.

"Moi aussi," I said.

"Watch out, she's speaking French again," Alex joked. "Good thing I'm ambidextrous."

"You mean bilingual?" Jane asked.

"No, ambidextrous. I've got to juggle a bottle of wine in one hand and glasses in the other."

"I think it would simplify matters if you put it all on a tray," I quipped as he poured some wine for Jane and me.

"Excellent idea," Alex agreed as he reached for the

tray. A couple of seconds later he was headed off toward the patio.

"Let's collect these recipes and put them away for today," I suggested to Jane. "It's time to head out to the patio!"

Alex had poured the wine and was getting the fire going on the grill. Mary and Anne were questioning Russell about the cards the children had with them in the playpen.

"There are different symbols on the cards," Russell explained. "Here, let me show you. See the triangle on this card? There are five different cards laid out in front of the children. They take turns identifying the card that has the same symbol on it as the card I'm holding. Watch."

Russell held the card with the triangle up in front of the children.

"Seth, please point to the card which matches the card I'm holding."

Seth looked at the card in Russell's hand, then looked down at the cards in front of him and pointed to the corresponding card with the triangle on it.

"That's right, Seth. Very good!" Russell praised. Hope was clapping and Seth was smiling.

Russell did another card, a square this time, with Hope. He obtained the same positive results.

"When did you start working with the cards?" I asked.

"This afternoon," he replied.

"And they've learned so fast!" Mary exclaimed.

"They are exceptional children," Russell reminded her. "A few weeks from now we'll still be using the cards, but by then the cards in front of them will be face down and I'll ask them to identify which card matches the card I'm holding. They'll be able to do that as well. Shortly after that I'll be holding the card facing myself, and they'll still be able to match it with the face down card in front of them."

"Remarkable!" Mary proclaimed as we all started chatting about the children's abilities.

In a short while Joshua arrived and we got dinner on

the grill. I warmed up the sauerkraut and sliced up some onions and tomatoes for the burgers. Dinner on the patio that evening was a treat, good company and good simple food.

The next morning Russell left early to pick up Jennifer via the portal. We were still working on our first carafe of coffee when they both walked though the back door.

"Hi, Mom!" Jennifer said as she walked over to me to give me a hug.

She made the rounds hugging everyone else and sat down at the table. She looked happy and self assured, and so very beautiful. She poured coffee for herself and Russell, who had deposited her duffel bag in the front hall and was now seated beside her.

"Mom, is it too late to put in a special request for a raisin cake for the party?"

"No problem, that's one of the easiest recipes Grandma had," I responded.

"I'd like white chocolate frosting on it; do you have a recipe for that?"

"Yes I do. I didn't know it until just yesterday when Jane and I were sifting through my recipe file. I wondered where it came from and why I had it. Now I know; you were going to ask for it!"

"I'll make the cake, okay? It's about time I learned how to do it," Jennifer stated.

"Okay, you'll see, it's a snap."

"So who is coming to this event?" Anne asked.

"A couple of people from work," Jennifer replied. "Remember Richard, the guy whose family sold me the cottage in Scotland? He's coming along with his girlfriend. Another co-worker, Sara and her husband are coming. Cynthia, my neighbor and very good friend in London will be here with her daughter. And two of my classmates from college that I have stayed close with over the years, Helen and Eric, will be coming. Russell's mentor, Joseph, will be here accompanied by the woman who is the portal travel agent of sorts at the

Center, Eleanor. That's it, except for Jane et al of course."

"I expect Joshua will be delighted to meet Eleanor. He'll be picking her brain about all the great portals of the world," Russell joked.

"Sounds like a title for a book... 'Great Portals of the World'," Mary laughed.

"And a best seller to boot!" Anne chuckled.

The next day dawned clear and mild. The forecast for the next couple of days was more of the same delightful weather. I was pleased that I'd be able to have the patio doors open so the guests could stroll out on the patio and lawn. I had the urns on the patio and on either side of the front door filled with my old standby combination of purple verbena, orange lantana and dark and chartreuse varieties of wild yam.

Everyone woke early and we gathered around the kitchen table sipping coffee, talking about what we needed to do and who was going to do what.

Jennifer was assigned the cake making and flower cutting and arranging responsibilities; she'd wait until the following morning to cut and arrange the flowers. Mary was to make the potato salad. Anne was responsible for a green pea and radish salad. I was going to prepare a pate' as well as asparagus vinaigrette. Alex was going to pick up the beverages, meat and cheese platters, crudités and dips, shrimp cocktail platter and bread and rolls and various last minute items such as good quality white chocolate and cream for the icing. Russell was going to weed and trim the flower beds. Hope was just going to sit around and watch.

We spent the rest of the day cooking, baking, gardening, running errands and tidying up the house a bit. Everything was ready and everything was perfect.

And then the day arrived; a glorious day in our little spot in Vermont. Jennifer said she was going to go out while the dew was still on the flowers and cut what she needed for the arrangements. Russell said he'd carry the basket for her, and off they went into the morning mist. We sat at the kitchen table looking out the patio doors at them as they made their rounds.

"It reminds me of the morning they met; she was cutting flowers and he ended up holding the basket for her just as he is now," Anne recalled with a catch in her voice.

As we sat there continuing to stare out at them, the silence was broken by Hope shouting "Mama" and pointing to me. Then she pointed to Alex and exclaimed "Papa!"

"That's right, Hope. That's 'Mama' and 'Papa' Mary said pointing to each of us. Very good!"

Hope had a very pleased look on her face and appeared to be delighted being the center of attention. Alex leaned over and gave her a kiss on her cheek and her little lips puckered up as he did so. She was so adorable.

We were still sitting there sipping coffee and eating bran muffins when Jennifer and Russell came in with the flowers.

"I've got all the vases out on the counter, Jennifer, so be just as creative as you always are," I advised. "There's going to be four tables out on the patio in addition to the wrought iron table, so it would be nice to have a smaller arrangement on each of those tables. Then I think a lower one for the coffee table in the living room and a nice tall one for the book table, one for the dining room table and one for the counter in the kitchen."

"I found spaces on the bookshelf for most of those books that had been piled on the table in the living room," Alex boasted.

"Yes, I noticed that," Jennifer said. "And I love that lovely old Persian rug you artistically draped across the table."

"It's a Beluchi design," Alex advised. "It's well over 100 hundred years old. It is beautiful; I'm glad you like it."

Russell poured himself a cup of coffee and joined us at the table as we watched Jennifer sorting and selecting the lilacs, peonies and mock orange that she had cut. She certainly had a flair for flower arranging.

Just before noon we were ready to receive company. Alex put a mix of instrumental old standards on the CD player. Russell and Jennifer had picked them out themselves the night before. They said they wanted the music to be soft and not intrude on conversation. Luckily, we had quite a few CDs that fit the bill.

Our guests had been advised that this would be an informal gathering and to come casually dressed. Russell was wearing light tan slacks and a white collarless shirt. He looked so handsome, but then again, I always thought he was handsome no matter what he wore.

I had no idea what Jennifer was wearing, and when she walked into the kitchen wearing the gauze dress, I was stunned. It was one of those cotton gauze dresses that were made in India and so popular in the 70's. I had several of them back then. They were cool, comfortable and so very beautiful. Hers was a collage of different complementary patterns, both floral and geometric, and all in various shades of pale pink and ivory. It had a simple round neckline with tiny little pearl buttons down the front to the waist. The sleeves were full and long with elastic at the wrists. The waist had a wide elastic band gathering the fabric which accented her tiny little midriff beautifully. The skirt was full and fell to about mid-calf. She had simple flat leather sandals on and no jewelry except for a pair of pearl stud earrings that I had given her when she graduated from high school.

"You look amazing," Russell whispered as he walked up to her and kissed her on the cheek.

"You really do," I said. "That dress is wonderful. It looks like the kind that was popular decades ago. Did it come from India?"

"Yes, Russell bought it for me," Jennifer replied. "And if you'll recall, I traveled with only a duffel bag. This fabric doesn't wrinkle. I just rolled up the dress and stuffed it in the bag and voila'. Actually Russell bought me several blouses and a couple other dresses all made of the same cotton material. I love them!"

"There's a couple walking across the back lawn," Anne announced.

"That must be Joseph and Eleanor arriving via the portal!" Russell exclaimed and he and Jennifer went out to greet them.

I watched out the door as Russell and Jennifer approached Joseph and Eleanor. Joseph was short and slight, with long grey hair pulled pack into a pony tail. Eleanor was significantly taller than Joseph, had severely cut short grey hair and a beautifully proportioned face. I saw Russell hug and kiss both and introduce them to Jennifer.

I reached the back door just as they approached. Russell introduced them to me and I felt an immediate and inexplicable closeness to them both.

"Thank you for coming," I welcomed them. "It's a pleasure to have you here."

When I shook Joseph's hand, I felt a slight electric shock, similar to what I felt when I first met Russell. And I was also drawn to this man as if there was something very special about him.

Russell briefly showed them the house and then brought them outside to the patio.

Jane et al had arrived and other guests were arriving on their heels. Jennifer and Russell were on hand to welcome all as they arrived.

We had the beverages set up for self service on the counter in the kitchen. Crudités, dips, shrimp cocktail and my pate´ arranged with cornichon pickles and cocktail rye slices were placed on the table near to the patio doors, formerly known as the book table.

"Did you make the pate´?" Jennifer's friend Cynthia asked me.

"Yes, do you like it?" I asked.

"It is amazing. I could make a meal out of this alone," she said as she spread a little mustard on a slice of cocktail rye and topped it off with a slice of pate´.

What's in it?" she asked.   Jane had joined us and was savoring a slice as well.

"It's a combination of veal, pork, ham and bacon along with onion, garlic, spices, egg and sherry," I replied.

Alex and Joshua were now sampling it, and I could tell it was a hit with them as well.

I made my way over to Joseph and Eleanor and offered to take them on a little tour of the gardens. I brought them over to the stone bench and showed them the carved "Meghalaya" in the seat.

"It is an amazing world, is it not?" Joseph asked. "We traveled here from Meghalaya only to arrive at another Meghalaya on the other side of the globe. You have a very special place here, Connie."

"Thank you. I've loved it from the start, and seem to appreciate it even more with every passing day. I'm curious, how did you know which way to turn once you emerged from the portal out back?"

"Remember that I was Russell's teacher when he was a child; I've been here before," Joseph replied.

"Right, I entirely forgot about that!"

"This is my first time here," Eleanor declared, "and it is an enchanting place. The setting with the lake and the mountains in the distance is spectacular."

We headed back toward the patio and I noticed how relaxed and happy everyone appeared. Anne was walking toward us holding Hope.

"I don't think you've met Hope," I remarked.

"Oh, yes, we have. Russell introduced us to both Hope and Seth shortly after we arrived," Joseph replied.

"Do you mind if I hold her for a while?" Eleanor asked.

"By all means; please do. There is a playpen set up in the far corner of the patio, so if you get tired you can place her in there," I responded.

"Can I help you do anything?" Anne asked as we walked into the house.

"I'll check with Jennifer to see when she wants the buffet put out. I could use your help then."

It was just then that I spotted a couple walking through the living room toward the patio doors. I couldn't believe my eyes; was that my brother and sister-in-law? I whispered to Anne, "Is that Stephen and Virginia heading this way through the living room?"

"Yes it is! I didn't know they were coming! I haven't seen them in years! Fantastic!" and she took off in their direction with me at her heels.

"Hello! What a lovely surprise to see you both," she exclaimed as she embraced Stephen and gave him a kiss, and then did the same with Virginia.

"I'm so happy you're here," I remarked to Stephen as I gave him a hug.

"Surprised, I bet. I asked Jennifer not to saying anything as I wasn't sure I could make it," he replied.

"Virginia, it's so good to see you!" I said and hugged her.

Mary and Jennifer had just made their way over to us. As Mary was busy greeting them, I said to Jennifer, "Boy, you know how to keep a secret!"

"Stephen wasn't sure he could make it and asked me not to mention it to you. He didn't want to disappoint you if he couldn't be here."

My brother worked for the federal government, the State Department to be exact. What his position was with them I didn't know and he didn't talk about it. He traveled extensively in connection with his job and had several apartments around the world. His home was located in Maryland's Eastern Shore, but I don't think he spent much time there. I hadn't seen him in years. He and his wife looked wonderful, so travel must agree with them.

Jennifer escorted them over to Russell who was

standing just inside the patio door. After a few minutes with Russell, I heard her say, "So do you want to meet your newest niece?" She took them out to the patio and headed over to the playpen where Jane and Joshua were with the children. I was looking out at them when Anne walked up next to me and said, "Quite a surprise, huh?"

"Amazing."

Russell was talking to a couple that I hadn't yet met. He turned to us and said, "Connie, Anne, I'd like to introduce you to Richard and Sandra," Russell said.

We shook hands and it dawned on me just who this Richard was. "You're Jennifer's co-worker from whom she purchased the cottage in Lamlash Bay, right?"

"Right, actually she bought it from my uncle's estate. Have you been there yet?"

"No, but we've seen pictures of it. It's absolutely breathtaking. We'll be going soon, I'm sure. I was just waiting for Hope to get a little older before we traveled."

"Actually my sister Mary and I were talking about maybe taking the trip over in September," Anne interjected.

"September is a spectacular month over there. Absolutely beautiful weather," Richard responded.

"I was admiring your art work," Sandra commented. "This 'Baptism of Christ' is quite thought provoking. Russell was telling us it was painted in the early 1700's. Makes you wonder what they knew back them that has been lost or suppressed today."

"It does make you wonder, doesn't it?" I replied.

"And the other painting on the other side of the window is fascinating. It really draws you in and makes you wonder about what is going on inside that cloud..." she continued.

"Have you met Jane yet?" Russell asked. "Jane is the artist."

"No, I don't think we have."

"She's out there on the patio with her son Seth. Come,

let me introduce you," Russell suggested. "Excuse us, ladies."

They walked outside and Anne and I headed into the kitchen. Jennifer's former classmates Helen and Eric as well as her friend Cynthia and her daughter, Julie, were standing by the bar area.

"Connie, what do you think? I was suggesting that Russell import clothes from India and I could sell them in the States. Doesn't that sound like a great idea? The dress that Jennifer is wearing is amazing. A line of clothes like that would be a sure winner," Helen announced.

Jennifer approached just in time to hear most of Helen's comment.

"Actually, those gauzy Indian print dresses and blouses were all the rage back in the 1970's," I responded.

"Then they are overdue for a comeback! The time is right. I'm serious about this. Where is Russell? I have to talk to him!" Helen exclaimed.

"He's out on the patio," Anne said.

"I'm heading out to have a little chat with him," Helen declared and off she went accompanied by Eric.

"Well, that is one determined woman," Cynthia said.

"I think the last thing Russell wants is to get involved with the import/export business," Jennifer chuckled.

"So, Jennifer, how did you even manage to reach Stephen?" I asked.

"Simple, I called the only phone number I had for him, which was the one down at the house in Maryland. I got his answering machine and left a message. He called me back within a couple of hours. He mentioned that they can't stay long; he's got to be in India tomorrow on business. There's a car and driver out front waiting to take them back to the airport."

"I'd like them to at least have a bite to eat before they leave. When do you think we should set up the buffet?" I asked.

"We could start right now. That way people can help

themselves whenever they want," she replied.

We started pulling the platters and bowls out of the refrigerator and arranged them on the dining room table. In a few minutes all was in place.

"I'll make the rounds and let everyone know that they can help themselves to lunch," Jennifer said and headed toward the living room. She stopped in her tracks, turned around, came back and gave me a hug. "Everything is perfect, Mom. Thank you so much." And with that she went to announce lunch was served.

"Well, I think I'm going to beat the crowd to the buffet table, how about you?" Cynthia asked Julie.

"Sounds good to me, Mom," was the response and off they went.

I poured myself a little wine and refreshed Anne's glass and we stood and watched as people began to filter into the dining room.

"So what's with this possible trip to Scotland in September?" I asked.

"Mary and I really wanted to get there this year," Anne replied. "I mentioned it to Jennifer and she said August and September were good months and to just let her know what worked for us."

"Well, would you mind it if we tagged along?" I asked.

"Mind it? I'd love it!"

"I'll speak with Alex and see what he thinks. Are you planning on a conventional mode of transportation or doing the portal?"

"I guess that depends on Russell. We'll see."

Cynthia walked up to me with a heaping plate of food and asked, "Did you make this potato salad?"

"Yes, I did."

"It is delicious. There's something different about it, what is it?"

"I used equal amounts of sour cream and mayonnaise. It was my mother's recipe."

"Equal amounts of sour cream and mayonnaise. I'll remember that easily enough. Anything else I should know?"

"It's seasoned with celery seed and salt, that's it. The celery seed gives it a unique flavor. And there's also sliced celery, but no onion."

"Thanks, Connie. I'll never make potato salad the same way again."

When there was a lull at the buffet table, Anne and I made dishes for ourselves and went out to the patio. Mary was sitting at a table with Stephen, Virginia, Joseph and Eleanor. Anne and I pulled up a couple of chairs and joined them.

"Everything is delicious, Connie," Joseph commented.

"Thank you. I had lots of help, though."

"Eleanor and I had an opportunity to spend some time with both Hope and Seth. They are exceptional children, but I know you are already aware of that."

"Yes, I was aware of that, but it wasn't until Russell started their training that I fully realized it," I responded. "What I mean is I couldn't fathom what he would be teaching them at such and early age. And he has taught them so much already. It's amazing!"

"Yes, it's between birth and 18 to 24 months of age that children really learn. Most people don't comprehend that and either ignore direct communication or talk down to their children. It is a real loss, unfortunately."

Joseph and Eleanor excused themselves and headed over to the table where Russell, Jennifer, Jane and Joshua were sitting.

"We met Hope; what a beautiful child she is," Virginia declared.

"Thank you. I'm fortunate to have her; she keeps me young!"

"And it's quite some coincidence that your friend Jane has a child about the same age," Stephen noted.

"Yes, isn't it? The children play together quite often," I responded.

Stephen knew nothing about the children's extraterrestrial heritage and I didn't want him to know. I can't say why I wanted to keep this from him, but I did. Perhaps it was because he was affiliated with the government of which I had an inherent distrust? I don't know.

"Did you see the UFOs the other day?" he asked.

"Yes, a group of them flew right over Lake Champlain. Did you see them?"

"No, I was in a remote area of Africa at the time and didn't see a thing. Before these two mass sightings, I had my doubts that they existed. Even now it's difficult for me to believe that they are not from this earth."

"The President has admitted that a UFO crashed at Roswell and that the government has been in communication and working in collaboration with certain of them."

"I've lived long enough to learn that you shouldn't believe everything you read and you shouldn't believe everything you hear," he replied. "Call me a skeptic, but I need to see a UFO in order to believe it, or at least start to believe in the possibility of it. Right now all I know is what others are telling me, and that's not enough."

Well, that was a surprising response coming from my brother, the high level State Department official!

When we arrived back inside the house it appeared that it was an appropriate time to serve the cake. Alex brought out the champagne, and I carried the cake out onto the patio. Before Russell and Jennifer cut the cake, Russell advised they'd like to say a few words. Jennifer went first.

"Even before I set eyes on Russell, I think I was already in love with him," she said. "My mother and aunts gushed about how wonderful he was, and even Alex admitted that he seemed to be a nice guy, and that is a glowing recommendation coming from Alex. I have to admit I was intrigued. I couldn't wait to meet him. And then he walked into my life. Literally, he walked down this driveway and walked into my life. I saw him approaching, and halfway down the drive I knew, without a doubt, that he was the man for whom I had been waiting. I knew he was out there somewhere and I found him in my mother's front yard! Thank you, Mom, for buying this very special house, Russell's boyhood home, which brought us together. As you say, 'there is a great force controlling my life' and all is exactly as it should be. I thank you all for being here today with us to participate in our celebration of love and commitment to each other."

Russell then spoke, "Connie, I raise my glass to you, as your actions brought Jennifer and me together. To Connie!"

Everyone raised their champagne glasses in a toast to me, and I was deeply moved. Some of the people in attendance didn't know the full extent of what 'your actions' meant. They assumed it was solely the purchase of this house. And yes, the purchase of the house and property started the ball rolling, but there was so much more that they didn't know.

"I thank you Connie and Alex for hosting this gathering today. All is perfection, from family and friends who have traveled here today to join us, the magnificent food and drink, lovely floral displays both within and without the house, to the warm and comfortable atmosphere that you both create just by being who you are. Anne and Mary, thank you both for your assistance; and thanks for 'gushing about how wonderful I was' to Jennifer before she met me. Happily, it had a very positive effect!

"I always felt that 'the' special someone was out there waiting for me. And of all places, I found her waiting for me at the end of the driveway to this house. It's hard to describe my emotions as I saw Jennifer standing there. 'Hello old friend' immediately came to mind as I walked toward her, as I felt for sure I knew her, not from this place and time, but from another. I was coming home; both to my boyhood home, Meghalaya, as well as home to the woman I loved."

Tears were falling down Jennifer's cheeks as well as mine. Actually, looking around, I don't think there was a dry eye in the place.

"I look forward to spending the rest of my life with my dear Jennifer. Thank you all for being here to witness my declaration of love and commitment."

"To Jennifer and Russell!" Alex exclaimed and we all raised our glasses in toast to the couple.

Just then the faint sounds of "Our Love is Here to Stay" filtered out onto the patio.

Russell looked at Jennifer and asked "Want to dance?"

She nodded and responded in a whisper, "I'd love to."

The timing of that song beginning at that very moment was incredible. They had mentioned it last night as they were searching through our CDs. They came upon a CD entitled "Gershwin Plays Rhapsody in Blue" and put it on to see if they liked it. They more than liked it, they loved it. One song they commented on that they especially liked was "Our Love is Here to Stay". This CD was George Gershwin at the piano actually playing his own compositions. It was taken from piano rolls that dated back as early as 1924. This CD went on their 'to play' pile. And now, hearing it again, it was the inspiration for their impromptu dance on the patio.

As the song ended, Russell and Jennifer kissed and embraced. It was a lovely sight to behold. A few seconds later Jennifer announced, "Okay, it's time for cake!"

Jennifer had made the cake in three graduated square layers. When she was a teenager she had taken a cake decorating class, which came in handy now. After she frosted it, she had piped trim and small rose decorations around the cake entirely in that same white chocolate frosting. This morning she placed the white mock orange blossoms and some of its green leaves around the base of the cake.

She began slicing the cake and Russell began passing the pieces around to the guests.

Stephen came over to me and asked "Is this Mother's raisin cake recipe?"

"Sure is."

"I haven't had this in decades, and it's as good as ever. Remember how she was always trying to improve on it? She put chocolate chips in it one time and peanut butter cups another and there was nothing that could compare to her original recipe."

Jane was standing next to me, savoring every bite. "This is amazing," she said. "It's so moist and the combination of spices and raisins works perfectly. The frosting is delicious, too! I remember these are two of the recipes we selected for the cookbook."

"Jennifer made the cake, and it was her idea to frost it with white chocolate icing. I think they compliment each other beautifully."

Shortly after we had the cake, Joseph and Eleanor left, via the portal of course. They wanted to leave while there was still daylight left in order to see their way out to the chamber. Joshua saw them saying their goodbyes to Alex and me and he insisted on walking them out there. I think he wanted to pick Eleanor's brain about the best spots to visit via portal. Of course, I might have entirely misjudged the poor boy.

"I hate to have to eat and run, Connie, but Virginia and I have to take a flight to India a little later today," Stephen advised.

"Yes, Jennifer told me. You have no idea how happy I am that you were able to be here today. Thank you."

They got up and said their goodbyes to Jennifer and Russell and then Anne, Mary, Alex and I walked them out to their limo.

"Oh, I should have brought some food out to your driver!" I exclaimed.

"Jennifer did. He's been well taken care of. Hey, I don't know what made me think of this, but you don't still have that old '64 Dodge Dart, do you?" Stephen asked.

"I certainly do!"

"Want to see it? It will only take a moment," Alex remarked.

"I'd love to!"

With that we walked over toward the garage. Alex opened the door and announced "There it is!"

"It looks as good as the day I sold it to you!" Stephen exclaimed as he walked around it and peered inside. "You've taken such good care of it. Do you still actually drive it?"

"Quite often, in fact."

"Incredible, absolutely incredible," he murmured as we walked back to the limousine.

We said our goodbyes and they drove slowly away.

"Well, that was quite a surprise, wasn't it?" I asked of no one in particular.

"A wonderful surprise," Anne murmured.

Jennifer's co-workers and friends left a little while later. They were all staying at the same hotel and had plans on continuing the party there.

Jane and Joshua stayed for a while longer with us out on the patio. The children had been so well behaved throughout the day, and even managed to take a nap in their playpen despite the party going on around them.

"What a lovely day this has been!" Jennifer exclaimed.

"The weather was wonderful, the company was exceptional and the food and hospitality were beyond compare," Russell remarked. "Thank you Connie."

"It wasn't just me; I think we are all to be congratulated on a job well done."

"And not a cloud in the sky," Alex murmured.

"Except for that one over there," Mary muttered.

"This feels like déjà vu all over again," Alex moaned. "What cloud, where?"

"Right there, straight ahead just coming over the mountains."

We watched as a relatively small cloud slowly travelled across the sky toward our house. As it got closer, the faint outline of a disc shaped object was visible within the cloud. I could see the rays of the setting sun glinting off of the metallic exterior. It was now directly overhead and I would estimate only a couple hundred feet above us. It remained stationary, and after a couple of seconds it produced an amazing light show of a myriad of colors. Hope and Seth were both looking up, taking it all in and seemingly mesmerized by it.

Russell stood up and Jennifer joined him. The lights stopped and the craft tipped slightly to one side as if it were bowing in recognition of them. The cloud reformed around the ship and it slowly moved off beyond the house and disappeared from view.

"I guess they like me," Jennifer murmured.

"I'm sure they do; they wouldn't put on a display like that for just anyone," Russell chuckled.

We sat on the patio for a while longer and reflected on what an amazing and perfect day it had been.

Chapter 28 – Scottish Sojourn

Jennifer and Russell left the next morning for places unknown. I don't know if they really didn't know where they were headed or if they just wanted to keep it to themselves. I didn't ask. All I knew was that for the next two weeks they would be together and taking a break from their normal work routines.

That morning before they left, we were all seated around the kitchen table and I brought up the subject of Scotland in September. Jennifer said she had more than enough room for all of us to visit at the same time as the cottage had 4 bedrooms and there was a 1 bedroom apartment out back.

"Actually, there'd even be plenty of room for Jane et al to join us. It would be fun, don't you think?" Jennifer asked.

"And I could take you there via portal," Russell said. "No cost, no airport, no passports, no customs hassle. Just take a walk out your back door and you're almost there!"

"Alex, what do you think?" I asked.

"I say let's go! Call Jane right now and see if she and Joshua can join us," Alex answered. "Oh, one thing. There's no problem bringing the children over that way? They'll only be 9 months old; is that too young?"

"The children will be fine. I was a little younger than that when Joseph first took me to Meghalaya. I'll have to take them separately, but it will be no problem, believe me."

"Okay, I'm calling Jane," I said and got up and dialed

her number. She was surprised to hear from me so early in the morning. I explained what we had been discussing and said there was plenty of room for them to join us. I don't think Jane was fully awake, as she didn't jump right on this and say okay. Jennifer asked me to hand her the phone.

"Jane, remember that I have 4 bedrooms and an apartment out back. You and Joshua can take the apartment. You'd have your own privacy and the rest of us would be just across the courtyard from you. Russell said he'd take you via portal. Come on, even Joshua would go for that."

Apparently Joshua was right there, listening on another line. When he heard the travel would be via portal he said "Come on, let's do it!" And that was that, we were all going to Scotland!

The summer came and was almost gone when my sisters were back, ready for their portal trip. I was out on the patio with Hope when Alex drove in with them from the airport. When Hope saw them walk out onto the terrace she waived to them and said "Hi!"

"She really remembers us!" Anne exclaimed as Mary picked up Hope and gave her a hug and kiss.

"Love you," Hope said to both Mary and Anne.

"I missed you so very much. You're growing so fast!" Mary sighed.

Alex walked out on the patio and proclaimed, "You ladies sure are travelling light; one duffel bag for each of you, amazing."

"That's how Russell and Jennifer travel, with just one duffel bag. We had to go out and buy duffel bags as all we had was traditional luggage. We packed very light. Jennifer has a washer and dryer, so how much does a person need?" Anne quipped.

"Right you are! Who says you can't teach old dogs new tricks?" Alex jested.

"Is that any way to speak to your elders?" Anne laughed. "I have to admit, though, it was wonderful not having to check in luggage at the airport."

"I'll get you ladies some wine. Are you hungry? Can I get you anything to eat?" he asked.

"I wouldn't mind some cheese and crackers," Mary answered. "They didn't even give us peanuts on the flight!"

"Sure thing, I'll be right back."

"What time are we planning on leaving tomorrow morning?" Anne questioned.

"Early, around 7 or so. Jennifer will be at the train station which is around the corner from the portal. She bought a couple of inexpensive baby strollers, or 'prams' as they call them over there. Russell will bring the children over one by one and leave them with Jane at the station. Then he'll come back for each of us."

Alex arrived with wine and cheese and we sat chatting about the upcoming trip for a while.

"How are the children's lessons progressing?" Anne inquired.

"Great. Remember that card thing Russell was teaching the children, the one where they had to match the symbol of the card in Russell's hand? Well, they progressed to being able to identify the symbol on cards that were face down in front of them. They could see the symbol on Russell's card, but they couldn't see the symbols on the other cards. And they do it!" I exclaimed.

"It would be interesting to see how much psychic ability we all have with similar cards, don't you think?" Mary asked.

"It's certainly something we can check out while we're at Jennifer's," I responded. "I think it would be fun."

"Who's watching Itzy while you're away?" Mary asked.

"Herbert and June, our neighbors down the road, remember you met them?"

"Yes, we had Old Krupnik with them after Thanksgiving dinner," Anne remarked.

"Right. They'll come in once a day and give her fresh water and wet food and top off her dry food. We'll only be gone 5 days, so she'll be fine."

"I think I'd better get the grill going," Alex remarked and headed off in that direction.

"What are we having for dinner?" Mary asked.

"Grilled tuna and Caesar salad. I've got the salad ready to be tossed and the tuna steaks brining."

"You brine the tuna?"

"I'm trying something new. They've been sitting in a brine of half salt and half sugar for several hours."

"What made you think to brine them?" Anne inquired.

"They were frozen, not fresh. It's not always easy to find fresh tuna, but frozen steaks are readily available. However frozen steaks seem tasteless and dry to me. I've had brined turkey and chicken and it was always flavorful and juicy, so I thought I'd try it with tuna. Actually, I should remove them from the brine and let them sit on the counter in marinade while the grill is getting hot. Excuse me, I'll be right back."

We had a relatively early dinner out on the patio as it was a lovely warm evening. And I had to admit I was very pleased with the way the tuna turned out.

"This tuna is out of this world!" Mary said.

"Trying to be funny, Mary? Out of this world..." Alex laughed.

"It's spectacular. It is so moist and it has wonderful flavor. What did you put in the marinade?"

"Lemon juice, olive oil, garlic and a touch of cayenne."

"I'd say your experiment was a success," Anne declared. "I hope you include this in your recipe collection. You can call it 'Tuna from Out of this World'."

"I like it; very catchy title!" I exclaimed.

Hope was sitting in her highchair happily feeding herself on steamed carrots and lentil and brown rice burgers that I formed into small stick shapes so she could pick them up easily. She loved those things! They were good for her, too, as they had egg, onion and garlic in them in addition to the well cooked lentils and brown rice.

The next morning I was up extra early. Hope was still sleeping, and as I peeked through the bedroom door it looked like Anne and Mary were still sleeping as well.

As I descended the stairs, I could hear voices in the kitchen. Was Russell here already? Sure enough, there he was sitting at the kitchen table with Alex, sipping coffee.

"Good morning, Connie! Ready for your trip?" he asked as he got up and gave me a hug and kiss.

"Sure am! We're all packed and ready to go."

I walked over to pour myself a cup of coffee and I heard Anne say "Could you pour one for me, please?"

"You're up! I thought you were still sound asleep," I replied in surprise.

"I heard you pass by the room and then I heard voices down here, so here I am! I made sure Mary was up, too. She'll be here any minute."

"What's the weather like on Arran Isle today?" I asked Russell.

"Beautiful. It should be in the high 60's when you get there. A lovely day for a ferry ride!"

Mary came down a few minutes later holding Hope.

"Look who I found awake in her crib," Mary proclaimed.

"Looks like the gang's all here," I said, "except for Jane et al. I expect they'll arrive within a half hour or so."

We had a quick breakfast and got dressed. Sure enough, Jane, Joshua and Seth arrived right on time and we were off!

"It's a good thing you cleared this pathway through the woods to the portal a while back," Jane said to Alex. "It would have been a little difficult carrying the children through the brush!"

"I know," Alex acknowledged. "It dawned on me just

before Jennifer and Russell's party that Joseph and Eleanor would be walking through those woods and it would be nice to have a path cleared for them."

We reached the portal and Russell took Seth first.

"Don't worry about him," Russell said to Jane. "When we get there Jennifer will be waiting. At first we were thinking she'd wait at the train station, but it's such a nice warm day, she's at the portal. That will speed things up a bit. I'll be there in back in no time. Alex, could you take both of the flashlights and accompany me inside the cave? I want to make sure I have a good grip on Seth, so I'll need two hands to hold him. Leave one flashlight on the bench, so I'll have it when I return. Okay?"

"Okay."

With that, the three of them entered the cave and a minute later Alex returned with flashlight in hand.

In just a few minutes Russell emerged from the cave and said "One down, seven to go!"

He took Hope from my arms and walked back into the cave with Alex in the lead holding the flashlights.

Again, in a few minutes he returned and took the remainder of us one by one through the portal.

The last to arrive in Glasgow was Alex. We were all standing there in the alley chatting with excitement when the outlines of Russell and Alex appeared in the recessed opening of the stone wall. Their bodies became semi-transparent at first and a second or two later there they stood, nice and solid!

I walked over, gave Alex a hug and said "Welcome to Scotland!"

"Okay, folks, let's get over to the train station. The next train leaves in 15 minutes," Russell said.

Jane pushed Seth in the pram and Jennifer was right next to her with Hope. We all followed and easily made the train to Ardrossan Harbor with minutes to spare. We settled into our seats and Russell asked if anyone wanted coffee or tea. We all wanted something, and he took our orders and headed off to the café car with Jennifer. A short while later they returned with beverages and crackers, or biscuits, as they called them over there.

Hope and Seth were really enjoying the biscuits and juice as we sipped our hot beverages.

"The Glasgow train station was really incredible," Joshua said. "What is it, something like one hundred years old?" he asked Russell.

"I think building was completed was 1879."

"Everything was so clean and efficient," Jane stated. "Even what I saw of the city streets was remarkably clean."

We finished our drinks and a short while later we arrived at Ardrossan Harbor.

"That was fast," Mary noted. "What was it, something like 45 minutes or so?"

"Just about," Jennifer said. "Not a bad trip, huh?"

"Very convenient from the portal, that's for sure," Joshua chuckled.

We departed the train and headed toward the dock, which was only a very short distance away. The ferry was much larger than I had envisioned. It held over 600 passengers and something like 60 cars. From the dock you could look across to Arran Isle and see Goat Fell, which was the highest peak on the island. Russell thought it was over 2800 feet tall.

We settled in for the 55 minute ride to the town of Brodick on Arran Isle. Both Hope and Seth had fallen asleep in their prams. We had plenty of time to take in the amazing scenery, as you could walk around the ship and see the mainland on one side and Arran Isle on the other. I was impressed that there was a cafeteria on board that served hot meals, breakfast, lunch and dinner. From what I saw, everything looked delicious! Very civilized country, Scotland!

As we approached Arran Isle, we noticed what looked like a castle not far from the dock. Russell confirmed that it was Brodick Castle which was built in the 16th Century.

We disembarked and Russell led us to the adjacent

parking lot or car park as he called it. He walked toward a two-tone Volkswagen bus and unlocked it.

"Don't tell me this is yours!" Joshua exclaimed.

"Jane and I felt we needed something other than a bicycle to get around and the neighbor lady was selling this," he responded.

"This is a classic! This is a Volkswagen Microbus!" Joshua gasped.

"And it's more than just a Microbus, it's a Sunroof Deluxe with canvas panel and roof lights, also known as the Samba," Alex chimed in. "What year is this, Russell?"

"1964. Only has 32,000 original miles on it. The husband of Jennifer's neighbor bought it when it was new, but how far can you travel on a tiny island like Arran? They hardly ever ventured off island and thus the incredibly low mileage."

"Don't you love the color combination?" Jennifer asked? "It's called sealing wax red on the bottom and beige grey on the top with basalt grey interior. Rose, the lady we bought it from, had the original brochure and gave it to us; that's how we know what the colors are."

"It's an eight seater. How convenient!" I said.

We piled in and were extremely comfortable in this vintage auto, which amazingly looked brand new.

"It's only about 4 miles south of here to the cottage, so it won't take long!" Jennifer said as Russell started up the bus and headed out of the car park onto the main road.

During the entire short trip, Alex and Joshua were talking about the VW bus. I was trying to take in the scenery and noticed that we went up a slight hill and past the Lamlash Golf Club on our left. As we descended I could see the bay in front of me and what I assumed to be Holy Isle looming out of the water. What a magnificent site.

Russell came to an intersection and turned left. The bay was now on our right side. He slowed down and turned into a driveway.

"Don't tell me this is your cottage!" I exclaimed.

"Yes, what do you think of it?" Jennifer asked.

"The location is amazing. I know I saw pictures, but it is really breathtaking!"

"Is that a palm tree over there in your front yard?" Mary asked.

"Weird, huh? The Gulf Stream passes by here and the weather is quite temperate. There are palm trees and tropical plants all over the island except for the higher elevations."

Russell parked the bus and we got out. It was a beautiful day and the temperature must have been close to 70 even now at close to 3 o'clock in the afternoon Scottish time. The front yard was a large expanse of manicured lawn. On what I assumed was the property line on both sides, tall trimmed hedges provided privacy. The palm tree was close to the left side looking toward the water and did not block the view. To the right of the front door was the patio that Jennifer had described with the wrought iron table and chairs.

To my surprise, the front door opened and Eleanor was standing there. "Hello everyone! Hope you had a pleasant trip!" she exclaimed.

I went over to her and gave her a hug and said how happy and surprised I was to see her.

"Eleanor knew you were coming for a visit and suggested that perhaps she could be here to act as a nanny for the children so you could really relax and have some time to yourselves," Russell explained.

"How thoughtful of you, Eleanor! Thank you so much," Jane said and went over and gave Eleanor a hug as well.

Anne had Hope in her arms and Mary was holding Seth. They made their way to the front door and greeted Eleanor and Jennifer piped, "Come on in!"

The foyer was large and gracious with a beautiful curved open staircase toward the rear. To the right was the living room and to the left was the dining room. We walked into the living room which ran the entire length of the house.

A fireplace was situated in the center of the far wall and a large bay window faced the front patio and water view. The furnishings were lovely and tasteful. The walls were a very pale buttery color. The two sofas facing each other on either side of the fireplace were a matching soft yellow brocade. Very pale aqua throw pillows and a corresponding crochet throw provided a little accent color. A vase of black-eyed Susan's sat on the coffee table in front of the fireplace. And one of Jane's paintings hung over the mantel!

"Jane sent you one of her paintings? I didn't know that!" I exclaimed.

"Yes, actually I received it just after I closed on the property. I don't know how she managed to select a painting that had the golden yellow and pale turquoise similar to that in this room, but she did. Doesn't it look spectacular above the mantle?"

"It's incredible! Nice selection, Jane!"

"It was purely luck. I had no idea what colors she had in this room, so I just chose one of my favorites and sent it along. I guess I chose the right one!"

We deposited Hope and Seth into the playpen which had been set up behind the sofa toward the back of the room. Jennifer had the blocks that they liked so much in there and they went right to work building whatever it was that they built.

"Come, let me show you the rest of the place," Jennifer suggested.

We followed her across the front hall into the dining room. The living room, hall and dining room all had hardwood floors with Persian rugs. I could tell Alex was making note of the rugs and I think he was impressed with their selections. The dining room window had a lovely view of Holy Isle as did the bay window in the living room. Directly behind the dining room was the kitchen which looked like it was very recently remodeled. There were stainless steel appliances, granite counter tops, updated cabinets and recessed lighting. It was very tastefully done and functional.

Jennifer took us upstairs and we saw the four bedrooms. One of the rooms had two cribs in it with a twin bed.

"This is where Eleanor will stay with the children," Jennifer advised. "I think this set up will work out well. As the children grow older, we can remove the cribs and have two twin beds in here for them."

"You went through so much trouble for us," Jane said. "You bought two prams, and two cribs, and the playpen. It was so generous of you."

"Hey, I want you to come back! And really, it was no big deal. The nice surprise was Eleanor offering her services as nanny."

We worked our way back downstairs and out the back door into the courtyard. At the far corner of the courtyard was the guest house. Beyond that was a walled garden. I peered through the gate and was surprised by the many flowers in bloom even at this time of the year. I could see the black-eyed Susan's that Jennifer had picked for the living room as well as roses, phlox and chrysanthemum among others.

The guest house was larger than I imagined and was what they called a story and a half high. We walked through patio doors into a large living area with fireplace and beamed ceiling. A comfortable looking sofa and chairs flanked the fireplace and a dining room table was situated just beyond the sofa. A compact kitchen area was tucked back into the far corner. At the opposite corner was a spiral staircase that took you to the bedroom on the second floor.

"This is one incredible spot you have here, Jennifer," Alex commented as we walked back to the main house. "If I were you, I don't think I'd ever want to leave."

"Actually, I feel the same way. We stayed here the entire two weeks after our party at your house back at the beginning of June," Jennifer responded.

"I wondered where you went," I said. "And I can't

blame you a bit for spending the entire two weeks here."

"I was hoping we could walk over to a local restaurant for drinks and early dinner tonight. Do you think you're up to it?" she asked.

"Sure, I know I am," Joshua declared and the rest of us agreed.

"Actually, it's five hours earlier Vermont time, so we're raring to go," Alex exclaimed.

"Let's not get carried away here," I murmured.

"I've got food for the children which I think they'll like, so they should be okay," Jennifer added.

"Do you have brown rice and lentils?" I asked.

"Yes. Why?"

"Tomorrow morning I'd like to make them the lentil and rice patties that they are fond of. Lentils are packed with nutrients and protein, fiber, complex carbohydrates and folic acid. Brown rice is rich in B vitamins, selenium, iron and fiber. And the kids love these patties."

"Hey, can you give me the recipe? Sounds like something Russell and I should be eating."

"Actually, they are delicious on a bun with a little mayo, lettuce and tomato."

A short while later we headed out the front door toward the local restaurant. I still couldn't get over the view. We walked down the driveway and made a right toward the village. Within minutes we were seated on the restaurant terrace, looking out at the bay and sipping our drinks.

I looked over at Jennifer and thought that I had never seen her look better or happier. She was sipping her club soda with a splash of cranberry juice and I saw Russell kind of raise his eyebrows and give her a strange look. I was wondering what that was all about when she said, "Now that we are all here, settled in and relaxed, I'd like to make an announcement." My heart was beating double time. "I'm pregnant!" she exclaimed.

A muted roar emanated from those at the table

followed by 'congratulations', 'fantastic', 'wonderful' and other exclamations of joy.

I got up, gave her a kiss on the cheek and said "I am so happy for you!"

"Thanks, Mom. I bet you had doubts about ever being a grandmother."

"The most important thing to me is your happiness."

"I never knew there could be this kind of happiness," she responded with tears in her eyes.

Russell got up and gave me a hug and I told him how delighted I was to hear the news.

"Connie, I know at times this appears to be hell on earth, but to me, right now, this is heaven."

"And I'm so happy for both of you. I never expected such wonderful news on this trip."

The rest of the evening was amazing. The announcement of Jennifer's pregnancy put us all in a euphoric mood and the setting, company and food were all without compare. What a delightful evening we had.

Jane and Joshua headed off toward the guest house after dinner and the rest of us settled into our respective bedrooms in Jennifer's cottage for the night. The bedroom was so comfortable and had a wonderful view of Holy Isle. There seemed to be a luminescence coming off the water that softly illuminated the bedroom. It was difficult for me to fall asleep as I was so excited by Jennifer's news. I was to be a grandmother! And the child would be part extraterrestrial heritage, one quarter to be exact. Talk about having good genes!

As I lay in bed, I could see reflections on the ceiling of ripples of light cast from the water outside. I got up to look out the window and I could see the dark mound of Holy Isle in the background which was made even darker by the illumination or glow emanating from the waters of Lamlash Bay in the forefront. I had never seen such play of light on the sea before; it was both calming and hypnotic. I climbed back into bed and soon fell asleep, knowing nothing else until the dawn's light woke me the following morning.

The next few days flew by. The Isle of Arran has what is called the "Coastal Way" which is a 65 mile long continuous trail that circles the island. We didn't walk the entire length of the trail, but we did walk quite a bit of it. The trail passes through most of the villages and provided us with the opportunity to stop and explore several villages to some extent as well as have lunch at various quaint eateries.

And, of course, we took the ferry over to Holy Isle. I was quite impressed with the organic vegetable garden they had on the grounds. And the view back to Isle of Arran and Lamlash Bay was spectacular from several points on the walking paths on the isle.

Our last night on Arran, Jennifer and Russell prepared us a wonderful dinner of poached salmon with cucumber dill sauce, potatoes au gratin and green beans Italian style. It was so good to have everyone together, including the children and Eleanor, savoring the wonderful meal. Hope and Seth especially were enjoying the beans which had been sautéed with onion, garlic, stewed tomatoes and Italian herbs.

"You know what puzzles me?" Joshua asked.

"What might that be?" Alex queried.

"How come they have a combination washer/dryer over here and back home you have to buy a separate clothes washer and separate clothes dryer? Here they have one appliance which does both. Are the Europeans that much smarter or are we Americans that much dumber?"

"Probably a little bit of both," Alex replied. "Corporate America wants us to buy two appliances, not one. They'll try to get away with it as long as they can."

"Ours is a Bosch, but I know Hotpoint and Hoover also make them," Jennifer advised. "I think they are so popular in the UK and Europe because there is limited space in many of the dwellings over here."

"We have limited space in some of our dwellings as

well," Joshua muttered.

"The drying feature is not on par with a separate clothes dryer though," Russell interjected. "The drying cycle is considerably longer in most models and there is a maximum weight capacity."

"Still, it would be nice to have the option of purchasing it," I admitted. Jennifer had hers tucked in under the counter in the kitchen and it was extremely convenient and actually attractive.

"I think they are now starting to be offered in the States to a very limited extent," Jane advised.

"Not to change the subject, Jennifer, but what are your plans for when the baby is born? Will you be having it in London?" Mary asked.

"I'm not sure yet, but I'm thinking I'll have it here in Scotland."

"You could always come to Vermont and have the baby there; I know a really good midwife," I offered.

"Thanks, Mom. The idea did cross my mind. However, if I did have the baby there, I wouldn't want to travel with it for the first few months, and then you'd be stuck with me for a while."

"I'd love to be 'stuck' with you! Russell is with Hope and Seth 4 days a week anyhow, so he'd be there with you. We have a computer, phone and fax so you'd be able to communicate with work from there as easily as you could over here. And if you need to travel to London or Scotland for whatever reason, for business or just to get away for a couple of days, there's a portal right out back and I'm your built-in babysitter. Will you just promise to think about it? That's all I ask. Okay?"

"Okay, Mom, I'll think about it. Thank you."

We headed home the following morning. Thanks to Russell, it was a pleasant return trip.

Chapter 29 – Signs in the Sky

"Well, that was a complete waste of time. It was just another Presidential press conference where nothing of any value was said," Alex muttered as he turned off the TV in exasperation and reached for his cup of coffee.

"Can you believe it's been months now and they have no more idea what group of extraterrestrials were involved in the last mass sighting than they did the day after it happened?" I complained.

"That was all a blatant lie!" Russell exclaimed. "They know exactly who orchestrated the whole thing. I have the feeling that they hope this just dies down and goes away. And if it doesn't go away, I think they're preparing a spin that will lead us even further from the truth."

"Gee, you sound just like Joshua," Alex joked.

"Have a little more coffee, Russell?" I asked.

"No thanks Connie. I have to meet Jennifer at the portal in London. We'll be back soon."

It was a Friday morning in early December. Russell had continued to teach the children 4 days a week and they were making tremendous progress. It was hard to believe that in a few weeks they would be a year old. They were able to speak in short sentences now and their telepathic abilities were amazing.

Russell headed out the back door to grab a ride on the portal and Alex headed out the front door to take a walk to the mailbox.

I put Hope in her playpen and started reviewing the final versions of the recipes which we had chosen for the cookbook. I thought my sisters would be very pleased with the finished product; they didn't know they were going to be spiral bound in book format. I was going to surprise them when they came up at Christmas with a copy for each of them.

Alex walked back into the kitchen and handed me the mail. I was very surprised to find a letter from my brother. It read as follows:

"What I am about to tell you is true. We have no idea what it was:

"Sunday evening November 8 was a mild night for that time of the year.

"Virginia and I decided to take a walk along the shore. During warm weather, we walked as often as possible and we thought that this warm evening might be the last opportunity for a walk this year.

"We had finished the first half of the walk and had turned to walk back toward where the car was parked. We weren't far from the car when Virginia noticed something in the sky. At first she saw a light moving toward us parallel to the shore, but slightly out to sea.

"Seconds later there was a second light, then a third and then a fourth – all evenly spaced. Then there was a slightly larger gap and a fifth light, then a larger gap still and a sixth light. The lights had a yellowish tint, about the color of candlelight. There was no sound. It was completely quiet.

"We stopped to watch the lights approach. Others near us did the same.

"As the first light reached a point about even with us, it made a right turn and headed out over the water. As they reached the same point, each of the other five lights made the same turn. As they proceeded out over the water, the lights went out one by one.

"We looked at each other and hurried toward the car.

"I just wanted you to know, Connie, that I'm not a

skeptic anymore."

I handed the letter to Alex and said "Here, I think you'll enjoy reading this."

I watched his face as he read and I could see a smile spread across his face.

"Well what do you know; Stephen and Virginia have seen something inexplicable in the sky. He didn't use the term 'UFO' but they were flying objects and he has no idea what they were. It was good of him to let you know."

"And they didn't just see one object, they saw 6 of them!"

It really pleased me to get that note from my brother. Maybe some day I could even tell him the truth about what's really been going on with our extraterrestrial friends. I wondered how he would respond if I told him Hope is half extraterrestrial, Russell is half extraterrestrial, Jennifer will be giving birth to a baby who is one quarter extraterrestrial, oh, and yes, we have an inter-dimensional portal in our backyard.

I heard the backdoor open and in came Jennifer and Russell. She was now 6 months pregnant and looked marvelous. Before I could say anything, Russell called for us to go outside. He seemed to be agitated.

We got up and followed Jennifer and him out on the patio.

"What is it? What's the matter?" I asked.

"Look up at the sky over your house," he instructed.

I looked up and saw contrails crisscrossing directly over the house, making and 'X' and a separate curved contrail spread completely across half the sky and terminating at the intersection of the two lines forming the 'X', almost as if it were pointing to the 'X'.

"Wow, how could that contrail just terminate like that?" I asked.

"Those aren't contrails, Connie," Russell answered.

"They're chemtrails," Alex announced.

"Right. I've seen them over the house several times

before, but I didn't want to alarm you. But I thought it was time that you should be aware of them. Especially since this is clearly an 'X' over your house."

"Like 'X' marks the spot?" Alex asked.

"Like 'X' marks the spot."

"Come on, it's cold out here, let's go inside," I urged and headed toward the house.

"I'm going to take a couple of pictures of that," Alex muttered and headed to grab the camera.

I put water on for tea for Jennifer and we all settled around the table.

"So what is the difference between a contrail and a chemtrail?" I asked.

"A contrail is normal condensation of ice crystals from jet engine exhaust. They are narrow plumes that dissipate in a relatively short period of time. However, chemtrails are something else entirely. Did you notice how the 'X' over your house was starting to billow out slightly? If you went out there now, it would still be visible, but the clear blue sky would now be filling in with the spread of the particles of the chemtrail."

"Funny, when I was heading back toward the house after getting the mail, I noticed how blue the sky was and I also noticed a couple of airplanes but I really didn't pay much attention to them," Alex murmured.

"I'm going to go outside for a minute and take another look at them," I stated and grabbed my coat as I headed toward the door.

Alex followed me outside and we stood there looking up at the 'X' which was wider than it had been previously with blurry edges that seemed to be spreading out across the sky as we watched.

"That is obviously not condensation," Alex said. "It is now spreading across the entire sky."

"I see what you mean; okay, let go back in."

Jennifer had poured herself a cup of tea and Russell was sipping coffee as we sat down again at the table.

"So what's the story with these chemtrails? Who's doing it and why? And from the name I would assume there are chemicals in those trails, right?"

"I don't think there are any real answers to your questions, Connie. I've read that toxin-laden aerosols are contained within the chemtrails. Who is doing it and why know one really knows. But there are those who would try to convince you that what you're looking at are just cirrus clouds. If you hadn't seen the very clear 'X' and the other strange curved line pointing toward it, you would probably go out there now and think they were cirrus clouds. Less than a half hour ago Alex noted the sky was clear and that there were a couple of airplanes flying by. Those planes formed that 'X' for a reason. What disturbs me is that it's over your house. I've heard that they might be using these 'X' chemtrails for satellite identification and tracking purposes."

"Are you saying that perhaps satellites are being positioned to watch the area below the 'X'? Do you think they're watching our house?" Alex asked.

"Possibly. I've also heard that they are beginning to watch intersecting grid lines or ley lines, so that might be another reason they have placed the 'X' above this location. Maybe they are monitoring possible portal locations. I don't know. There's quite a bit on the internet on chemtrails, but it's all speculation."

"You know what I'm going to do? I'm going to ask the other women on my blog to keep their eyes open for these chemtrails and let me know if they start seeing them as well."

"Good idea," Russell agreed. "That should be interesting."

"So, Jennifer, how are you?" I asked. "You look marvelous!"

"I feel marvelous!" she exclaimed. "And I've reached a decision; I'll take you up on your offer to have the baby here."

"Fantastic! I'm so thrilled! You made the right

decision."

"As you said, Russell works here 4 days a week anyway. And the computer, phone and fax connect me with work from here as easily as it would from Scotland. With the portal out back I can be in London for a meeting in about a half an hour. And, the most important thing of all, I have a built-in babysitter!" she giggled.

She finished her tea, went over to Hope and picked her up out of her playpen.

"Pretty soon she's going to be too big for a playpen. Actually, I think she's too big for it now. I think she could probably climb right over the side of it if she wanted to," she laughed.

"You're right about that. She is such a good child. She sits in there and 'reads' her books or plays with her cards and doesn't put up a fuss. But she can walk fairly well. Put her down and watch."

Jennifer put her down on the floor. A little unsteady at first, Hope held on to the back of the chair, and then took a few steps over to Itzy who was near Alex.

"Itzy pretty," Hope said and slowly reached over to pet the cat's head. Itzy had never shown any fear of Hope. If anything, she seemed to be fascinated by the tiny human. And somehow Hope knew enough not to make any fast moves to startle her. They got along very well together.

"Papa, pick up!" Hope exclaimed.

Alex bent over and picked her up and put her on his lap.

"She can walk; she can talk! Russell you are some incredible teacher!"

"I'm not teaching her to walk; she figured that out for herself."

"She can also count and read to some extent," I added.

"Her first picture is framed and hanging over there by the computer, see it?" Alex asked.

"It looks like the sun or the moon with rays of light

shining down," Jennifer speculated.

"I think it's the moon. She reads 'The Moon Shines Down' every day and I think that's where she got the inspiration for the picture."

"I'm going to check out the internet for info on chemtrails," Alex advised.

"Let's take Hope into the living room," Russell remarked to Jennifer, "and we'll demonstrate her telepathic capabilities."

"Sounds good!" Jennifer exclaimed and the three of them headed off toward the living room.

I sat down and continued to review my recipes. I had only made slight headway when I heard Alex say "Oh, no!"

"Find something interesting?"

"I don't know if 'interesting' is the right word, but I did find a connection between chemtrails and Rh negative blood."

"Seriously?"

"Seriously. The site I'm on now is saying that the toxins in the chemtrails are preventing our DNA from activating. Rh negative individuals are being targeted first because they, as a group, have ascended to a level where their DNA could spontaneously activate new strands. Whether this is being orchestrated by humans, extraterrestrials or a combination of the two is unknown.

"And here's another site that talks about the 'X' chemtrails over strategic locations such as intersecting ley lines, just as Russell mentioned. The proposition is that possible inter-dimensional portals in such areas are being monitored by satellite tracking, again by unknown entities."

"In both cases, we'd be at the top of the list. Remember Russell said that those with Rh negative blood have a distinct advantage as their DNA can mutate as they evolve to higher levels? Maybe someone doesn't want that to happen. Maybe they want us to be on a level playing field when the battle takes place. Make sure you keep those sites up for

Russell to see."

Later that day I entered a post to my blog describing what a chemtrail was and how it varied from a contrail. I asked my 'sisters' to advise if they had noticed chemtrails in the sky over their homes and if so, to describe their appearance. By the next morning I had responses from 7 of them. All 7 reported that they had observed unusual 'X' shaped marks formed by chemtrails.

"I've heard back from 7 women on my blog so far, and all 7 have seen 'X' shaped chemtrails over their homes."

"So, including you that would mean one-third of the 24 women have experienced the 'X' shaped mark," Russell murmured. "That's more than a coincidence, I think."

"And many of the women no longer check the blog every day as they're busy with the children and life in general," I added.

"Something is definitely going on," Alex concluded. "I wish we knew what it was."

We kept our eyes to the sky more frequently now. More chemtrails were observed over the house in the next couple weeks but no additional 'X' marks were spotted.

My sisters arrived for Christmas around noon on Christmas Eve. They were only staying a couple of days this time as they had booked a Nile River cruise and needed to get back home to prepare for that. Jennifer and Russell were already with us when Alex arrived from the airport with Anne and Mary.

"Jennifer, how wonderful you look!" Mary exclaimed as she walked through the front door.

Hope walked over and hugged Anne's leg.

"Hope! Hi! You're really walking now!" Anne gasped.

"Hi, Annie!" Hope replied.

"And you're talking too!"

We settled in around the kitchen table as Jennifer and I were in the midst of making strudel.

"What kind of strudel are you making?" Mary asked.

"Two kinds, apple cranberry and raisin nut."

"That sounds delicious. I haven't had homemade strudel in years, actually decades," Anne declared. "Is there something else we can help you with?"

"No, thanks. We're having a more or less traditional Christmas brunch tomorrow with fresh kielbasa, hurka, baked ham, scrambled eggs, home fried potatoes and pickled beets. Jane is bringing a couple of quiches and homemade bread. So there's really nothing else to do."

"Where did you get the fresh kielbasa and hurka?" Mary asked.

"Believe it or not, I bought them on-line! It had to be shipped overnight mail and I received it yesterday. It certainly looks and smells fantastic."

"Okay, I know I'm a relative newcomer here, but what is 'hurka'?" Russell asked.

"It's a Slovak sausage made with pork, pork liver, rice, onion, garlic and spices. Have you ever had haggis?" Anne asked.

"Yes, actually I have."

"And did you like it?"

"It wasn't bad."

"Then you'll love hurka!"

"Did you get fresh horseradish to go with the kielbasa?" Mary asked.

"Of course," I replied.

"I've never had horseradish either," Russell commented. "What's it like?"

"Hot, similar to wasabi. Want to try a little taste on a spoon?" I asked.

"Okay!"

I went to the refrigerator, took out the horseradish and put a little on a spoon for him. He put the spoon in his mouth and we watched and waited. He was nodding as if he liked it. We continued watching and saw the tears come to his eyes and his face turn a bright red. I could almost see the smoke coming out of his ears.

He was speechless for several seconds and then he said "Wow, that's great stuff!"

"Welcome to the family!" Anne proclaimed.

We spent the rest of the day relaxing and being entertained mainly by Hope and Russell. Russell would hold up a card to his forehead, only showing the back of the card, not the front. Six cards were placed face down in front of Hope. She would sit there quietly for several seconds, supposedly picking up Russell's thoughts. Then she'd reach for a card and turn it over. Without fail, she was always correct.

We all gave it a try as well, with less than stellar results. By the look on Hope's face, it appeared she found us very amusing.

Christmas morning was crystal clear. It was very odd that there was no snow yet this season. I put the ham in the oven to bake and heard Mary and Anne describing the ports of call on their upcoming Nile cruise.

"You know, ladies, if you wanted to see Egypt, I could have escorted you over there via the portal," Russell reminded them.

"Thanks, Russell, but it's the whole 'cruise' experience that we love. Looking out at the water and the scenery as we pass by, being waited on hand and foot, exquisite food, gorgeous staterooms..." Anne was explaining when Mary interrupted by saying, "Let me show you the ship on the internet."

In a minute or two she had the website up on the screen and we were all peering over her shoulder, looking at the stateroom they would be occupying. I have to admit it was larger than any stateroom I had ever seen and very luxurious.

"Well, I could have at least brought you over to Egypt via portal and then you could have picked up the boat there," Russell commented.

"But we have considerable luggage; a duffel bag just wouldn't do it for us on a trip like this," Anne chuckled.

A couple of hours later the aroma of kielbasa and hurka in the skillet along with home fried potatoes and baked ham wafted through the house. Alex had the fireplaces lit, the little white lights twinkled on all the trees and all was ready.

Right on cue, the old Volvo pulled up to the front door. Russell and Alex went out to the car and we watched through the window. I saw Joshua pointing up toward the sky and saw Russell and Alex look up. Something wasn't right. I grabbed my coat and went outside. Anne and Mary came out with me and Jennifer stayed behind with Hope.

I looked up and there in the sky were three intersecting chemtrails. They formed something that looked similar to a giant asterisk hanging over the house. The older line was spreading out across the sky making a milky looking mess of what had been a beautiful cloudless blue sky just a little earlier. But there was something else; in addition to the white chemtrail lines, there was a dark line. It didn't appear to be composed of chemtrail spray. It looked like a black beam which wasn't quite centered on the middle of the asterisk. As we stood and watched the beam didn't appear to be spreading as the white chemtrails were.

"Do you see that black beam?" I asked.

"Yes; I've never seen anything like that before!" exclaimed Alex.

"There's something else up there," Mary murmured.

"What?" Jane questioned.

"Look just above the intersection of the chemtrails. There's a face there. Do you see it? Do you see the two huge dark eyes looking down? The oldest contrail almost appears to be a nose..."

"I see it," Russell chimed in. "But do you know what it looks like to me? It looks like a gasmask."

I could see it now, the face or gasmask or whatever it was. I felt a coldness sweep through me and it wasn't the weather causing it.

We went inside and Joshua explained that he and Jane had just commented on how beautiful the sky was; they hadn't seen one cloud when they started out, and then they could see the lines being laid as they got closer to our house. When they drove down our driveway into the courtyard, the asterisk was looming above.

Alex grabbed the camera and went back out to take a few pictures. Jennifer went with him to take a look for herself.

"That is unsettling, to say the least," she commented when she came back in. "It's evil, that's what it is. At least that's how it feels to me."

"Is that black beam still out there?" Anne asked.

"Yes, and it's not spreading as are the regular chemtrails," Alex responded.

Despite the chemtrails and black beam positioned over the house, we had a delightful brunch. Russell enjoyed the hurka very much and even had a second helping of it. .

In the lull between brunch and coffee and dessert, Alex and Joshua went on-line to see what they could discover about black beams. A short while later when we reassembled at the dining room table for strudel, Alex filled us in on what he had found.

"Several sites suggest that the black beam is a guide for the pilot of the chemtrail plane, telling them where the line should be placed. Some of the pictures which we saw show the chemtrail right next to or even on top of the dark beam."

"But that's not what happened here," Jennifer observed. "That black beam was almost another spoke in the wheel of that asterisk. It was not immediately next to nor part of a regular chemtrail line."

"Right you are," Joshua agreed. "But there was another theory that we came across. The chemicals contained in the chemtrails alter our DNA so that we can be controlled by the aliens."

Under normal circumstances (whatever normal

circumstances were, I couldn't remember that far back) I'm sure Joshua's comments would have triggered hysterical laughter from us. However now we just sat there in silence, sipping our coffee, eating our strudel and contemplating malevolent extraterrestrials orchestrating the application of chemtrails to alter our DNA.

"Oh, I almost forgot!" I exclaimed a few minutes later. I jumped up and handed the two wrapped presents on the sideboard to Anne and Mary.

"What's this?" Anne asked. "We don't exchange Christmas gifts any more!"

"They're not Christmas gifts," I replied.

"It's your cookbook!" Mary proclaimed after quickly ripping off the paper. "Connie's Cookbook, Out of this World Recipes; catchy title! And the UFO on the cover is great!"

Chapter 30 – Double Negative

Jennifer never experienced morning sickness during her pregnancy. She gave birth to a baby boy that following March. The delivery was relatively easy and she was assisted by Cheryl, the same midwife that I had hired. In retrospect, I recalled that none of the 24 women had experienced morning sickness and all of our deliveries were fairly easy. There must be something about that extraterrestrial DNA that is very compatible with us Rh negative individuals.

Jennifer and Russell named the baby Michael.

It was a wonderful experience having Jennifer with me during this time. I felt closer to her now than ever. And Russell, how can I even begin to describe my feelings for Russell? He was by Jennifer's side during the delivery and was with her whenever he was not teaching Hope and Seth. The love they felt for each other was palpable.

My sisters came to visit for Easter, which was a few weeks after Michael's birth. When they arrived from the airport, Hope ran to greet them.

"Hi, Annie. Hi, Mary!" she called from the open door.

As they greeted her with hugs and kisses, Hope asked, "Do you want to see Michael?"

"I'd love to see Michael. Where is he?" Anne asked.

"I'll show you," she replied and walked into the house making sure that Anne and Mary were following right behind her.

"Here he is!" she exclaimed as they walked into the kitchen. Jennifer was seated at the kitchen table feeding the baby. Russell walked over to my sisters and gave them each a hug and a kiss.

"He has a full head of dark hair!" Mary exclaimed.

"I think he has your eyes," Anne said to Russell.

"And you look wonderful, Jennifer," Mary remarked. "Motherhood agrees with you!"

"That's because Mother, Russell and Alex are taking such good care of me and Michael. All we do is sleep and eat!"

The next morning, Easter morning, everyone was busy with their assigned chores. Anne was slicing the Easter meatloaf, kielbasa and ham. Alex and Russell were performing taste tests on samples of the meat. According to them, everything was delicious.

"You know, it was last Easter that you and Russell met," I reminded Jennifer.

"And here I am, the mother of his little extraterrestrial baby!" she joked.

"Do you need flowers picked?" Russell asked me.

"Actually, yes I do."

"How about it, Jennifer; want to pick some flowers with me?" he asked.

"I'd love to," she replied.

"Here, I'll take Michael," Mary offered.

"Thanks. He should be sleepy. Just put him in the cradle if he dozes off."

"Can I go?" Hope asked.

"Sure," Russell responded. "Go find your sweater."

Hope went to the back hall and came back holding her sweater.

"Good girl, Hope. Let me help you put the sweater on," I offered.

Jennifer grabbed the snips and basket and headed out the front door with Hope and Russell. I watched them walk over toward the driveway and saw Russell take the basket from Jennifer. It appeared that she asked Hope to select the flowers, as I saw Hope pointing to individual daffodils, narcissus and hyacinths which Jennifer would then clip. I was standing there lost in thought when I heard Alex call "Connie, want me to make the vinaigrette for the asparagus?"

I walked back into the kitchen and replied "That would be great. Thanks."

Jane et al arrived promptly at noon and a little while later we were all seated around the dining room table. Seth and Hope took an immediate liking to the Easter meatloaf. And I was sure to have fresh horseradish on the table for Russell as it was now his condiment of choice. He routinely put it on veggie burgers and make-believe hot dogs.

"Has anyone noticed that there are more and more articles on the internet about Rh negative blood being connected with Reptilians?" Joshua asked of nobody in particular.

There was no immediate reply which might be due to the fact that we all had our mouths full and munching away.

Undaunted by the lack of response, Joshua continued, "And what they're saying about Reptilians is pretty negative. It's almost as if someone were trying to infer that Rh negative blooded individuals are evil or something."

"Actually, I have noticed that myself," Alex agreed. "It's almost as if someone wanted to start a witch hunt."

"And I would think it would be fairly easy to do that. The sheep will pretty much swallow anything that's fed to them," Joshua bellowed.

"What do you know about Reptilians, Russell? Are they malevolent?" Jane asked.

"There is good and there is bad in every species," Russell replied. "The same applies to the Reptilians."

"Well, that was a definitive response!" Joshua laughed.

"There are Reptilians that belong to the federation," Russell continued.

"You mean Seth or Hope might be Reptilian?" I asked.

"Would you have a problem with that?" Russell queried.

"No, if they are benevolent extraterrestrials and accepted by the federation, I guess not," I replied.

"Well that didn't sound too positive," Russell chided.

"There's something about the word 'reptilian' that is repulsive," Mary admitted.

"And why is that?" Russell asked.

"I don't really know. Could it be that the snake in the Garden of Eden was evil and a reptile?" she proposed.

"Do you know for sure the snake was evil?" he questioned.

"Since everything else I had previously assumed about the bible was pretty much way off target, maybe I was wrong about the snake as well," Mary speculated.

"Think about the Old Testament god, Yahweh. Remember Jesus called Yahweh a murderer, liar and the devil? We have determined that the god of the Old Testament was a malevolent extraterrestrial. And along comes the snake who tells Eve she will not die if she eats an apple from the Tree of Knowledge. It certainly seems as if the snake were an adversary of Yahweh's. That doesn't necessarily indicate that he was a benevolent extraterrestrial nor does it indicate he was malevolent. All it indicates is that you can't assume the snake was evil."

Somehow we managed to get the dinner discussion off evil extraterrestrials and on to more pleasant topics after a while.

The next morning Russell accompanied Jennifer to the portal as she had a meeting in London. Jane et al came over right after breakfast as they didn't have any opportunity to visit with my sisters that often. Hope and Seth were at a wonderful age. They could walk and talk and amuse the heck out of us. Anne and Mary had so much fun with them. They even tried to do the telepathic card thing with them. Hope and Seth took turns holding the card up to their foreheads and my sisters tried to determine which face down card matched. It even appeared they were making some progress with it!

Mid afternoon I heard the back door open and Jennifer call "Hello".

"Hi! How'd it go?" I asked as I entered the kitchen.

"My meeting went fine, but you won't believe what we saw in the chamber out back!" she proclaimed.

Alex, Jane, Joshua and my sisters filtered into the kitchen with looks of anticipation on their faces.

"What did you see in the chamber?" Alex asked.

"First of all, the third triskele has been completed. The center has been filled in. We think that is because of Michael's birth," Jennifer disclosed.

"And what else did you see?" I asked.

"There's been a new triskele carved above the others," Russell reported. "It's one large triskele, as large as the three smaller ones grouped together. As with the others, the center is not completed."

"What do you make of that?" Jane asked.

"This is just conjecture on my part, but I think it indicates that there will be another extraterrestrial birth, and this one will overshadow the others. This one will be of major importance."

"Do you have any idea of when or how this will happen?" Joshua asked.

"No."

"Do you have any guess as to why this will happen?" I asked.

"I think it's all part of the battle for this planet. The dark forces must be tremendously powerful and this is the federation's response. The ships that Alex saw in his dream, the ships that appeared in the skies around the globe, belong to extremely malevolent extraterrestrials. They are a branch of Reptilians that are violent, conniving and evil."

"So, since they are Reptilians, it might even help world leaders make the case that the Rh negative individuals on this planet are linked to them. And, if the populace believes that, then it will be a simple task to convince them that we need to be eliminated," I conjectured.

"It's entirely possible," Russell responded. "These malevolent Reptilians have underwater bases around the globe."

"Underwater! Their ships come up out of the water?" Jane asked.

"Yes. Think back when we had that last sighting. Where did you first see the large ships? Connie, you saw them over Lake Champlain. Anne and Mary you saw them over Calibogie Sound, Jennifer you saw them over the Thames River. I saw them over the Atlantic Ocean. They all originated from the water.

"The battle for this planet has already begun. Toxins in chemtrails could possibly be blocking the activation of DNA strands and groundwork is already being laid to link Rh negative individuals with malevolent extraterrestrials. Since these same malevolent beings control the media, it will be a simple matter to brainwash the populace.

"But the real battle won't begin until our children and their children have become adults. Isn't that correct? Jane asked.

"Yes, but that time will be here in the blink of an eye."

* * * * * * *

And, as Russell said, in what seemed to be the blink of an eye, years had passed. Hope and Seth were now 14. They had continued their lessons with Russell over the years and had often traveled to the Center for additional training. In all appearances they were average teenagers. They attended local public schools and they excelled in their studies.

Michael was 13, and Jennifer and Russell's only child. He, too, received instruction from Russell and traveled to the Center for training. He attended public school on the Isle of Arran. Jennifer opened a satellite office out of the apartment on her property in Lamlash Bay and her business was thriving.

There had been no other mass UFO sightings in all the intervening years. There had been no identification of the extraterrestrials responsible for the prior UFO sighting, at least not acknowledged by any government. Chemtrails still appeared in the skies around the world but the masses still didn't acknowledge them as a threat of any sort. The 'X' chemtrail and black beams frequently appeared over my house as well as over the houses of the other 23 comradettes. A darker and darker picture was being painted about Rh negative blood. We waited for something to happen, but we weren't sure exactly what that would be.

And then one night in March I was awakened by a bright light shining through my bedroom window. Was that the full moon? Although my eyes were open, I discovered that I couldn't move. This was the first sleep paralysis episode that I experienced since just before Hope was conceived. From my vantage point lying in bed, I didn't see anything out of the ordinary other than the unusual illumination all around me. I tried to focus my mind on a simple meditation, hoping that I would fall back to sleep. And then I heard a voice. Maybe it wasn't an actual voice; maybe it was a thought that entered my head. Whatever it was, it told me that Hope was to conceive a child, a very special child.

I awoke the next morning and just vaguely remembered what I thought was a dream. Alex was still asleep, which was unusual for him. Hope was sitting at the kitchen table sipping orange juice.

"Hi, sweetie," I greeted her. "Sleep well?"

"Not really."

The vague memory of my dream came to mind and my heart started to pound.

"Anything wrong?" I asked.

"Something strange happened last night. A bright light was shining through my window, so bright that it woke me up. And I realized I couldn't move. I couldn't move any part of my body. And then I gazed over toward the edge of my bed and the figure of a beautiful luminous woman was standing there, telling me not to be afraid. Instantly I became calm and continued to stare at her. She told me that I was to give birth to a very special child. The thought of the Virgin Mary and the Annunciation came immediately to mind. And that was all I remember. I must have fallen asleep after that."

I tried to keep my voice even and controlled when I said to her, "I had a dream last night; at least I thought it was a dream. I also was told that you were to conceive a very special child. Hope, I know you are aware that a great force is controlling our lives. We need to accept that."

"I know, Mom. I'm not afraid."

* * * * * * *

Nine months later Hope gave birth to a beautiful baby girl. She named her Krista.

Epilogue:

Weeks before Hope gave birth, scientists reported an object in the sky which they thought might be a comet. After prolonged observation and in spite of all their sophisticated satellites, telescopes and equipment, they were unable to identify it. They tracked its path across the sky and speculated on what it might or might not be. Then on the night before Krista's birth, it became stationary very high up in the sky directly over our house. The fact that it became fixed in its location and was of unknown origin caused considerable panic. World leaders issued statements in an attempt to alleviate growing alarm. The day after Krista's birth, it disappeared from view. A press release was issued a few days later advising that scientists identified it as an asteroid which harmlessly burned up in the atmosphere.

To be continued...

www.ingramcontent.com/pod-product-compliance
Lightning Source LLC
Chambersburg PA
CBHW030246030726
47493CB00023B/869